# DOUGIE'S WAR

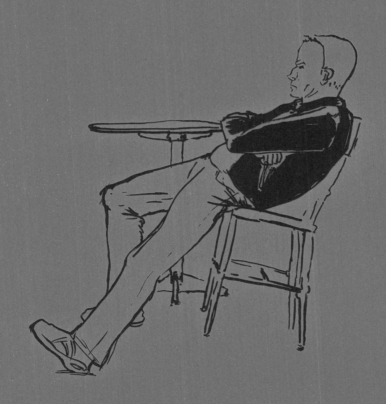

## A graphic novel about one soldier's return from Afghanistan

the publisher acknowledges investment from
**Creative Scotland** towards the publication of this book

First published 2010 as **Dougie's War**

Published by **FREIGHT**
49-53 Virginia Street
Glasgow
G1 1TS

British Library Cataloguing in Publication Data

A catalogue record for this book is available from the British Library

ISBN 978-0-9544024-8-8

# DOUGIE'S WAR

## A graphic novel about one soldier's return from Afghanistan

STORY BY
### RODGE GLASS

ARTWORK BY
### DAVE TURBITT

Design, layout and lettering by **Derick Carss**

Photography by **Nick Collins**

Additional contributions by **Adrian Searle**

# Introduction

**D**ougie's War is not a true story. Dougie Campbell doesn't exist, nor does his sister, nor his dubious friends. This graphic novel is, by nature, a fiction, a cautionary tale of the damage the trauma of war can inflict on servicemen and women, not just to their bodies, but also on their minds. While it's Dougie's story alone, it's also an amalgamation of a wide range of experiences of real veterans as told to the author, Rodge Glass. It deliberately presents a worst-case-scenario: what can happen if those injured emotionally are unable, for whatever reason, to seek help.

Post Traumatic Stress Disorder (PTSD) only affects a small number of people and is not solely a military condition (other members of society can be affected through working in stressful conditions, for example the police and fire service). The symptoms can appear while people are still in military service but sometimes problems don't reveal themselves until years later. Veteran case histories show that PTSD can result from one single traumatic event, or from years of working in a high pressure, high stress environment. However, the effects can be debilitating, if not crippling, to both sufferers and their families.

Our armed forces are undoubtedly among the best trained and most professional in the world. Recent conflicts in Iraq and Afghanistan have seen them operating in some of the most difficult and testing conditions experienced since the Second World War. They are taught to push themselves to the limits of human capability, for their country and for each other.

> *While it's Dougie's story alone, it's also an amalgamation of a wide range of experiences of real veterans as told to the author, Rodge Glass.*

The Services are better than ever at identifying and offering support to those with symptoms of PTSD. But in a culture which, by necessity, places great emphasis on personal endurance and mental strength, it can be difficult for individuals to admit to having issues. In a job where camouflage is a vital skill, service men and women can be adept at hiding how they truly feel. Sometimes it is after leaving the forces that problems really develop. Life after military service, without the day-to-day support of colleagues, can be when things get really tough.

Great work has been done in recent years to improve understanding and available support in the NHS. Over and above this, there are a number of charities who provide vital support to veterans with a range of needs. The Scottish Veterans Fund, which partially funded this graphic novel, aims to find innovative ways of raising awareness of debt we all owe to our Armed Forces and to promote understanding of the particular needs of those adjusting to life after leaving the Services.

The hope is that in reading this graphic novel, the accompanying interviews with veterans and the extracts from *Charley's War*, the first graphic novel to explore the psychological impact of battle, that you feel you have gained insight into, and understanding of, just some of the challenges facing the men and women of our Army, Royal Navy and Royal Air Force as they try to cope with the legacy of their military experiences.

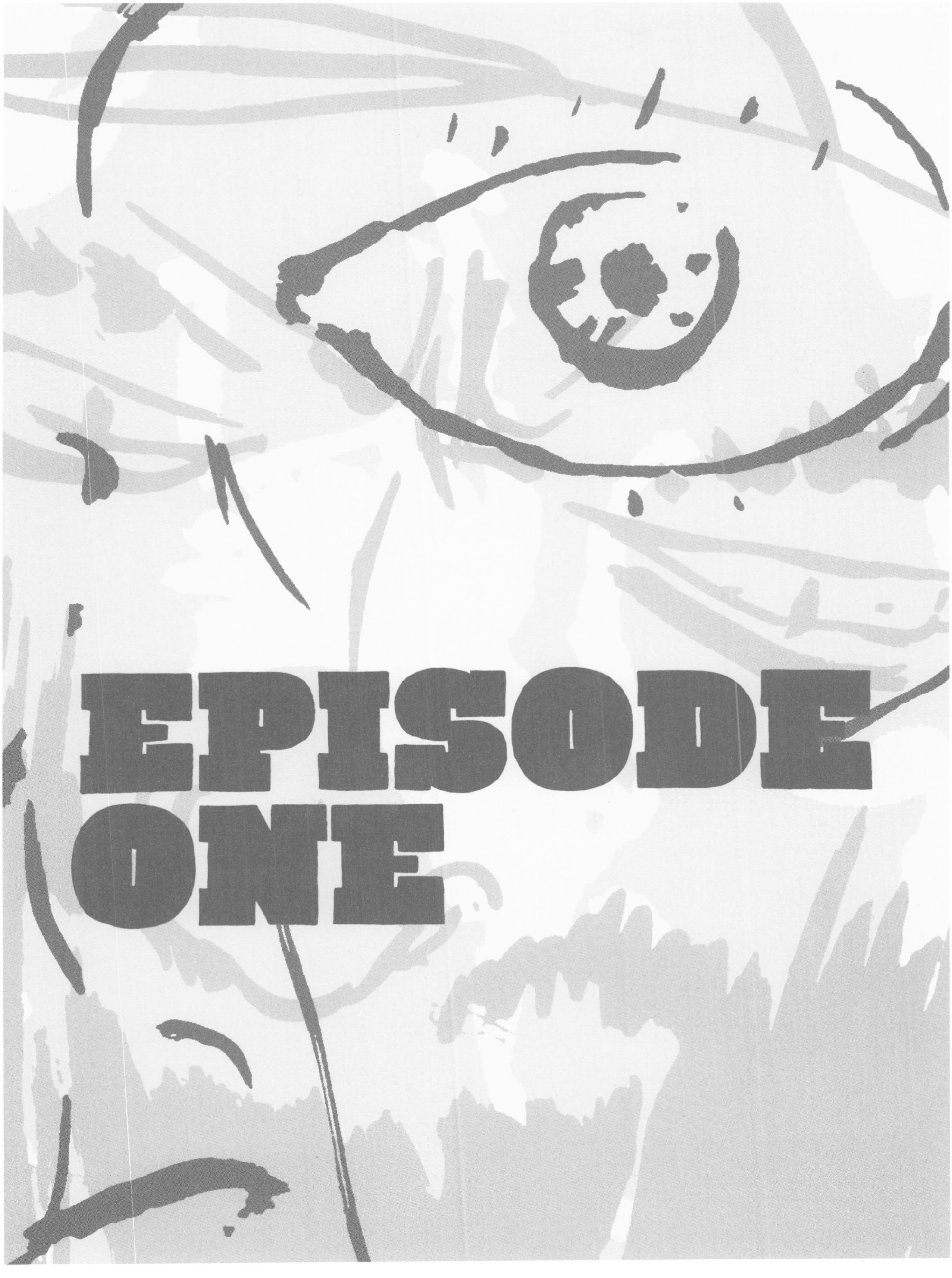
EPISODE
ONE

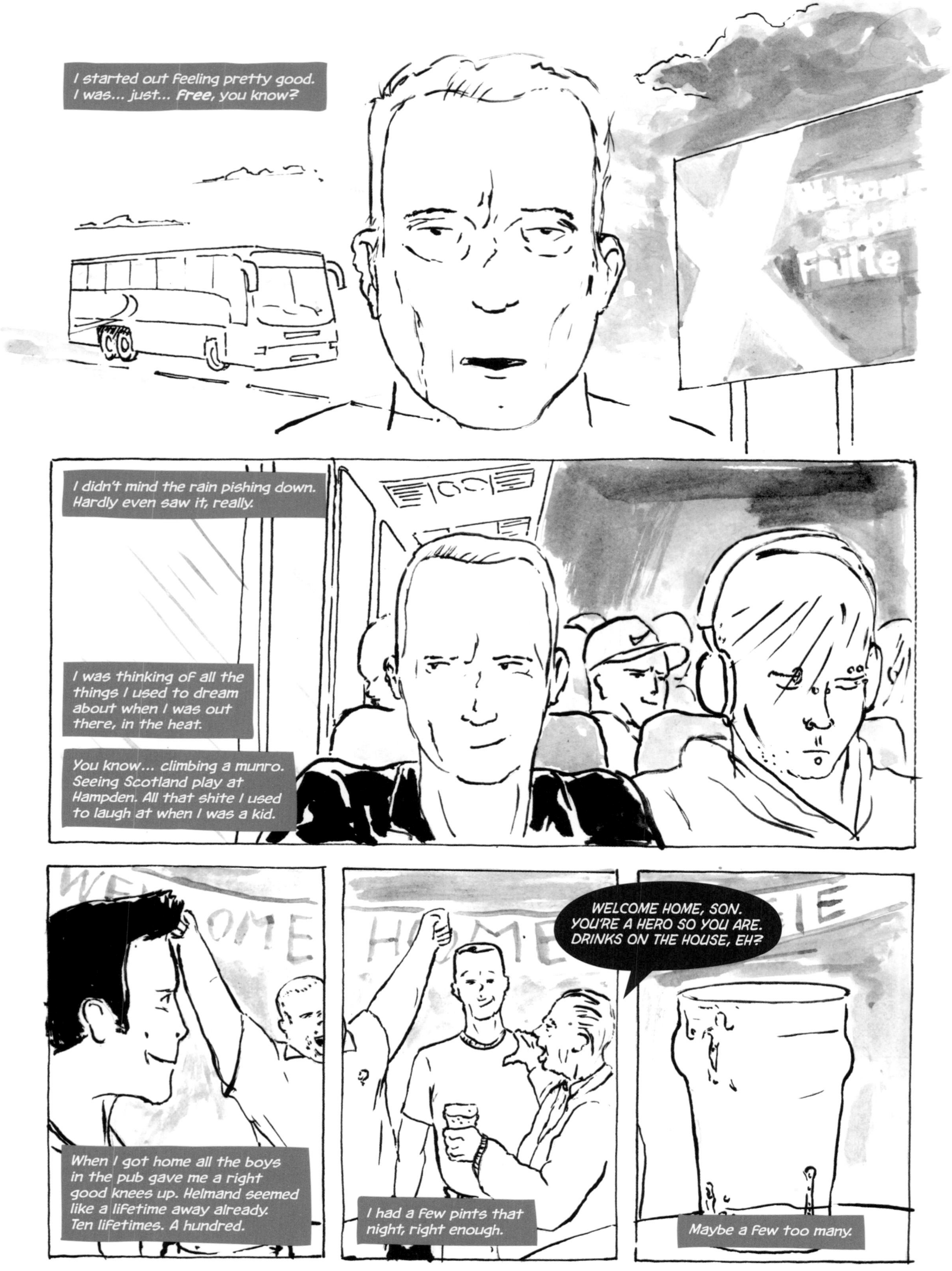

I started out feeling pretty good. I was... just... *free*, you know?
I didn't mind the rain pishing down. Hardly even saw it, really.
I was thinking of all the things I used to dream about when I was out there, in the heat.
You know... climbing a munro. Seeing Scotland play at Hampden. All that shite I used to laugh at when I was a kid.
When I got home all the boys in the pub gave me a right good knees up. Helmand seemed like a lifetime away already. Ten lifetimes. A hundred.
I had a few pints that night, right enough.
WELCOME HOME, SON. YOU'RE A HERO SO YOU ARE. DRINKS ON THE HOUSE, EH?
Maybe a few too many.

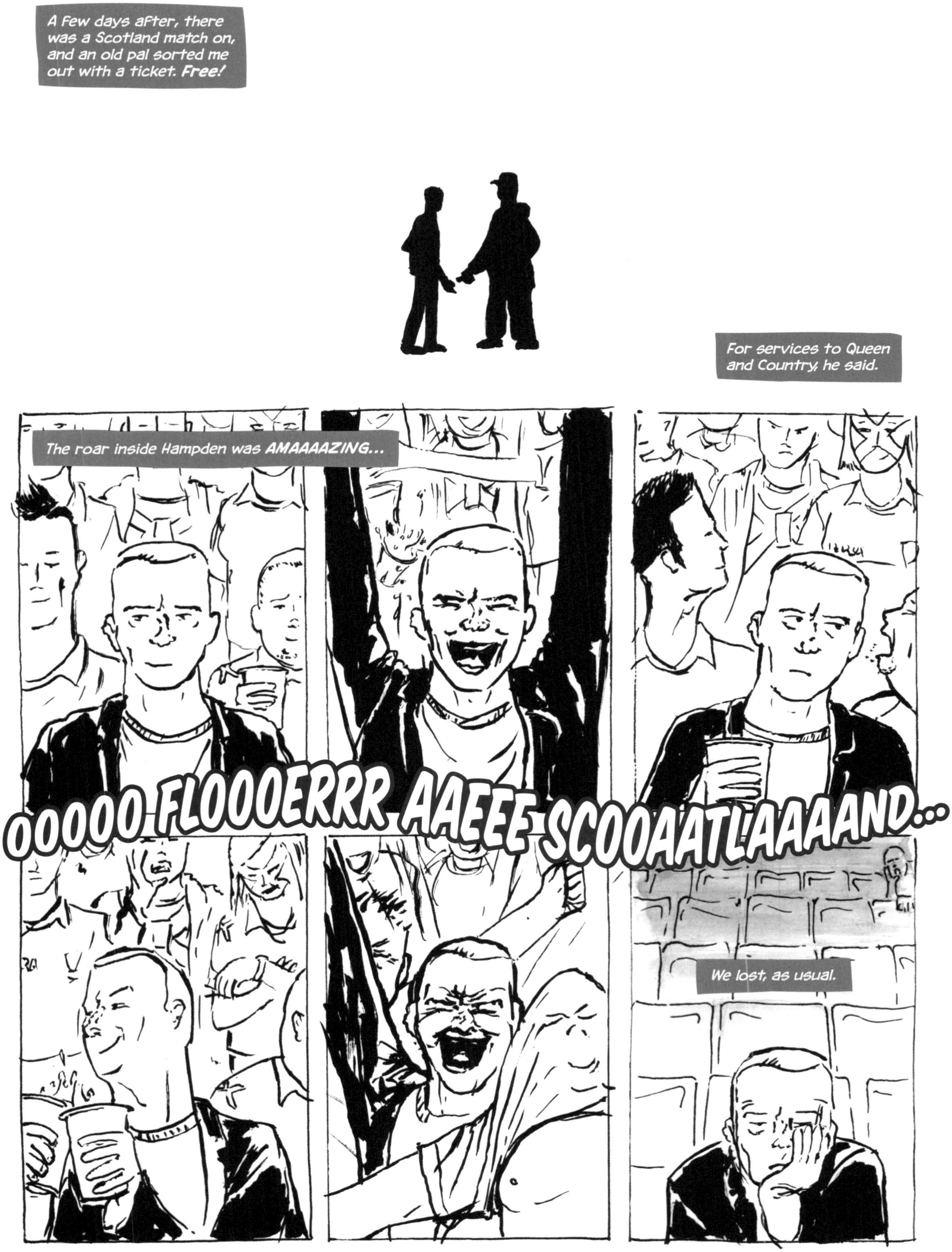
A few days after, there was a Scotland match on, and an old pal sorted me out with a ticket. Free!
For services to Queen and Country, he said.
The roar inside Hampden was AMAAAAZING...
OOOOO FLOOOERRR AAEEE SCOOAATLAAAAND...
We lost, as usual.

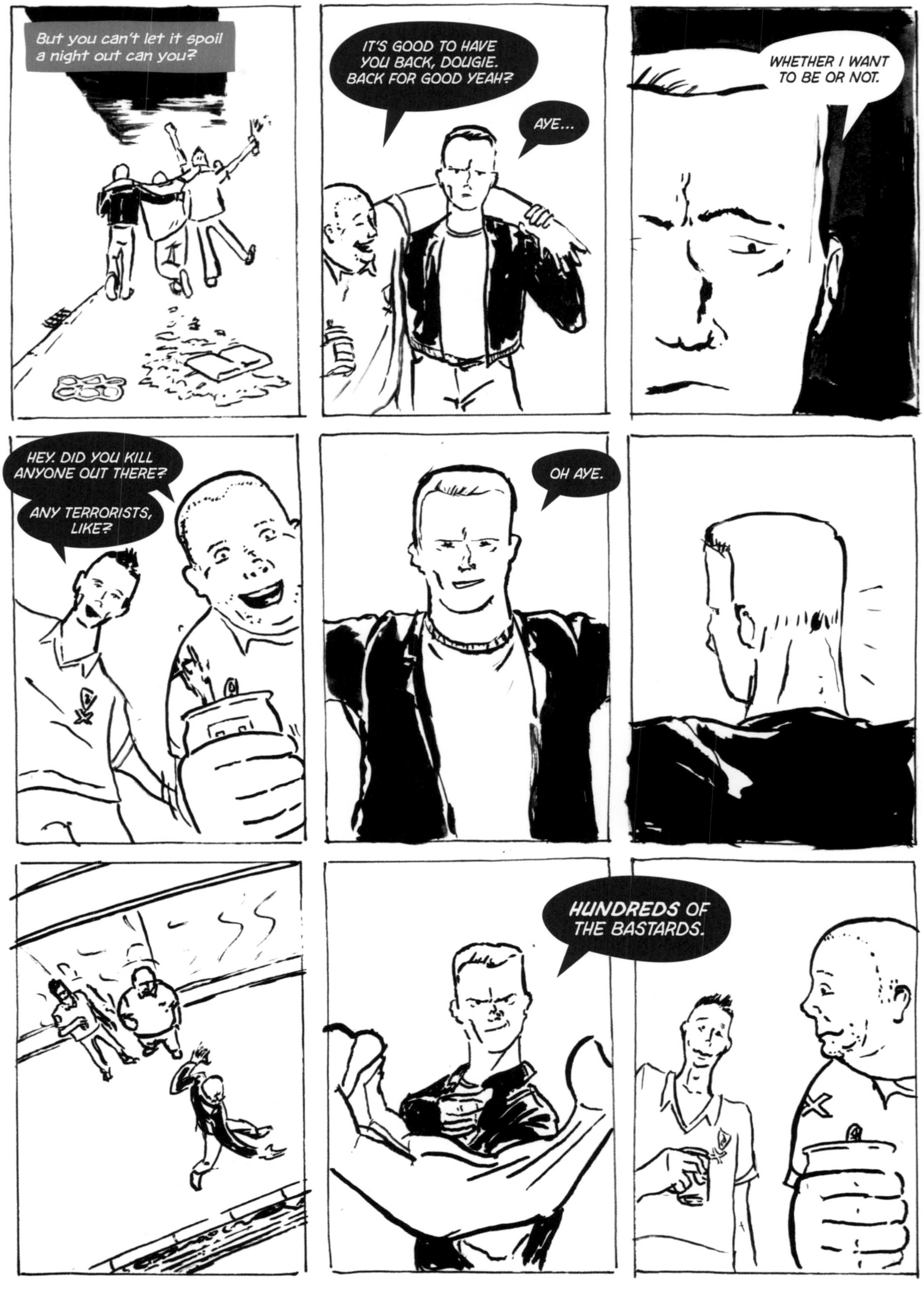

But you can't let it spoil a night out can you?
IT'S GOOD TO HAVE YOU BACK, DOUGIE. BACK FOR GOOD YEAH?
AYE...
WHETHER I WANT TO BE OR NOT.
HEY. DID YOU KILL ANYONE OUT THERE?
ANY TERRORISTS, LIKE?
OH AYE.
HUNDREDS OF THE BASTARDS.

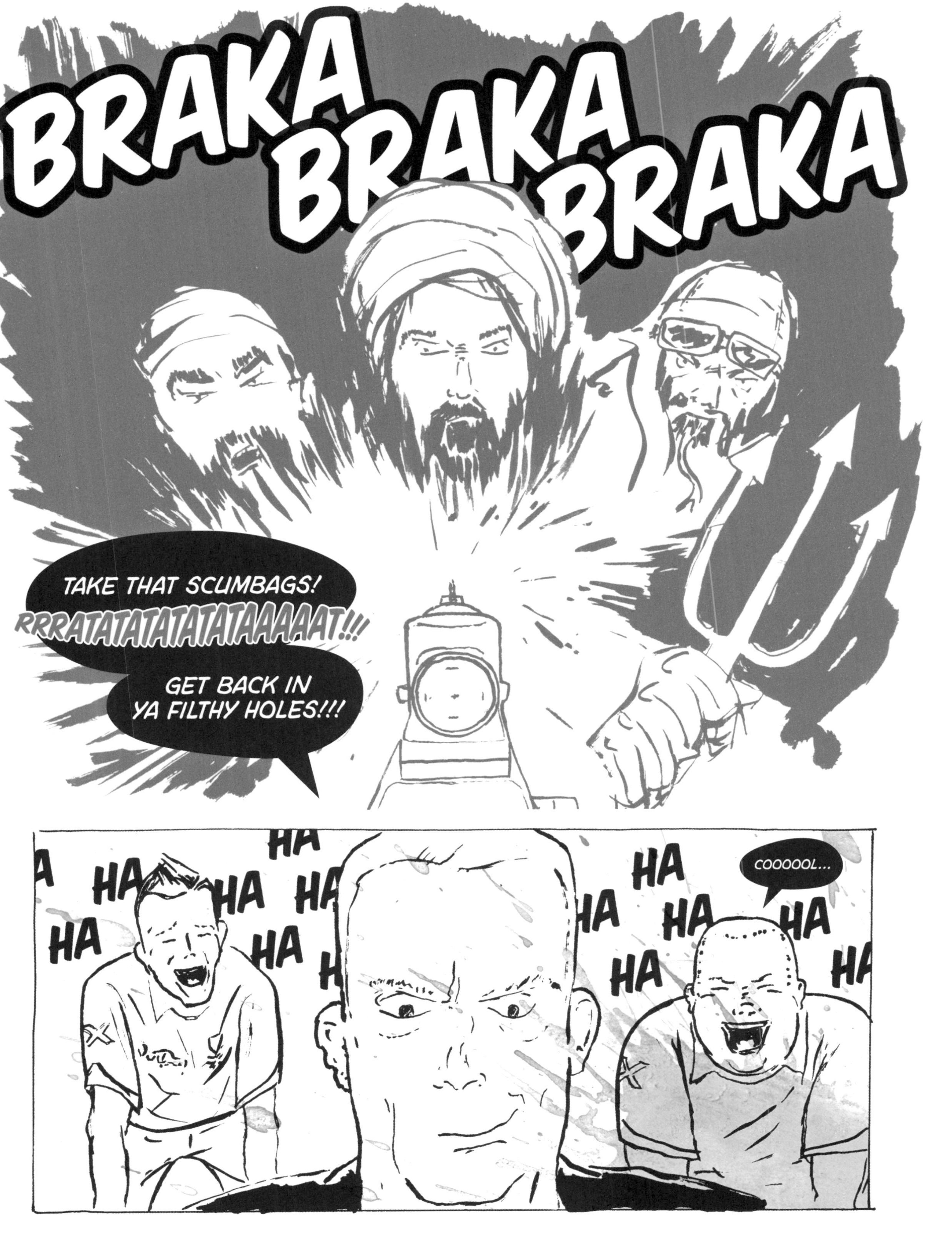

BRAKA BRAKA BRAKA
TAKE THAT SCUMBAGS!
RRRATATATATATATATAAAAAT!!!
GET BACK IN YA FILTHY HOLES!!!
HA HA HA HA HA HA HA HA HA HA HA HA
COOOOOL...

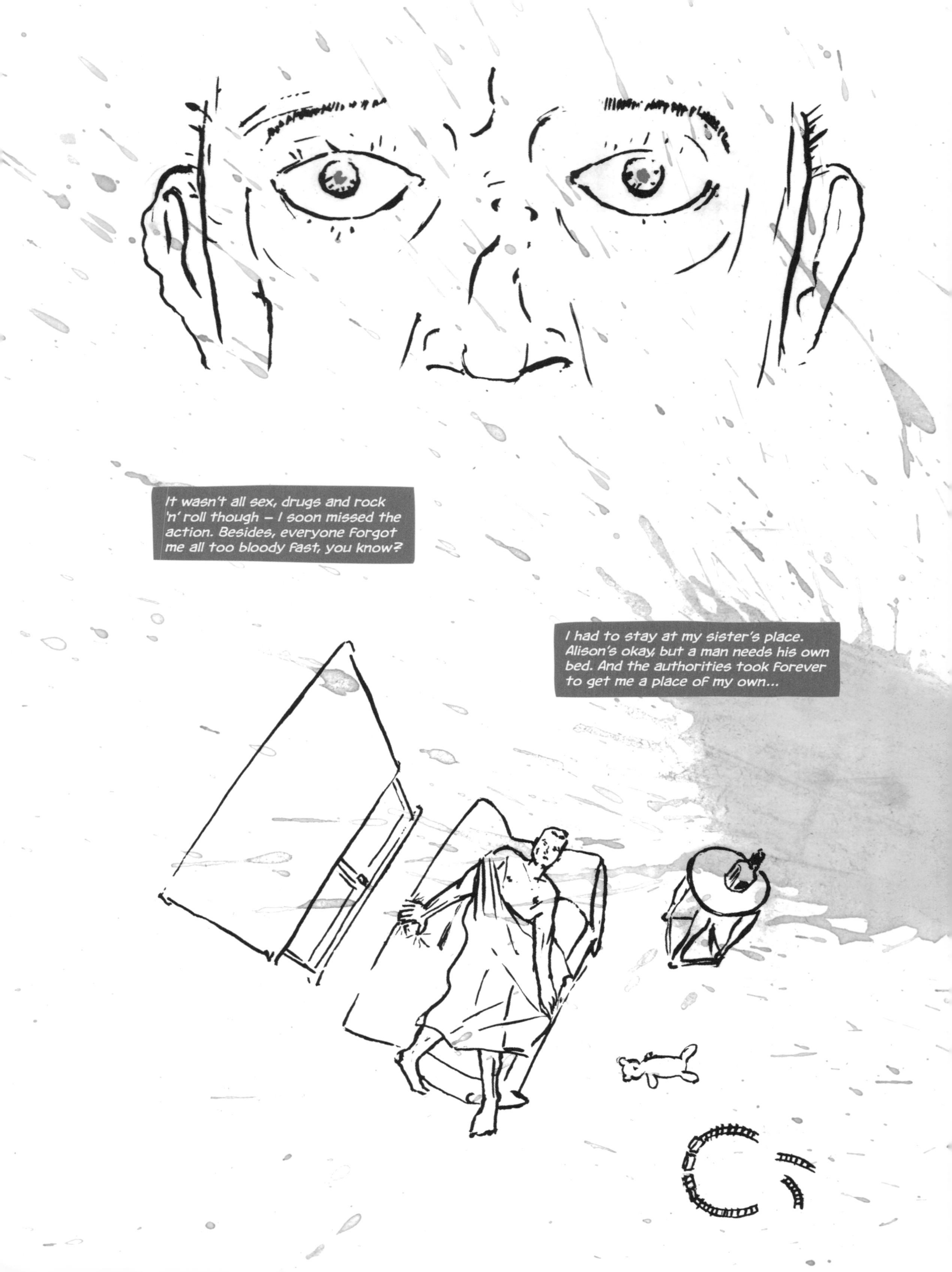
It wasn't all sex, drugs and rock 'n' roll though – I soon missed the action. Besides, everyone forgot me all too bloody fast, you know?
I had to stay at my sister's place. Alison's okay, but a man needs his own bed. And the authorities took forever to get me a place of my own...

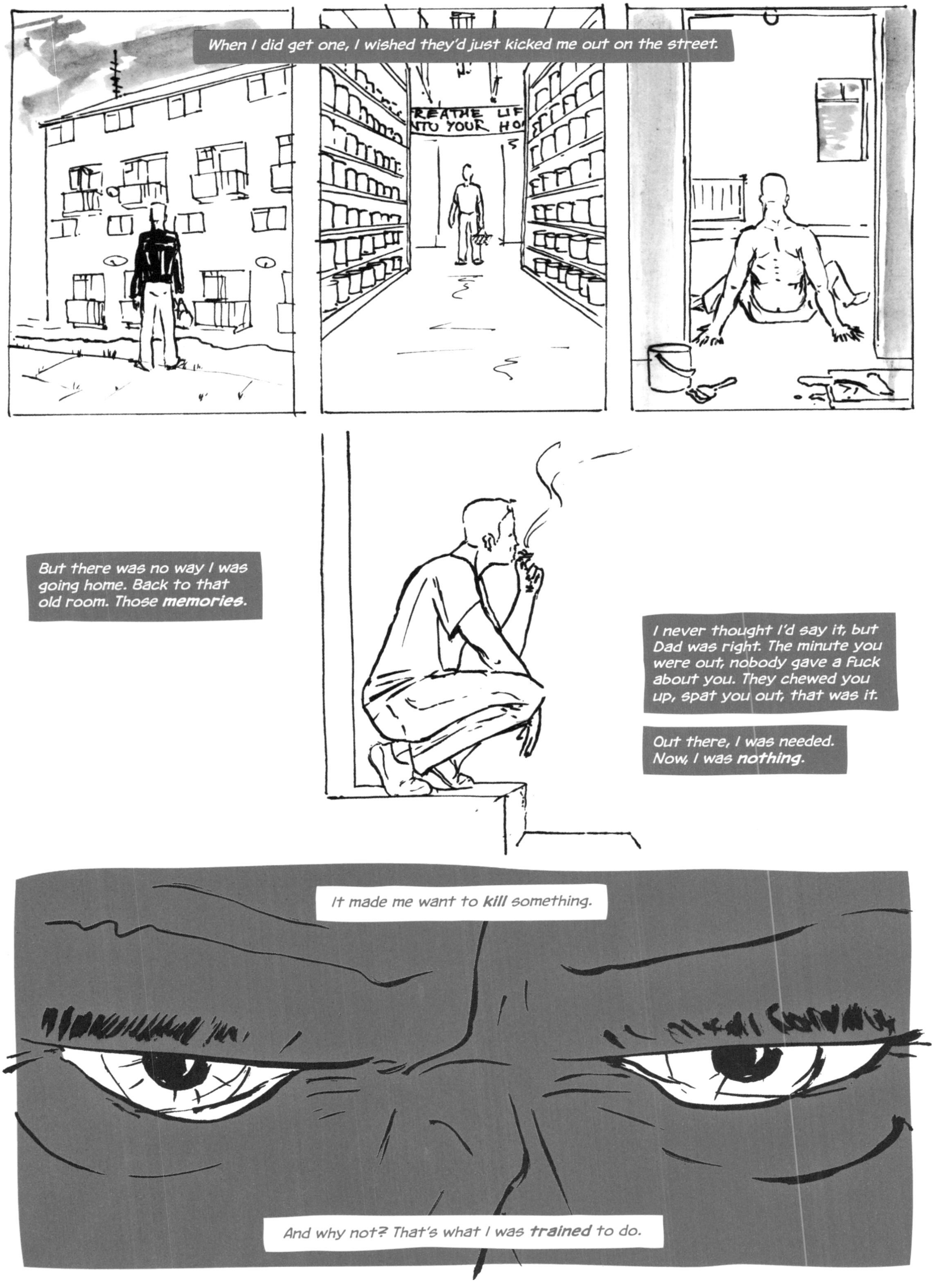
When I did get one, I wished they'd just kicked me out on the street.
BREATHE LIF
INTO YOUR HO
But there was no way I was going home. Back to that old room. Those **memories**.
I never thought I'd say it, but Dad was right. The minute you were out, nobody gave a fuck about you. They chewed you up, spat you out, that was it.
Out there, I was needed. Now, I was **nothing**.
It made me want to **kill** something.
And why not? That's what I was **trained** to do.

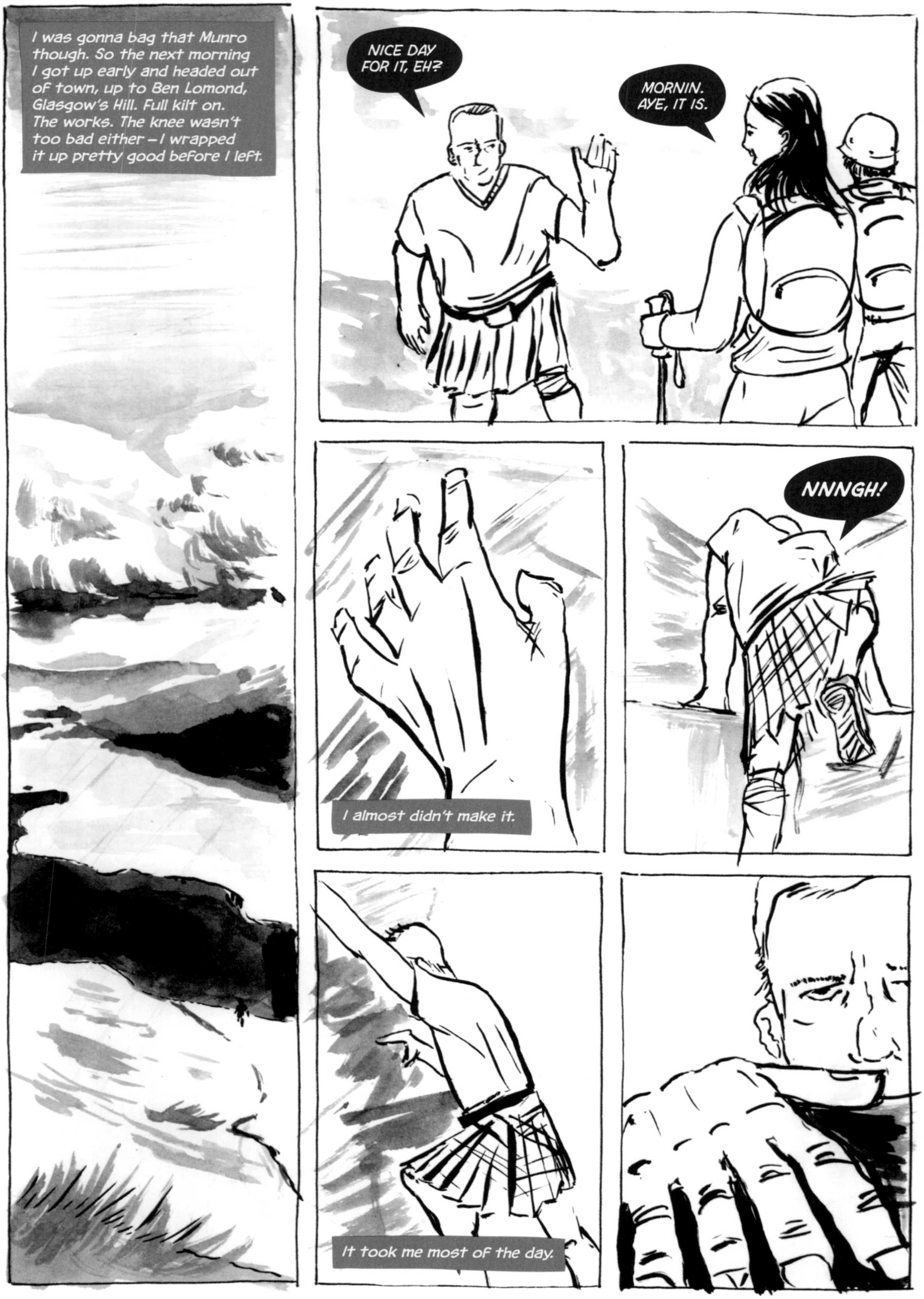

I was gonna bag that Munro though. So the next morning I got up early and headed out of town, up to Ben Lomond, Glasgow's Hill. Full kilt on. The works. The knee wasn't too bad either – I wrapped it up pretty good before I left.
NICE DAY FOR IT, EH?
MORNIN. AYE, IT IS.
I almost didn't make it.
NNNGH!
It took me most of the day.

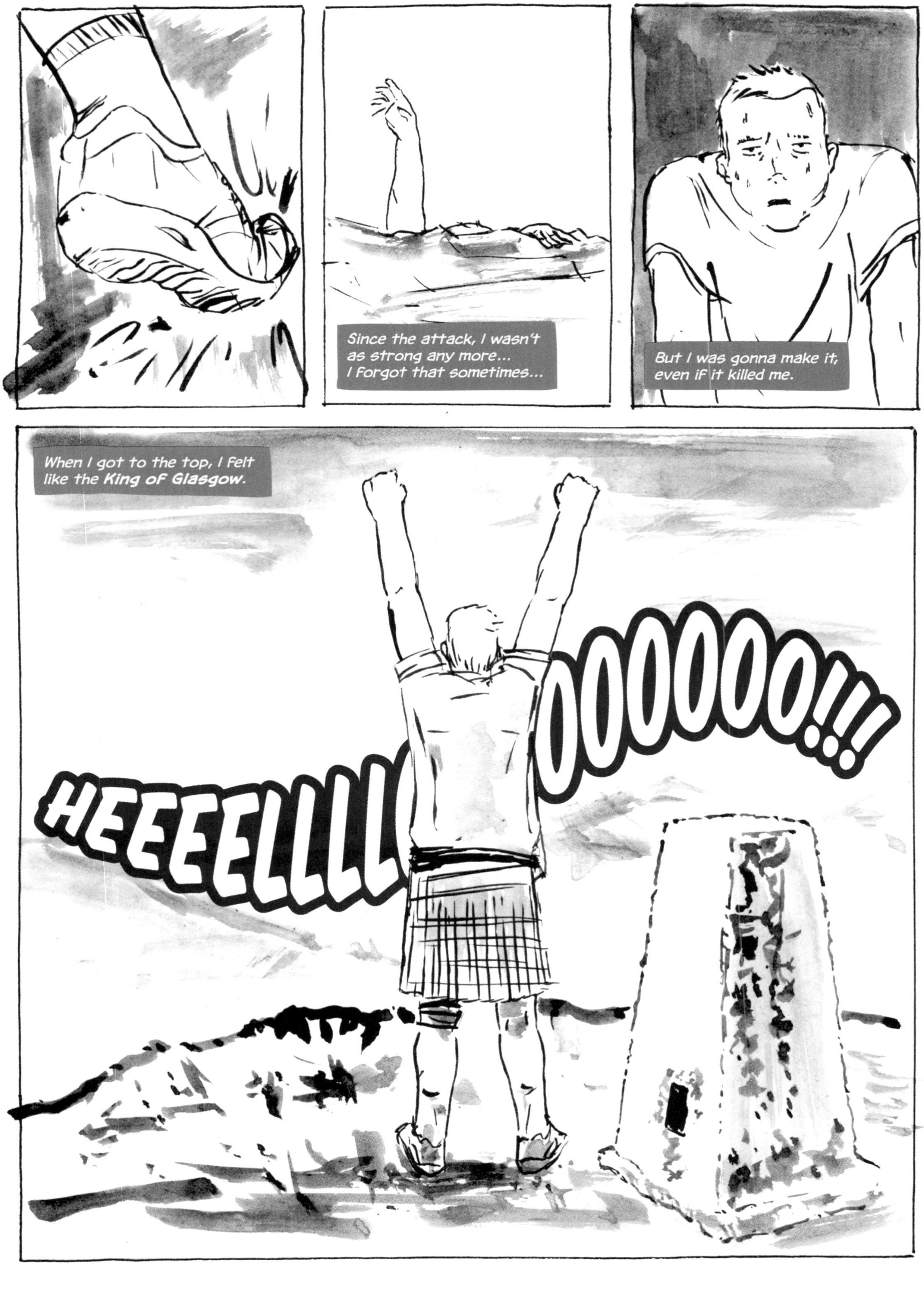
Since the attack, I wasn't as strong any more... I forgot that sometimes...
But I was gonna make it, even if it killed me.
When I got to the top, I felt like the **King of Glasgow**.
HEEEELLLLOOOOOOO!!!

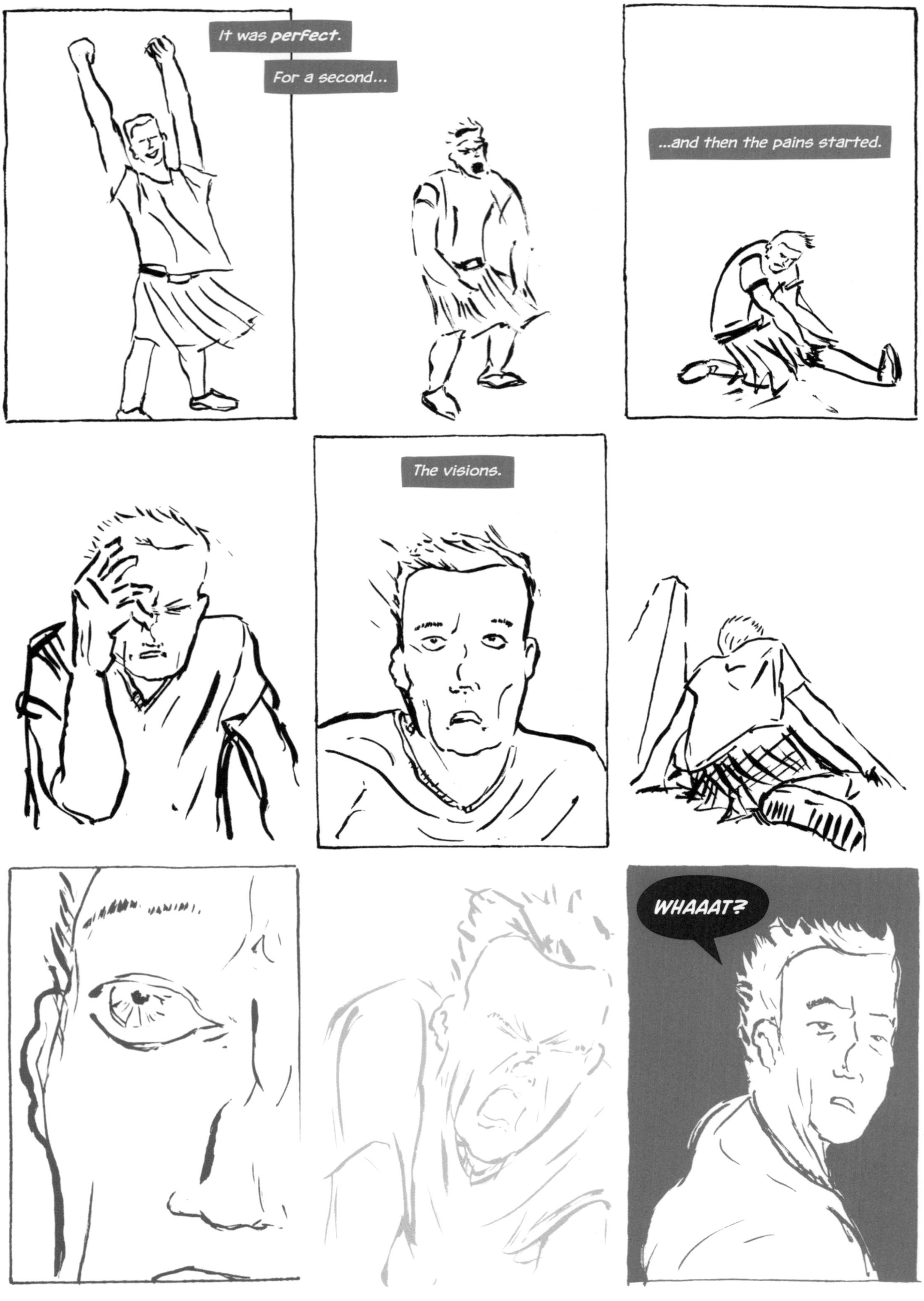
It was perfect.
For a second...
...and then the pains started.
The visions.
WHAAAT?

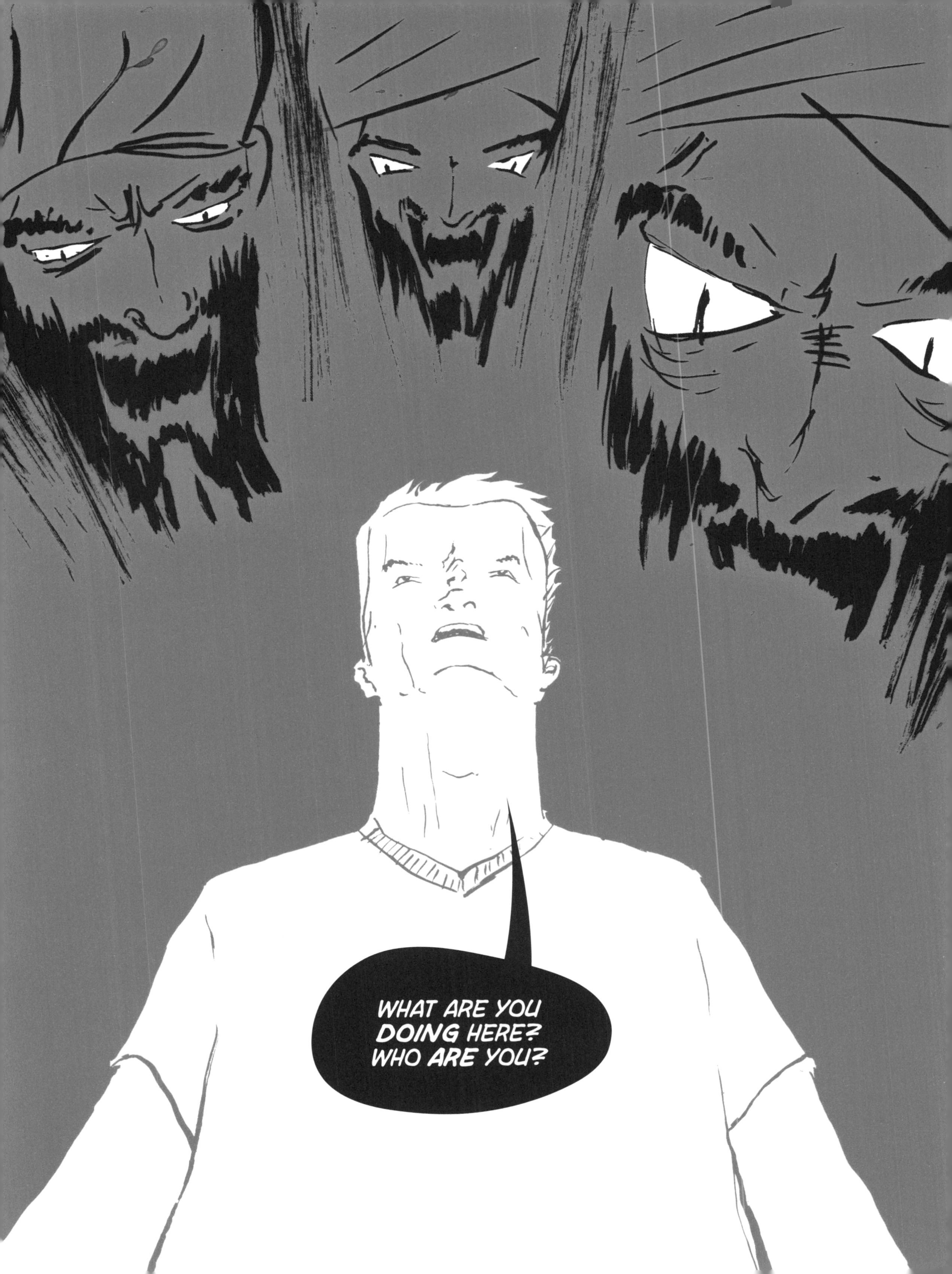
WHAT ARE YOU DOING HERE? WHO ARE YOU?

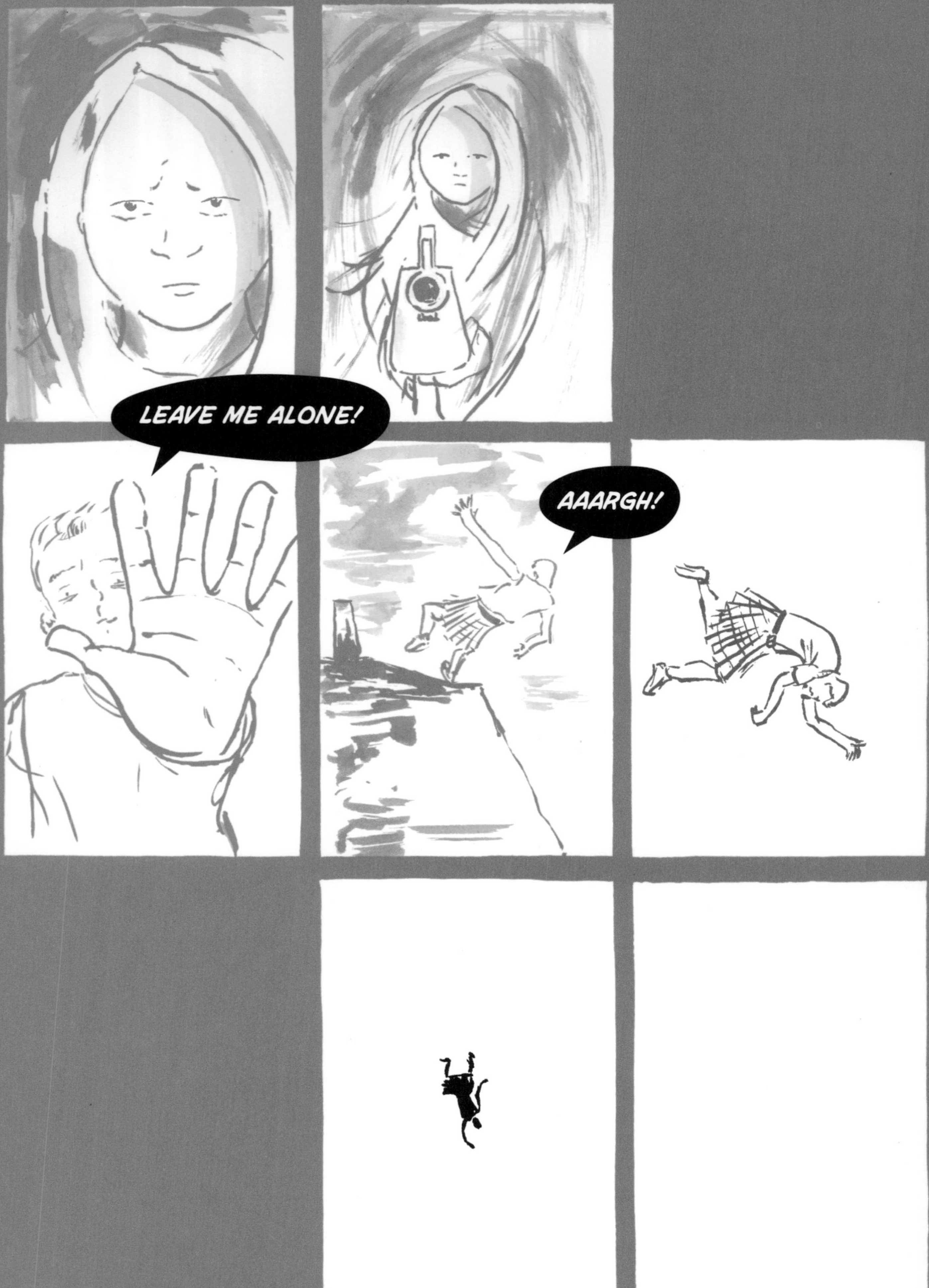
LEAVE ME ALONE!
AAARGH!

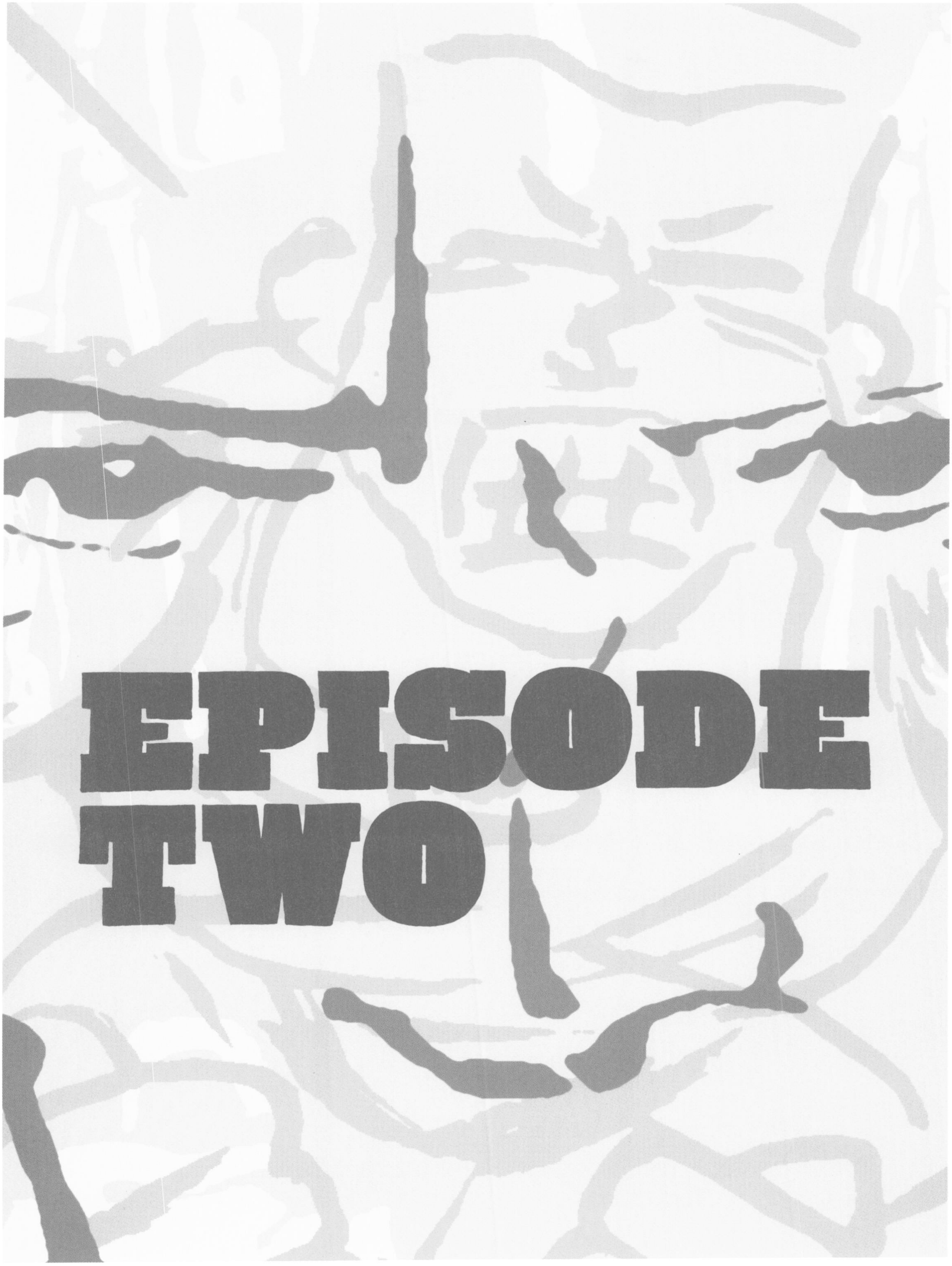

# EPISODE TWO

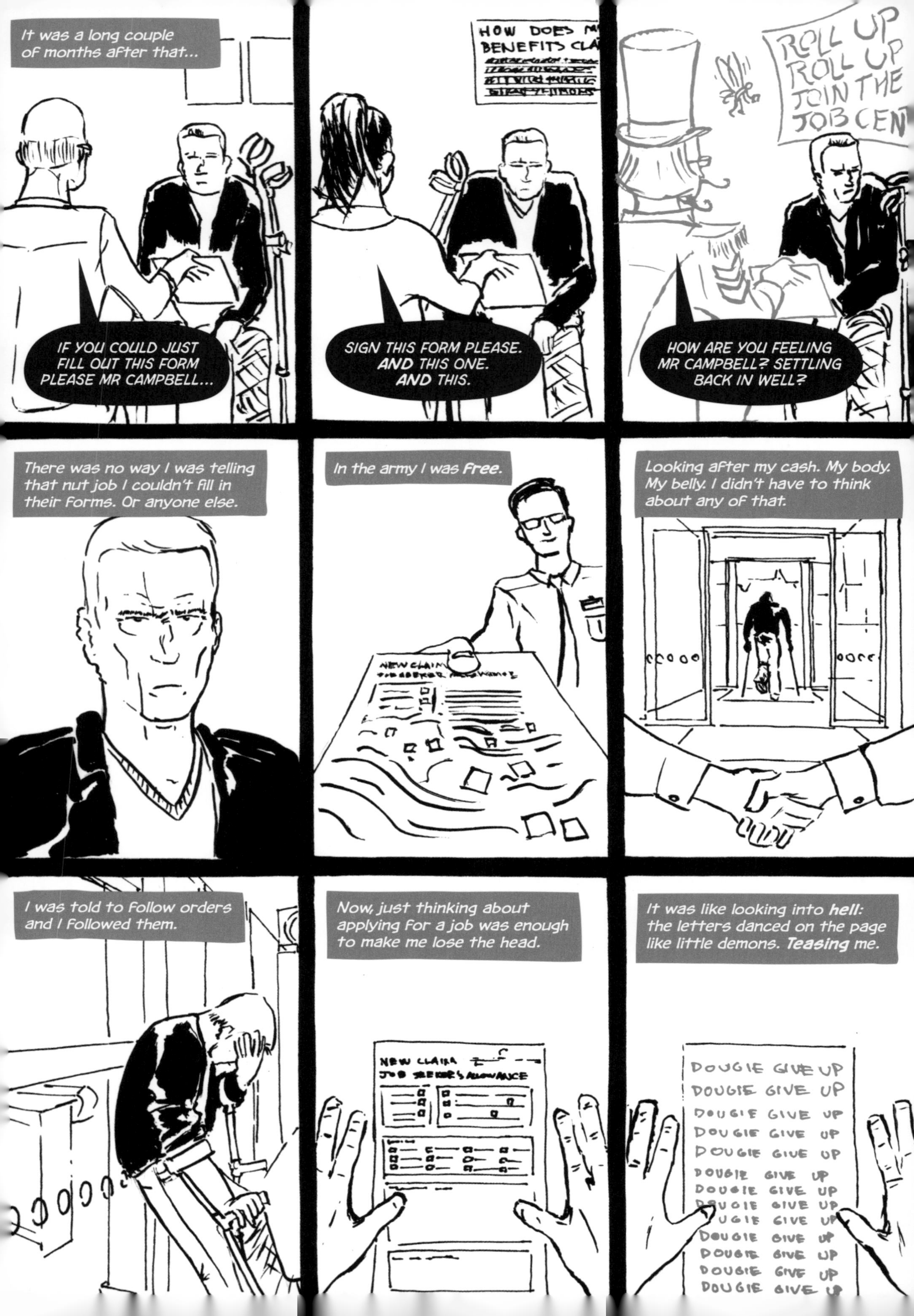
It was a long couple of months after that...
IF YOU COULD JUST FILL OUT THIS FORM PLEASE MR CAMPBELL...
HOW DOES MY BENEFITS CLA
SIGN THIS FORM PLEASE. AND THIS ONE. AND THIS.
ROLL UP ROLL UP JOIN THE JOB CEN
HOW ARE YOU FEELING MR CAMPBELL? SETTLING BACK IN WELL?
There was no way I was telling that nut job I couldn't fill in their forms. Or anyone else.
In the army I was free.
Looking after my cash. My body. My belly. I didn't have to think about any of that.
I was told to follow orders and I followed them.
Now, just thinking about applying for a job was enough to make me lose the head.
NEW CLAIM
JOB SEEKER'S ALLOWANCE
It was like looking into hell: the letters danced on the page like little demons. Teasing me.
DOUGIE GIVE UP
DOUGIE GIVE UP
DOUGIE GIVE UP
DOUGIE GIVE UP
DOUGIE GIVE UP
DOUGIE GIVE UP
DOUGIE GIVE UP
DOUGIE GIVE UP
DOUGIE GIVE UP
DOUGIE GIVE UP

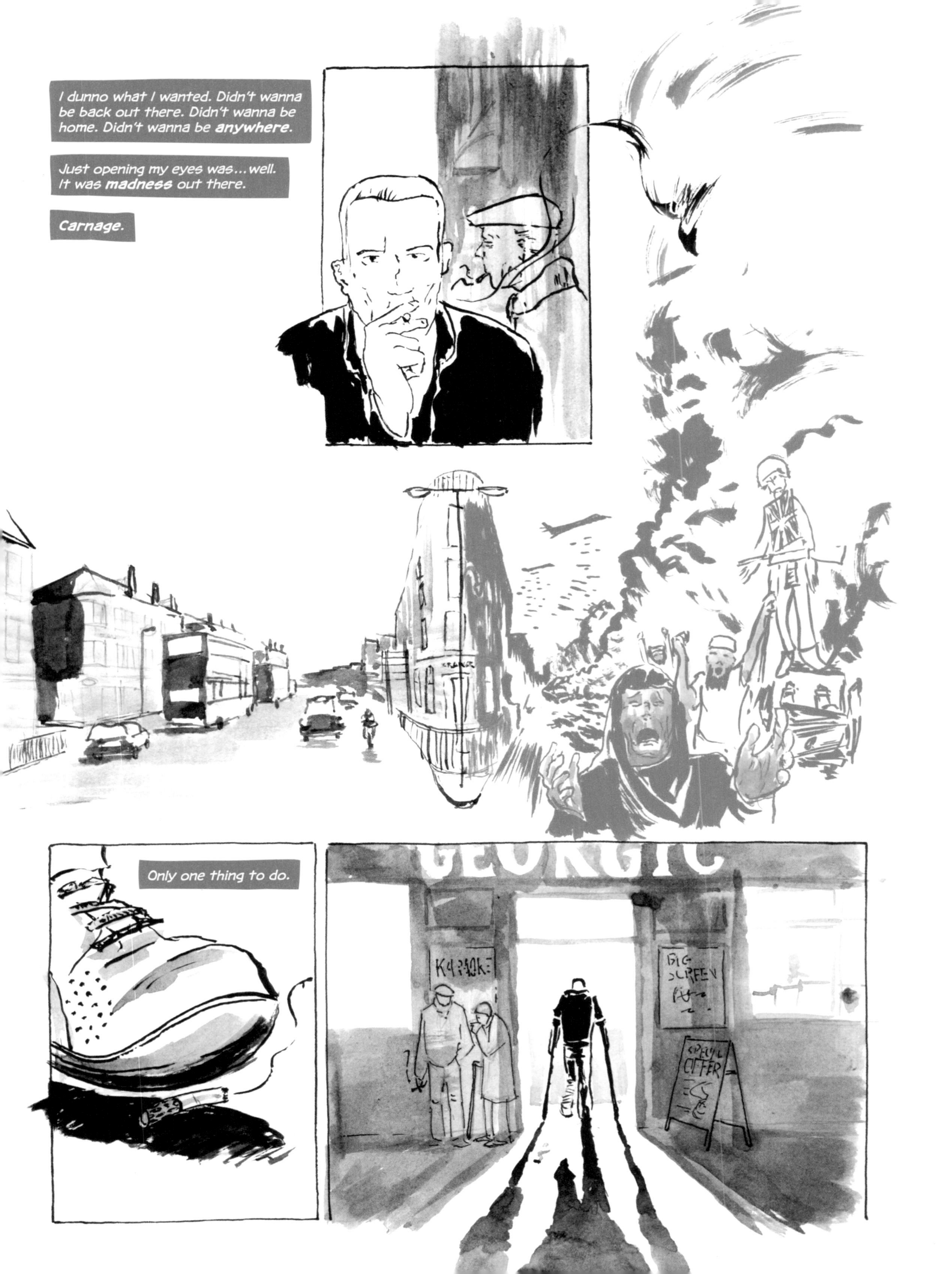
I dunno what I wanted. Didn't wanna be back out there. Didn't wanna be home. Didn't wanna be **anywhere**.
Just opening my eyes was... well. It was **madness** out there.
**Carnage.**
Only one thing to do.
GEORGIC
KARAOKE
BIG SCREEN
SPECIAL OFFER

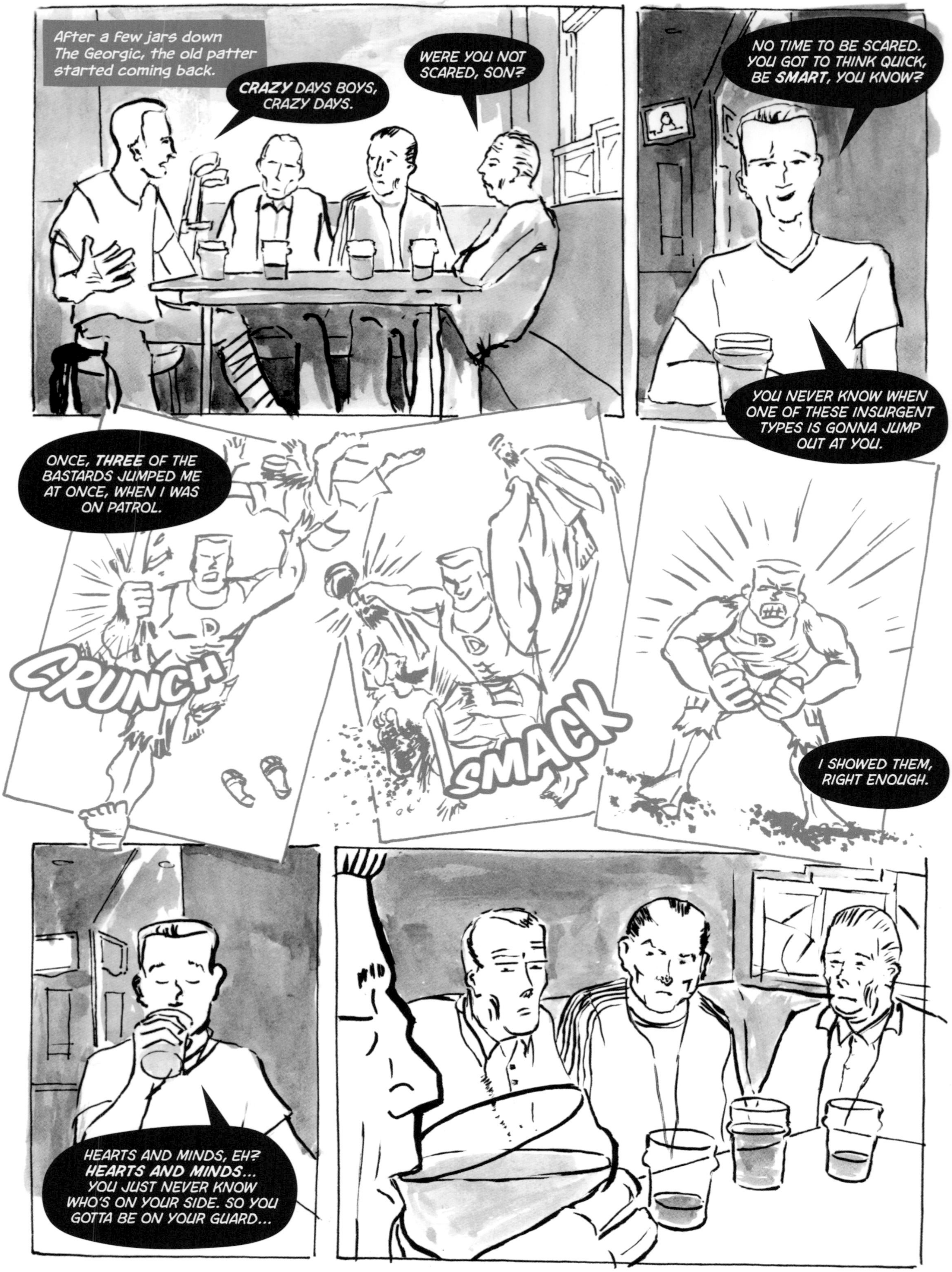
After a few jars down The Georgic, the old patter started coming back.
CRAZY DAYS BOYS, CRAZY DAYS.
WERE YOU NOT SCARED, SON?
NO TIME TO BE SCARED. YOU GOT TO THINK QUICK, BE SMART, YOU KNOW?
YOU NEVER KNOW WHEN ONE OF THESE INSURGENT TYPES IS GONNA JUMP OUT AT YOU.
ONCE, THREE OF THE BASTARDS JUMPED ME AT ONCE, WHEN I WAS ON PATROL.
CRUNCH
SMACK
I SHOWED THEM, RIGHT ENOUGH.
HEARTS AND MINDS, EH? HEARTS AND MINDS... YOU JUST NEVER KNOW WHO'S ON YOUR SIDE. SO YOU GOTTA BE ON YOUR GUARD...

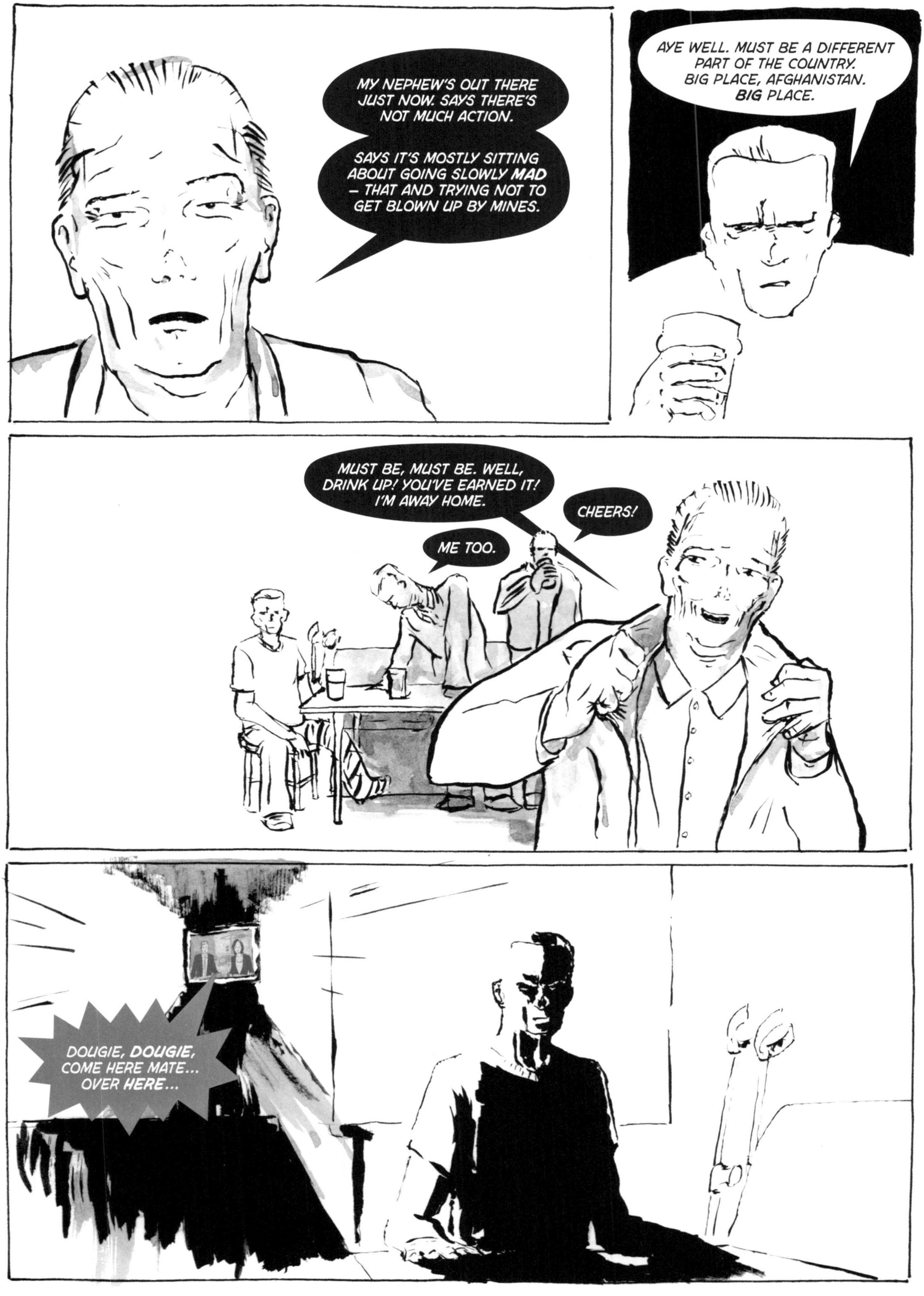
MY NEPHEW'S OUT THERE JUST NOW. SAYS THERE'S NOT MUCH ACTION.
SAYS IT'S MOSTLY SITTING ABOUT GOING SLOWLY MAD – THAT AND TRYING NOT TO GET BLOWN UP BY MINES.
AYE WELL. MUST BE A DIFFERENT PART OF THE COUNTRY. BIG PLACE, AFGHANISTAN. BIG PLACE.
MUST BE, MUST BE. WELL, DRINK UP! YOU'VE EARNED IT! I'M AWAY HOME.
CHEERS!
ME TOO.
DOUGIE, DOUGIE, COME HERE MATE... OVER HERE...

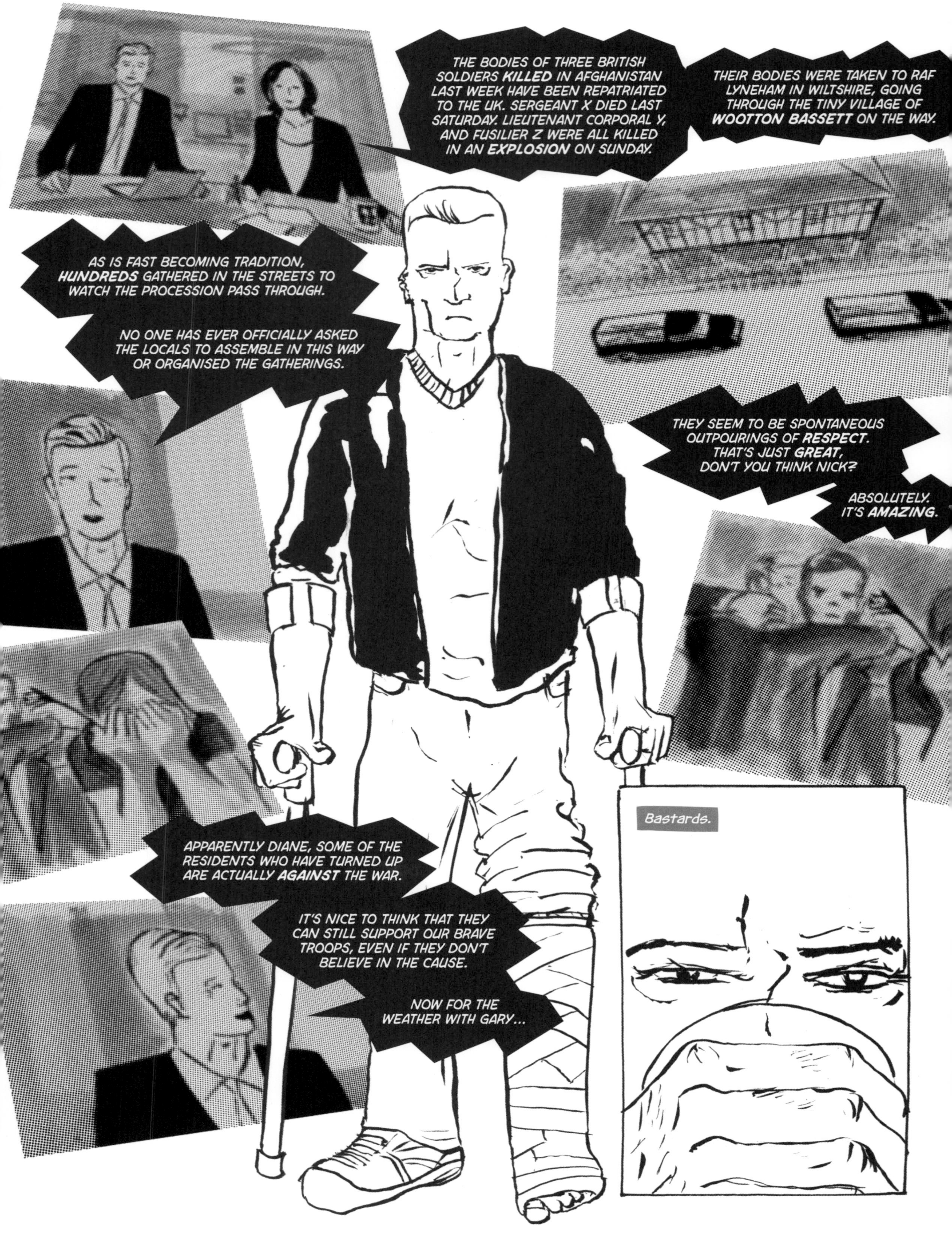
THE BODIES OF THREE BRITISH SOLDIERS **KILLED** IN AFGHANISTAN LAST WEEK HAVE BEEN REPATRIATED TO THE UK. SERGEANT X DIED LAST SATURDAY. LIEUTENANT CORPORAL Y, AND FUSILIER Z WERE ALL KILLED IN AN **EXPLOSION** ON SUNDAY.
THEIR BODIES WERE TAKEN TO RAF LYNEHAM IN WILTSHIRE, GOING THROUGH THE TINY VILLAGE OF **WOOTTON BASSETT** ON THE WAY.
AS IS FAST BECOMING TRADITION, **HUNDREDS** GATHERED IN THE STREETS TO WATCH THE PROCESSION PASS THROUGH.
NO ONE HAS EVER OFFICIALLY ASKED THE LOCALS TO ASSEMBLE IN THIS WAY OR ORGANISED THE GATHERINGS.
THEY SEEM TO BE SPONTANEOUS OUTPOURINGS OF **RESPECT**. THAT'S JUST **GREAT**, DON'T YOU THINK NICK?
ABSOLUTELY. IT'S **AMAZING**.
APPARENTLY DIANE, SOME OF THE RESIDENTS WHO HAVE TURNED UP ARE ACTUALLY **AGAINST** THE WAR.
IT'S NICE TO THINK THAT THEY CAN STILL SUPPORT OUR BRAVE TROOPS, EVEN IF THEY DON'T BELIEVE IN THE CAUSE.
NOW FOR THE WEATHER WITH GARY...
Bastards.

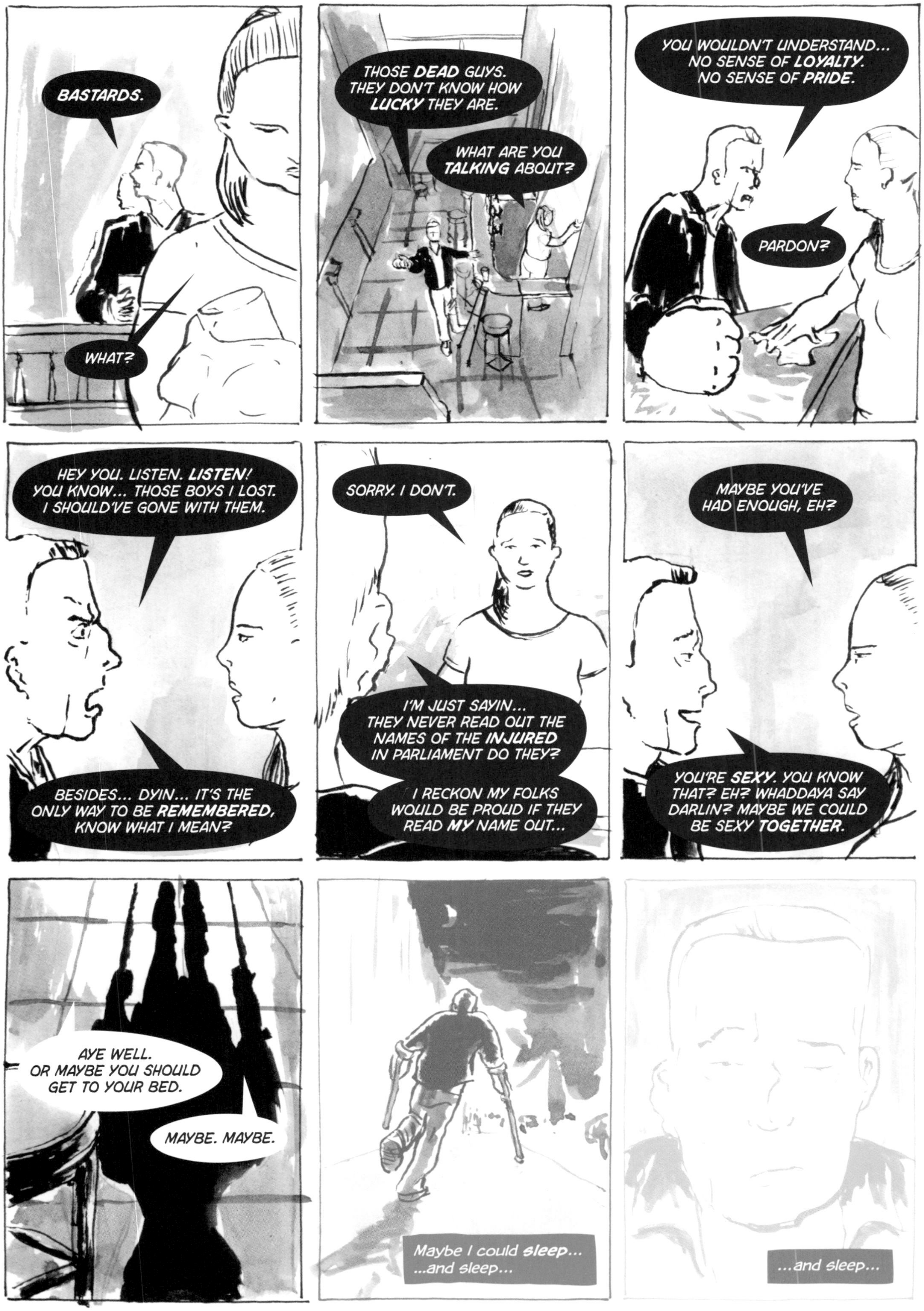
BASTARDS.
WHAT?
THOSE DEAD GUYS. THEY DON'T KNOW HOW LUCKY THEY ARE.
WHAT ARE YOU TALKING ABOUT?
YOU WOULDN'T UNDERSTAND... NO SENSE OF LOYALTY. NO SENSE OF PRIDE.
PARDON?
HEY YOU. LISTEN. LISTEN! YOU KNOW... THOSE BOYS I LOST. I SHOULD'VE GONE WITH THEM.
BESIDES... DYIN... IT'S THE ONLY WAY TO BE REMEMBERED, KNOW WHAT I MEAN?
SORRY. I DON'T.
I'M JUST SAYIN... THEY NEVER READ OUT THE NAMES OF THE INJURED IN PARLIAMENT DO THEY?
I RECKON MY FOLKS WOULD BE PROUD IF THEY READ MY NAME OUT...
MAYBE YOU'VE HAD ENOUGH, EH?
YOU'RE SEXY. YOU KNOW THAT? EH? WHADDAYA SAY DARLIN? MAYBE WE COULD BE SEXY TOGETHER.
AYE WELL. OR MAYBE YOU SHOULD GET TO YOUR BED.
MAYBE. MAYBE.
Maybe I could sleep...
...and sleep...
...and sleep...

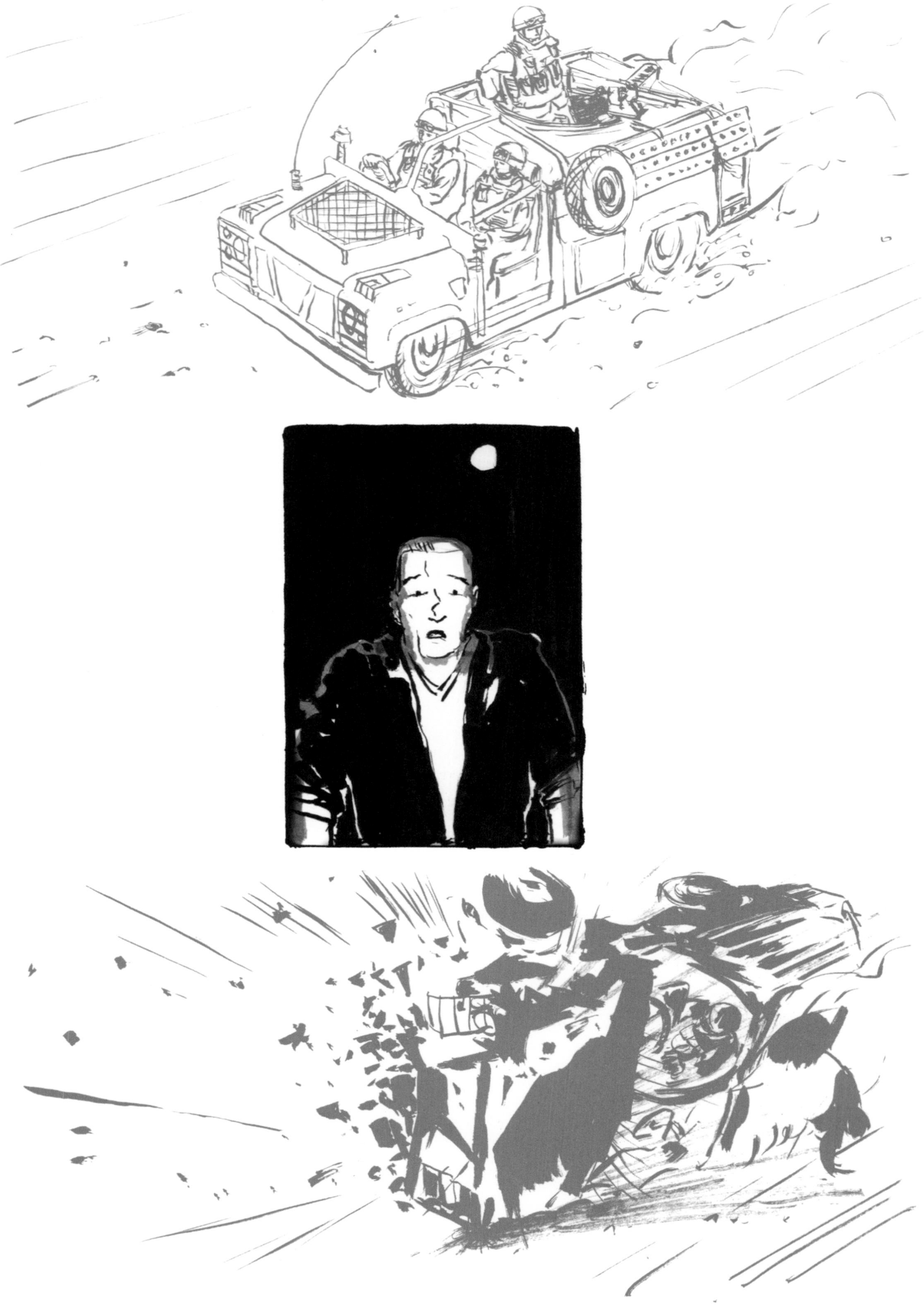

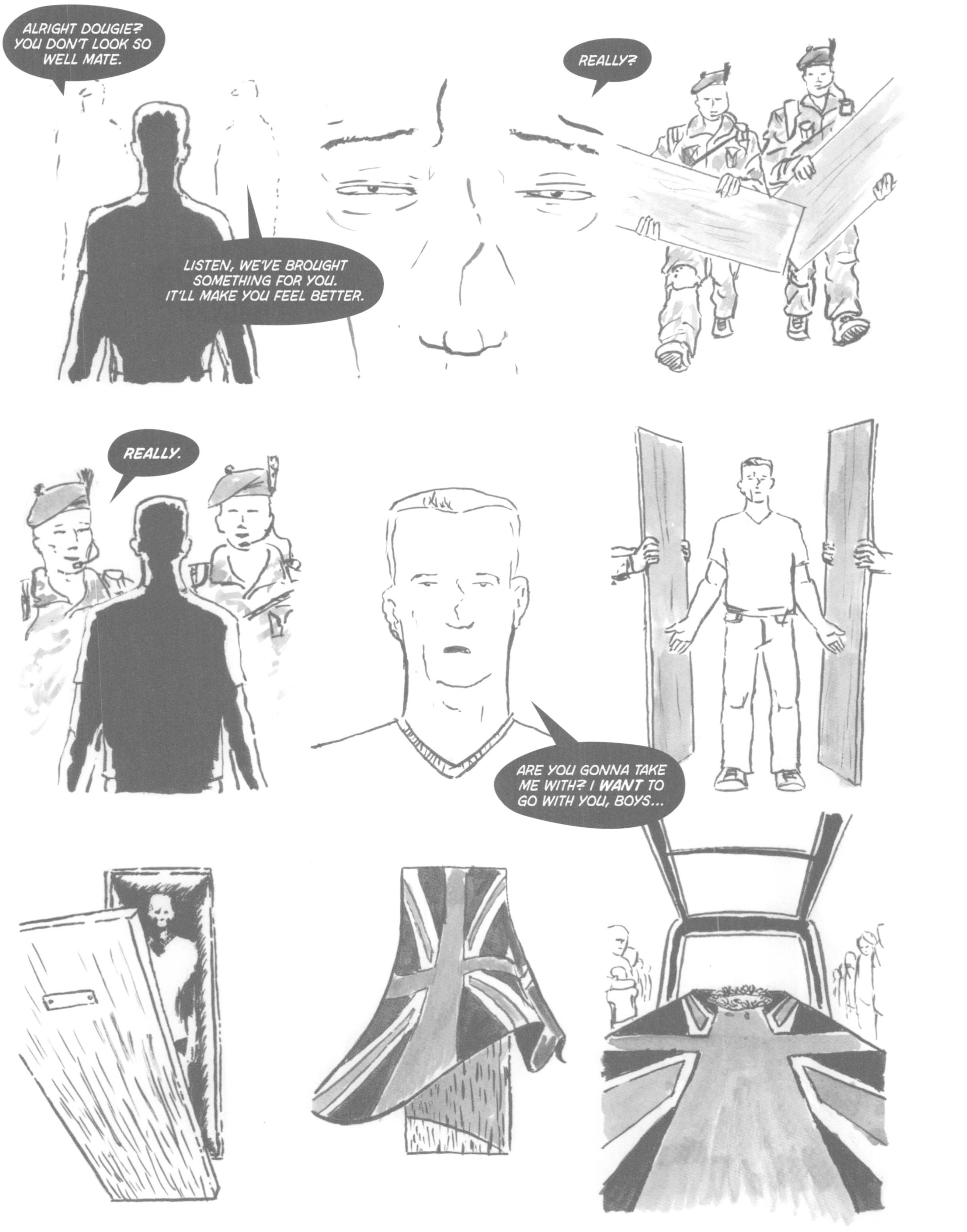
ALRIGHT DOUGIE? YOU DON'T LOOK SO WELL MATE.
LISTEN, WE'VE BROUGHT SOMETHING FOR YOU. IT'LL MAKE YOU FEEL BETTER.
REALLY?
REALLY.
ARE YOU GONNA TAKE ME WITH? I **WANT** TO GO WITH YOU, BOYS...

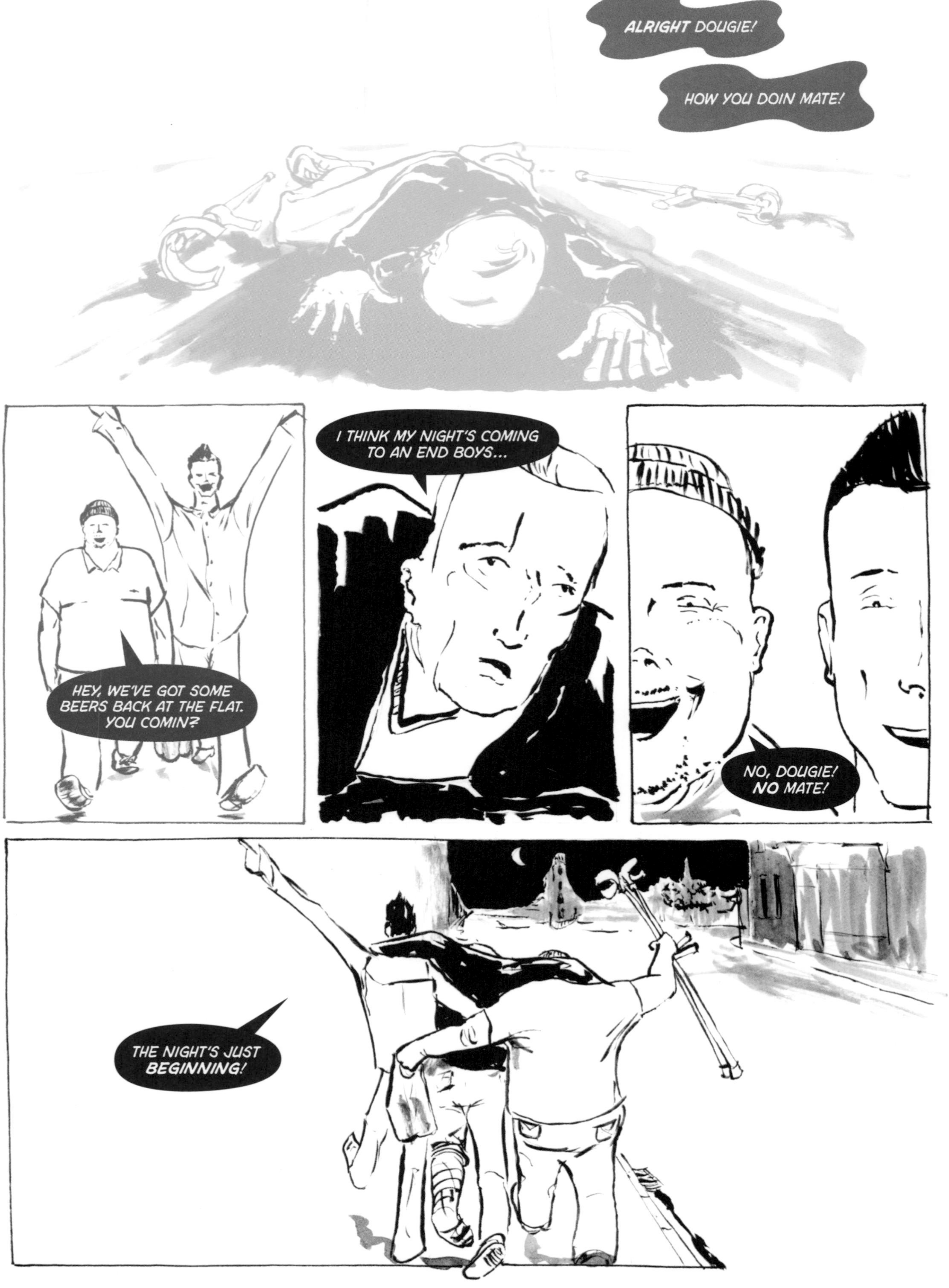
ALRIGHT DOUGIE!
HOW YOU DOIN MATE!
HEY, WE'VE GOT SOME BEERS BACK AT THE FLAT. YOU COMIN?
I THINK MY NIGHT'S COMING TO AN END BOYS...
NO, DOUGIE! NO MATE!
THE NIGHT'S JUST BEGINNING!

# EPISODE THREE

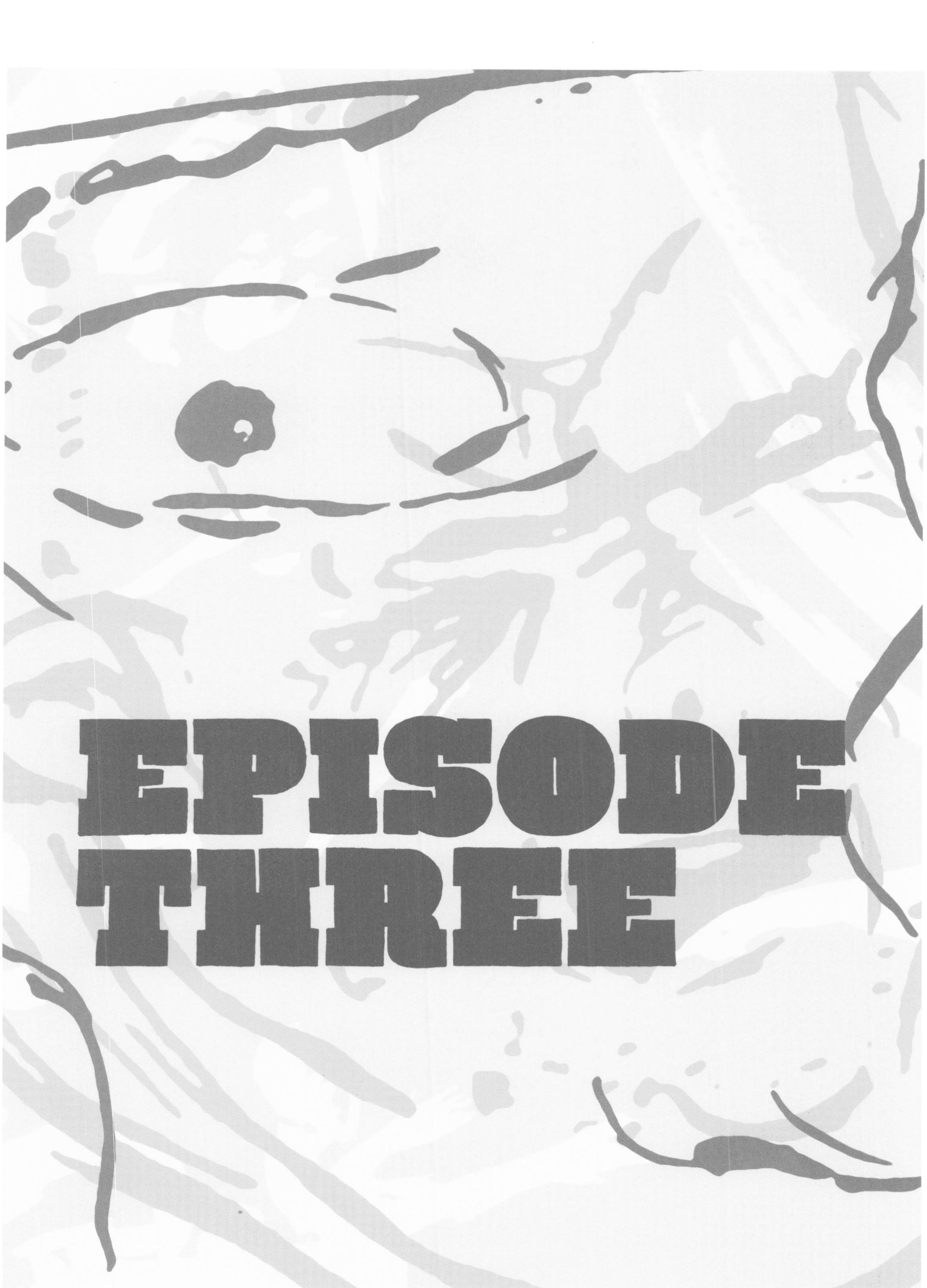

And that night was one of plenty.

Same deal, again and again. Staggering back home early doors...

...avoiding bad shit...

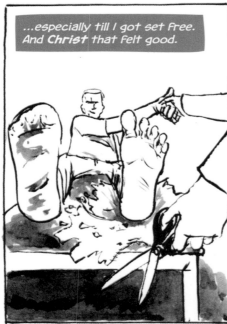

...especially till I got set free. And **Christ** that felt good.

But nothing much else did.

And I was never just left in peace.

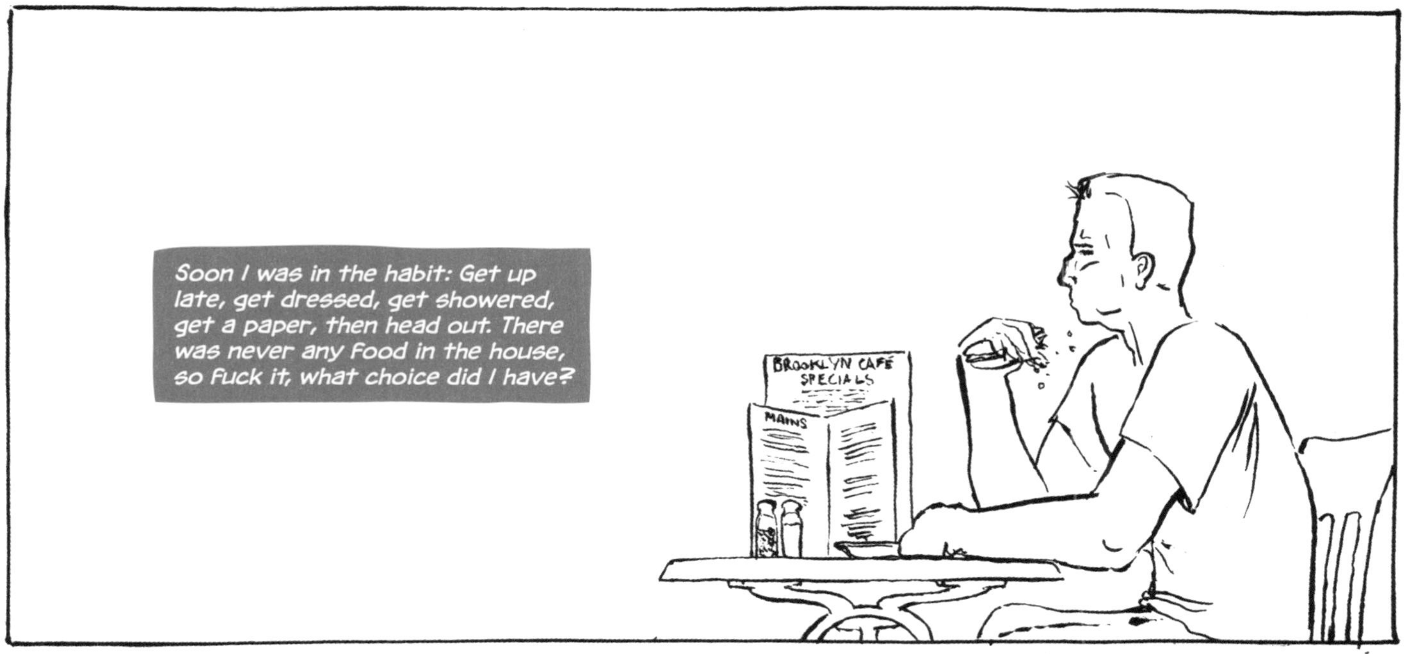
Soon I was in the habit: Get up late, get dressed, get showered, get a paper, then head out. There was never any food in the house, so fuck it, what choice did I have?
BROOKLYN CAFÉ SPECIALS
MAINS

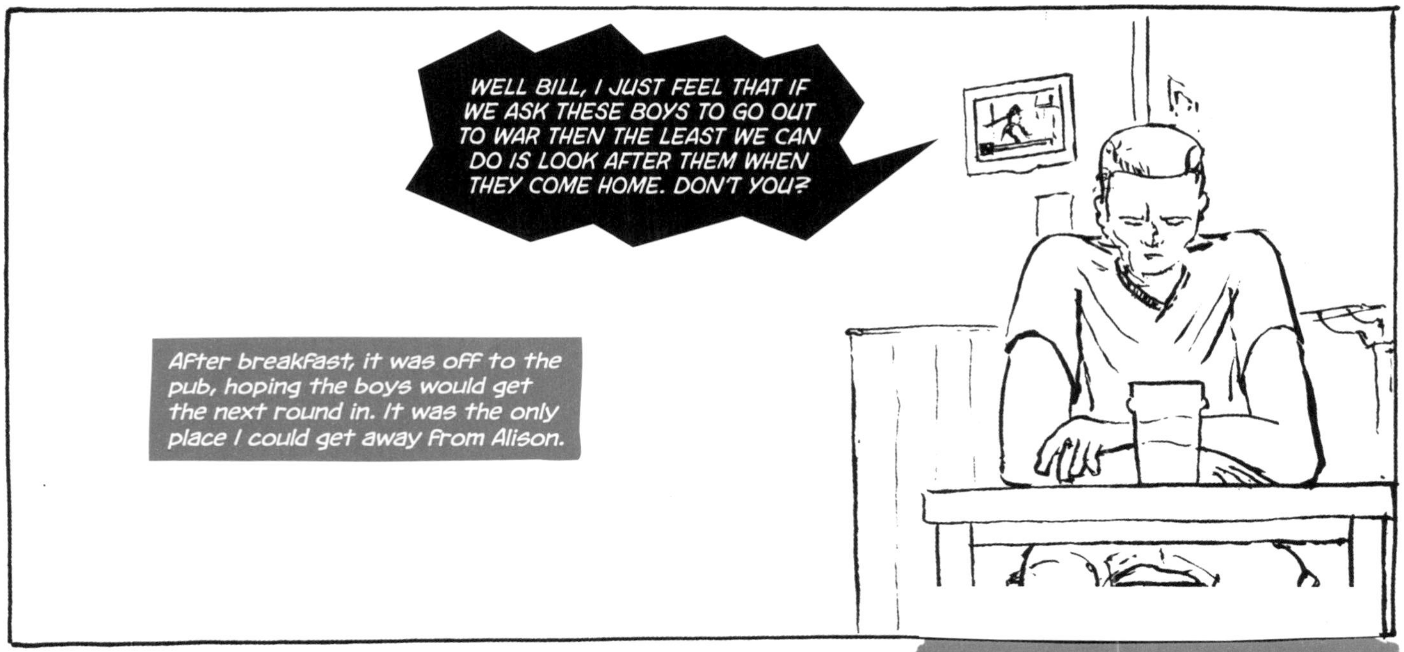
WELL BILL, I JUST FEEL THAT IF WE ASK THESE BOYS TO GO OUT TO WAR THEN THE LEAST WE CAN DO IS LOOK AFTER THEM WHEN THEY COME HOME. DON'T YOU?
After breakfast, it was off to the pub, hoping the boys would get the next round in. It was the only place I could get away from Alison.

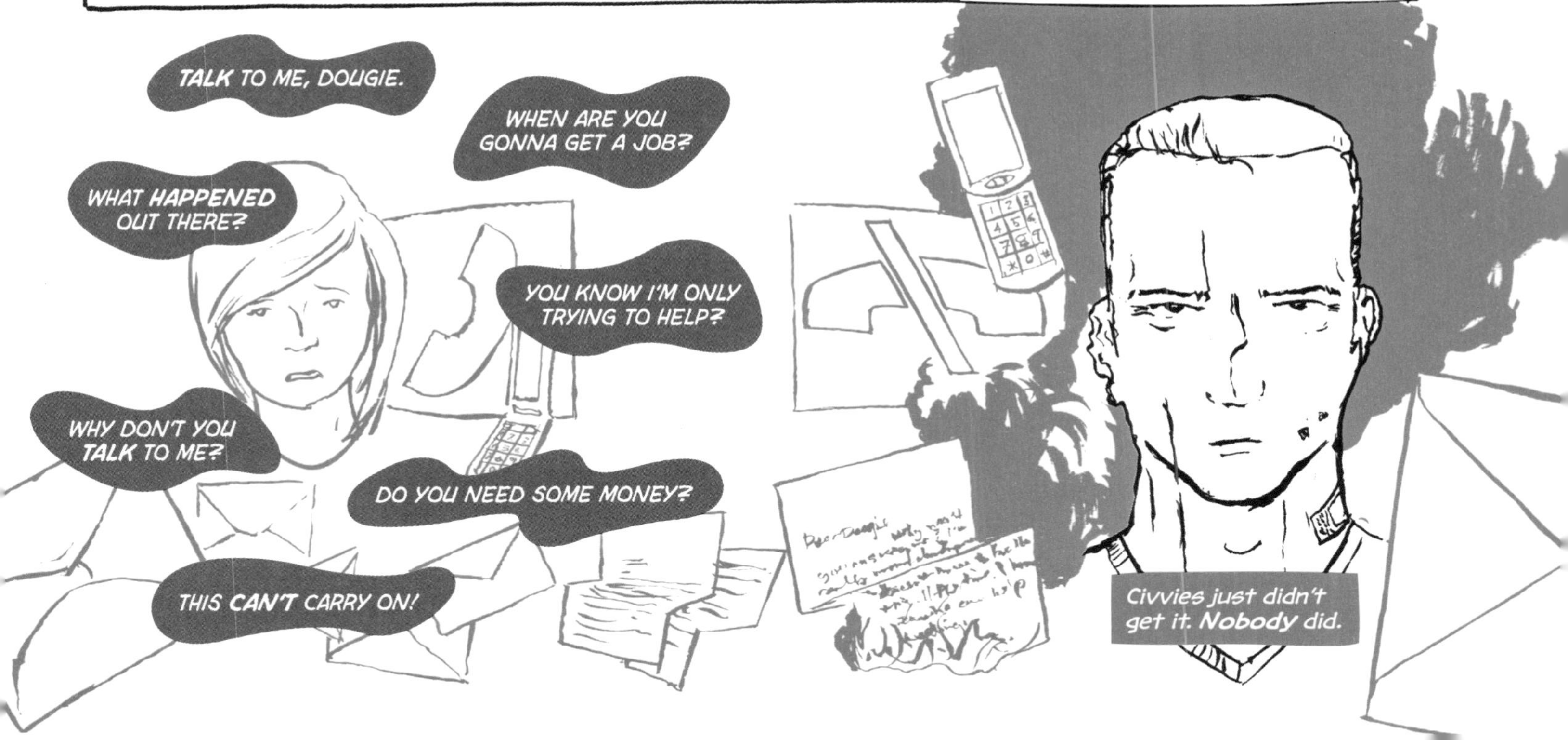
TALK TO ME, DOUGIE.
WHEN ARE YOU GONNA GET A JOB?
WHAT HAPPENED OUT THERE?
YOU KNOW I'M ONLY TRYING TO HELP?
WHY DON'T YOU TALK TO ME?
DO YOU NEED SOME MONEY?
THIS CAN'T CARRY ON!
Civvies just didn't get it. Nobody did.

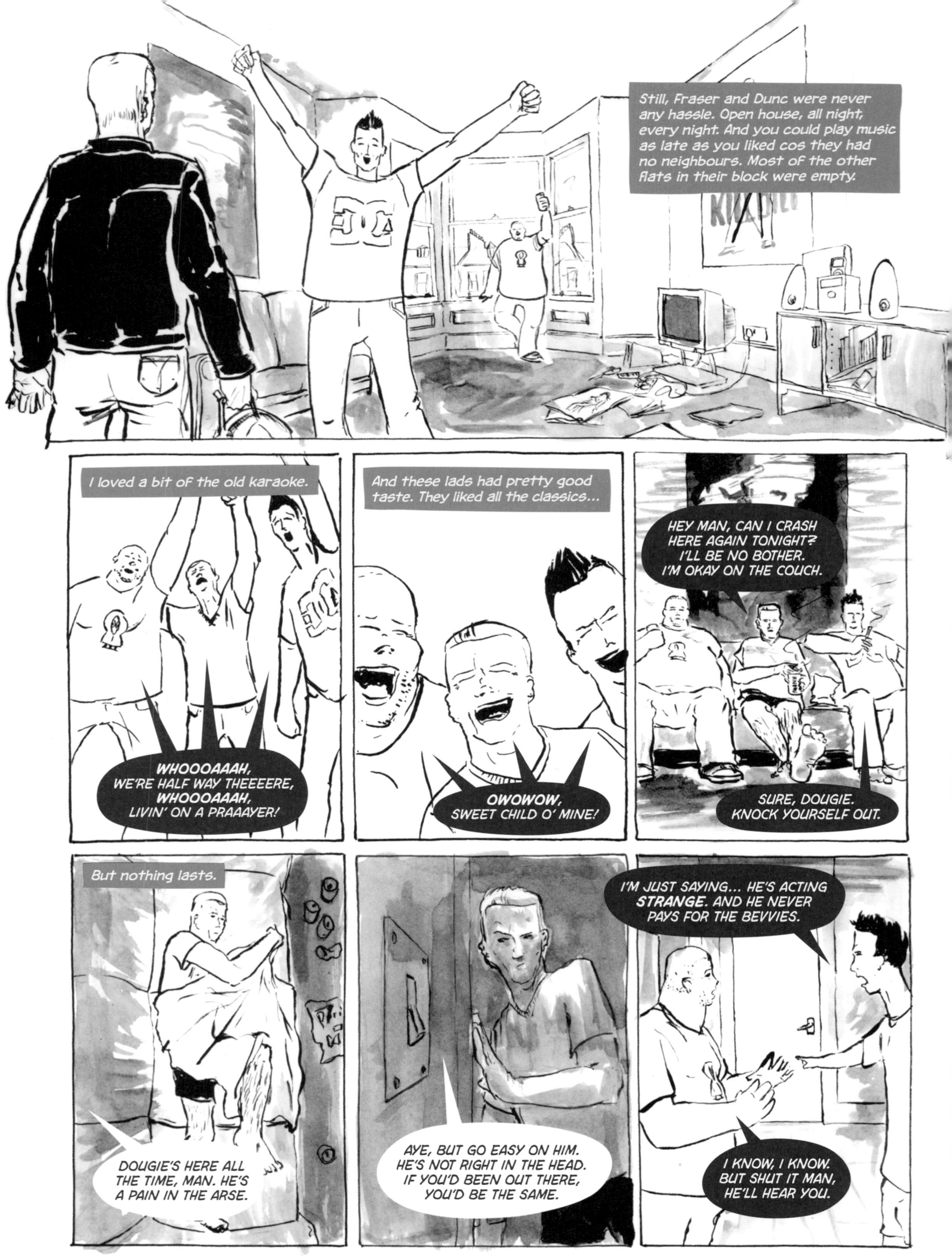
Still, Fraser and Dunc were never any hassle. Open house, all night, every night. And you could play music as late as you liked cos they had no neighbours. Most of the other flats in their block were empty.
I loved a bit of the old karaoke.
WHOOOAAAH, WE'RE HALF WAY THEEEERE, WHOOOAAAH, LIVIN' ON A PRAAAYER!
And these lads had pretty good taste. They liked all the classics...
OWOWOW, SWEET CHILD O' MINE!
HEY MAN, CAN I CRASH HERE AGAIN TONIGHT? I'LL BE NO BOTHER. I'M OKAY ON THE COUCH.
SURE, DOUGIE. KNOCK YOURSELF OUT.
But nothing lasts.
DOUGIE'S HERE ALL THE TIME, MAN. HE'S A PAIN IN THE ARSE.
AYE, BUT GO EASY ON HIM. HE'S NOT RIGHT IN THE HEAD. IF YOU'D BEEN OUT THERE, YOU'D BE THE SAME.
I'M JUST SAYING... HE'S ACTING STRANGE. AND HE NEVER PAYS FOR THE BEVVIES.
I KNOW, I KNOW. BUT SHUT IT MAN, HE'LL HEAR YOU.

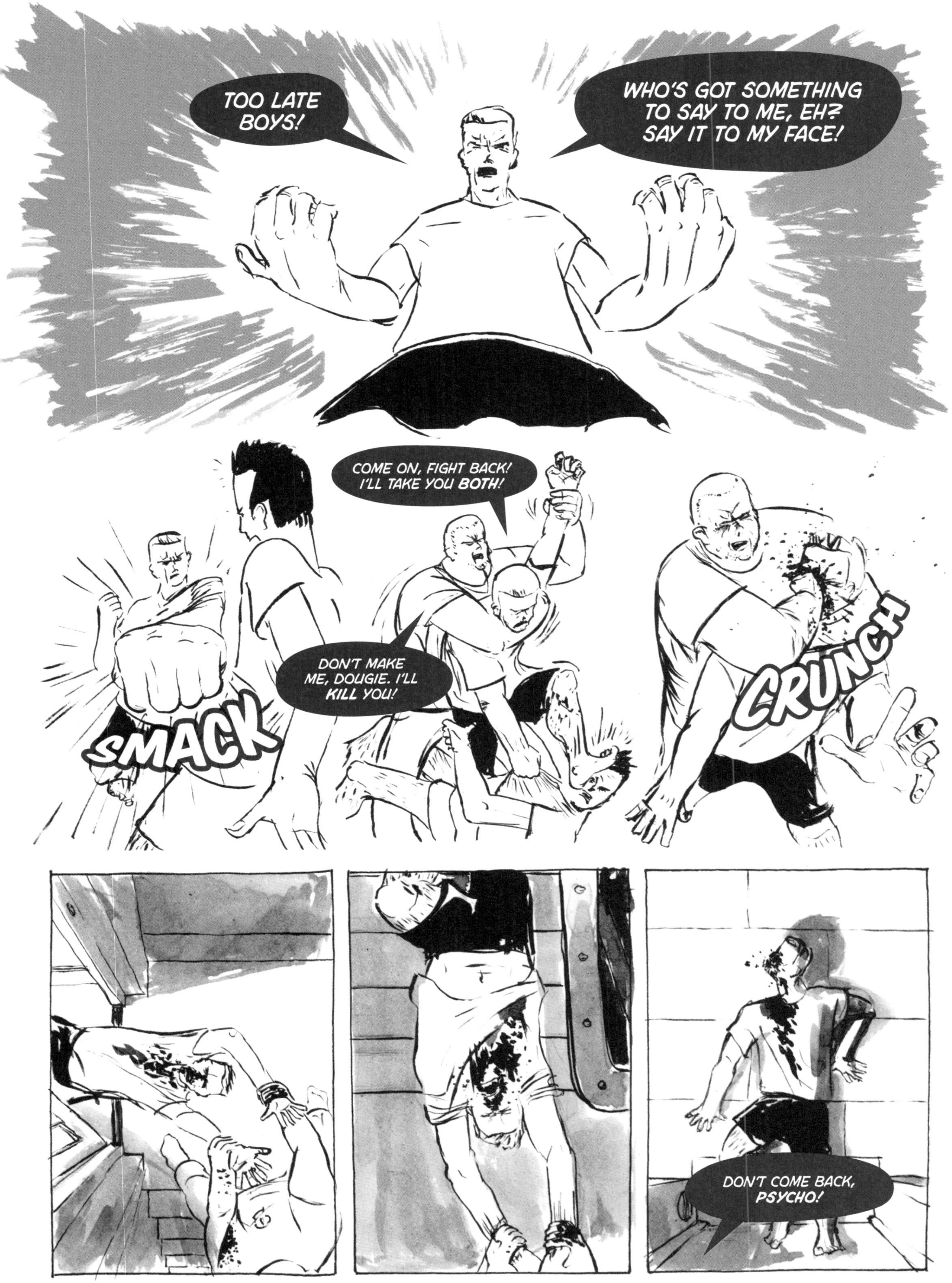
TOO LATE BOYS!
WHO'S GOT SOMETHING TO SAY TO ME, EH? SAY IT TO MY FACE!
SMACK
COME ON, FIGHT BACK! I'LL TAKE YOU BOTH!
DON'T MAKE ME, DOUGIE. I'LL KILL YOU!
CRUNCH
DON'T COME BACK, PSYCHO!

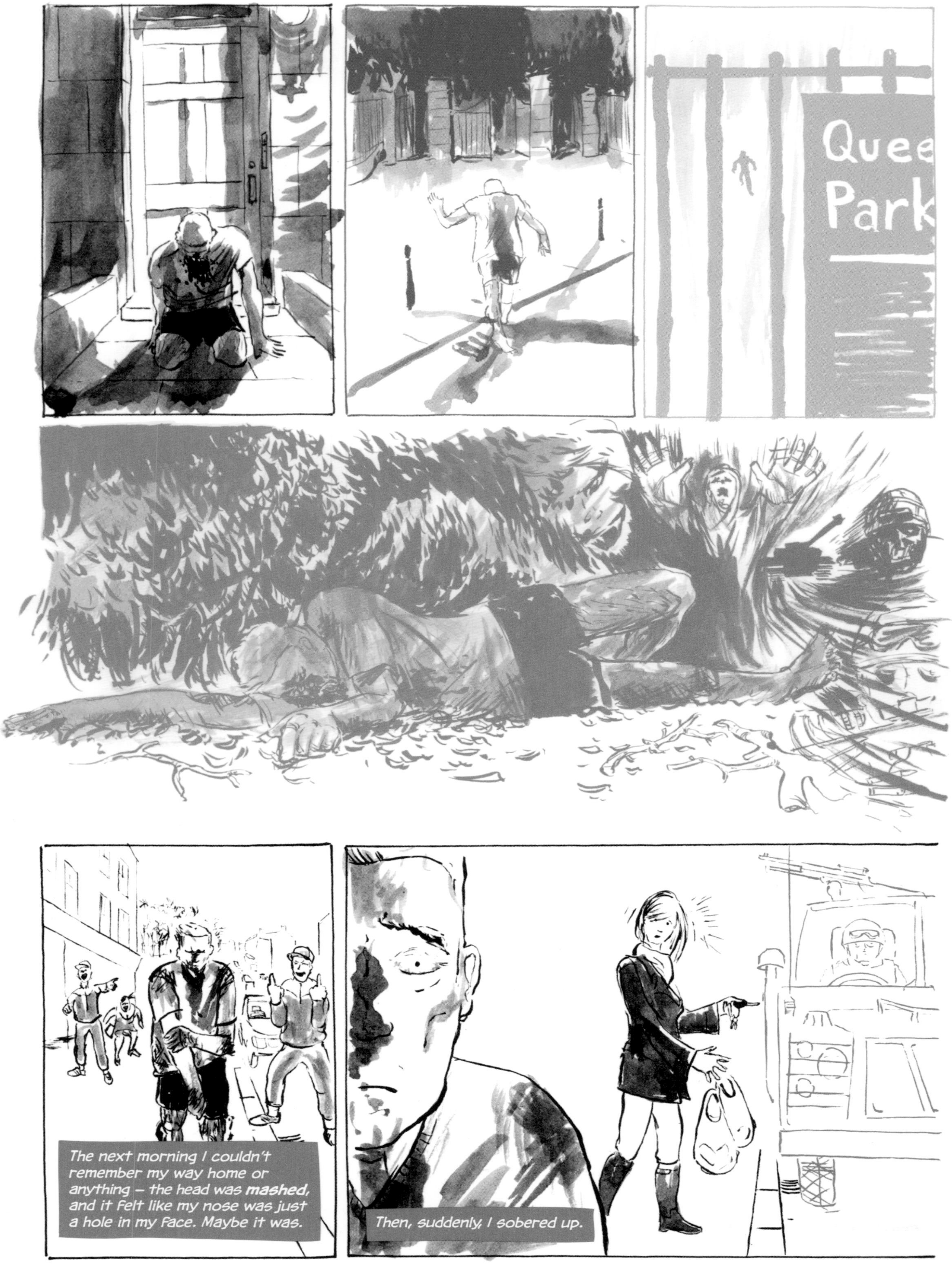

Quee
Park
The next morning I couldn't remember my way home or anything – the head was **mashed**, and it felt like my nose was just a hole in my face. Maybe it was.
Then, suddenly, I sobered up.

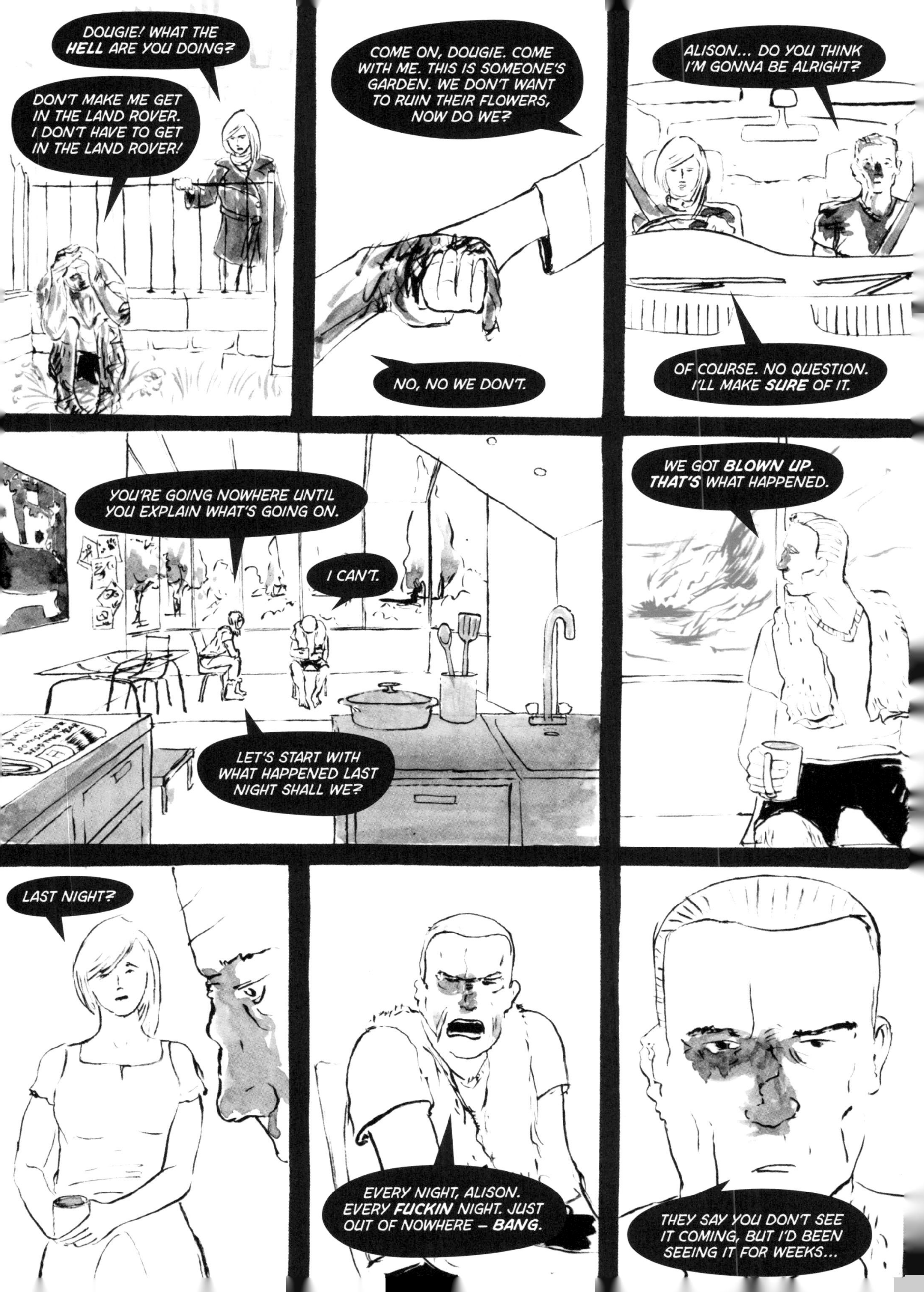

DOUGIE! WHAT THE HELL ARE YOU DOING?
DON'T MAKE ME GET IN THE LAND ROVER. I DON'T HAVE TO GET IN THE LAND ROVER!
COME ON, DOUGIE. COME WITH ME. THIS IS SOMEONE'S GARDEN. WE DON'T WANT TO RUIN THEIR FLOWERS, NOW DO WE?
NO, NO WE DON'T.
ALISON... DO YOU THINK I'M GONNA BE ALRIGHT?
OF COURSE. NO QUESTION. I'LL MAKE SURE OF IT.
YOU'RE GOING NOWHERE UNTIL YOU EXPLAIN WHAT'S GOING ON.
I CAN'T.
LET'S START WITH WHAT HAPPENED LAST NIGHT SHALL WE?
WE GOT BLOWN UP. THAT'S WHAT HAPPENED.
LAST NIGHT?
EVERY NIGHT, ALISON. EVERY FUCKIN NIGHT. JUST OUT OF NOWHERE – BANG.
THEY SAY YOU DON'T SEE IT COMING, BUT I'D BEEN SEEING IT FOR WEEKS...

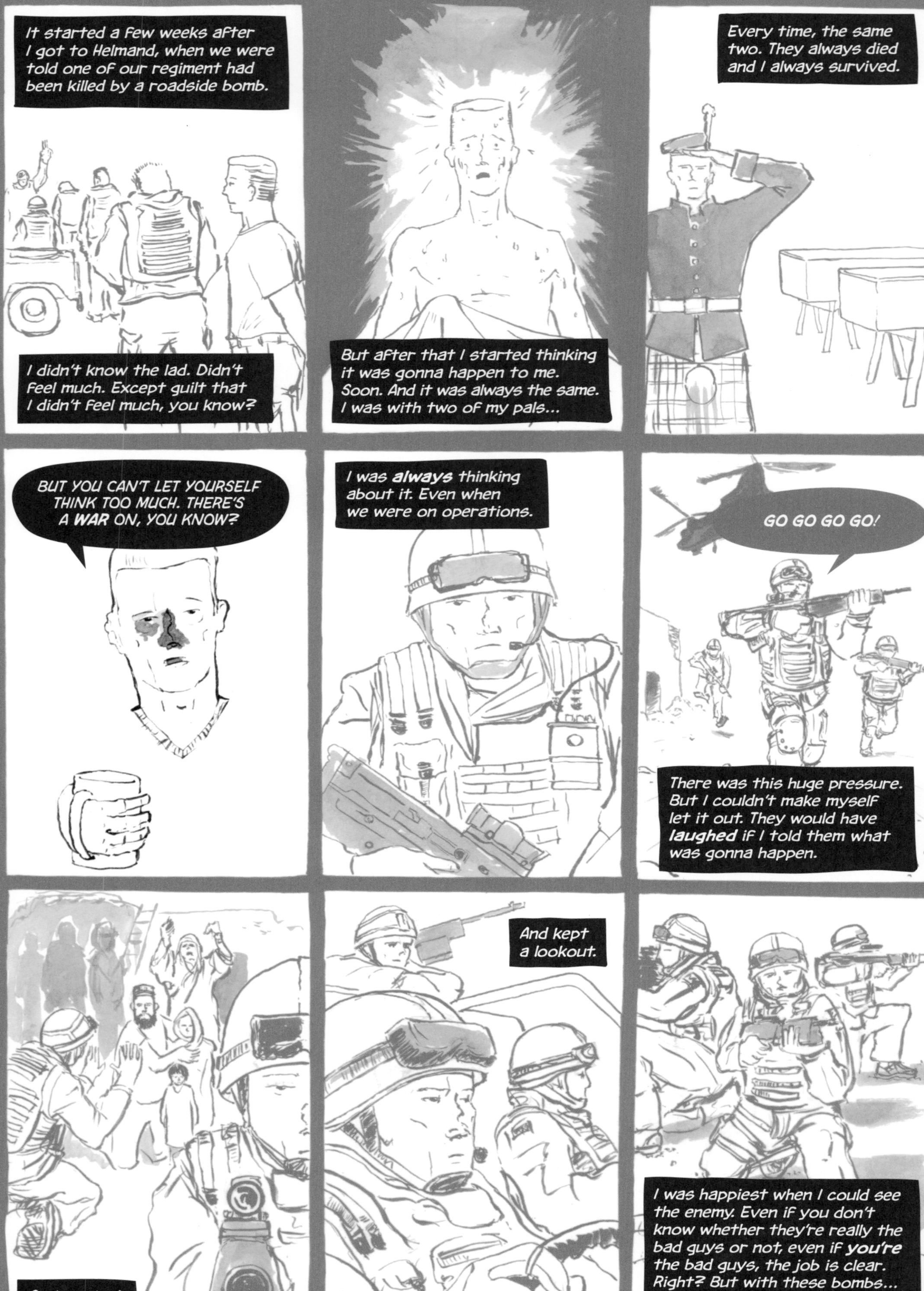

It started a few weeks after I got to Helmand, when we were told one of our regiment had been killed by a roadside bomb.
I didn't know the lad. Didn't feel much. Except guilt that I didn't feel much, you know?
But after that I started thinking it was gonna happen to me. Soon. And it was always the same. I was with two of my pals...
Every time, the same two. They always died and I always survived.
BUT YOU CAN'T LET YOURSELF THINK TOO MUCH. THERE'S A **WAR** ON, YOU KNOW?
I was **always** thinking about it. Even when we were on operations.
GO GO GO GO!
There was this huge pressure. But I couldn't make myself let it out. They would have **laughed** if I told them what was gonna happen.
So I worked.
And kept a lookout.
I was happiest when I could see the enemy. Even if you don't know whether they're really the bad guys or not, even if **you're** the bad guys, the job is clear. Right? But with these bombs... they can hit anyone, anytime...

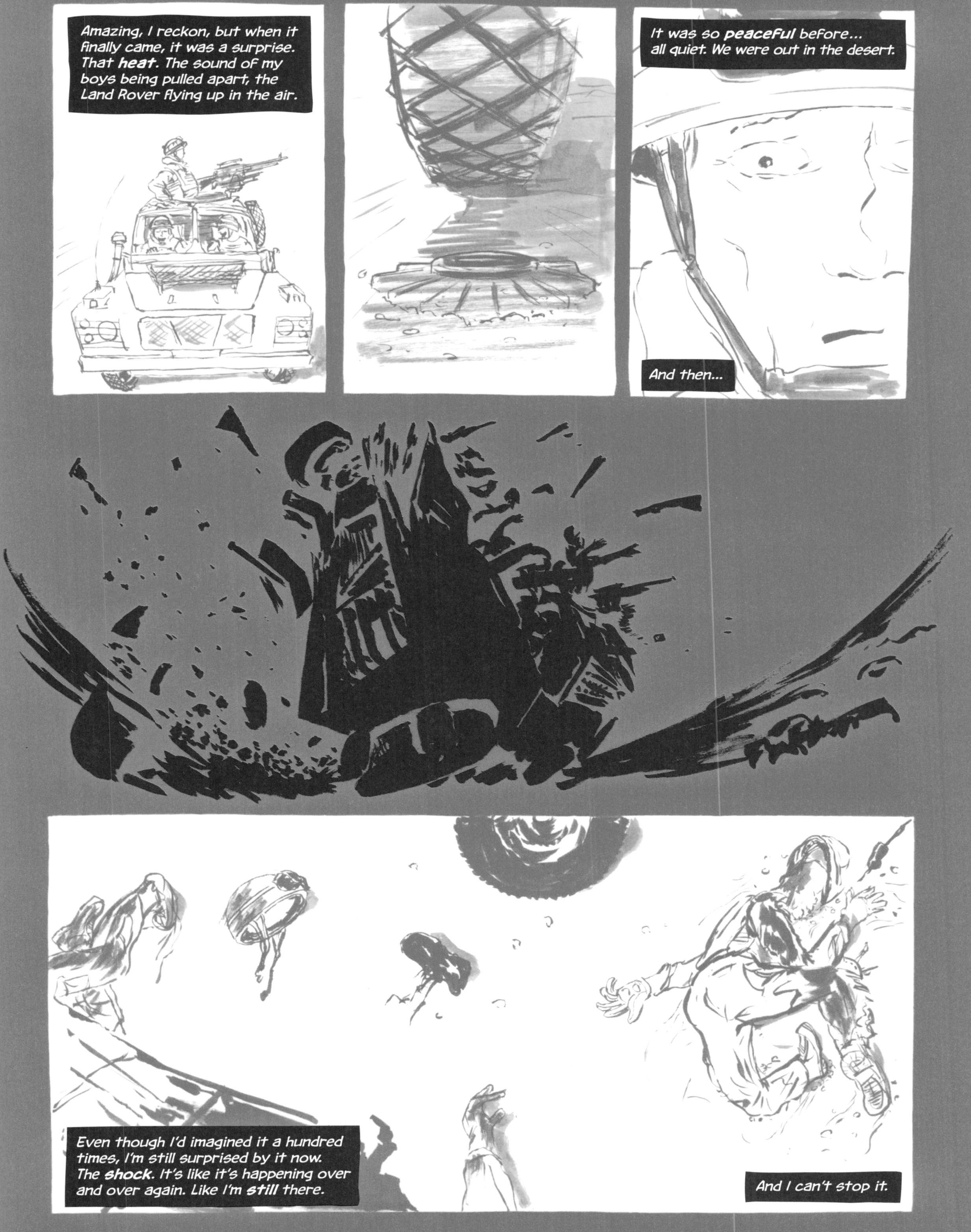
Amazing, I reckon, but when it finally came, it was a surprise. That **heat**. The sound of my boys being pulled apart, the Land Rover flying up in the air.
It was so **peaceful** before... all quiet. We were out in the desert.
And then...
Even though I'd imagined it a hundred times, I'm still surprised by it now. The **shock**. It's like it's happening over and over again. Like I'm **still** there.
And I can't stop it.

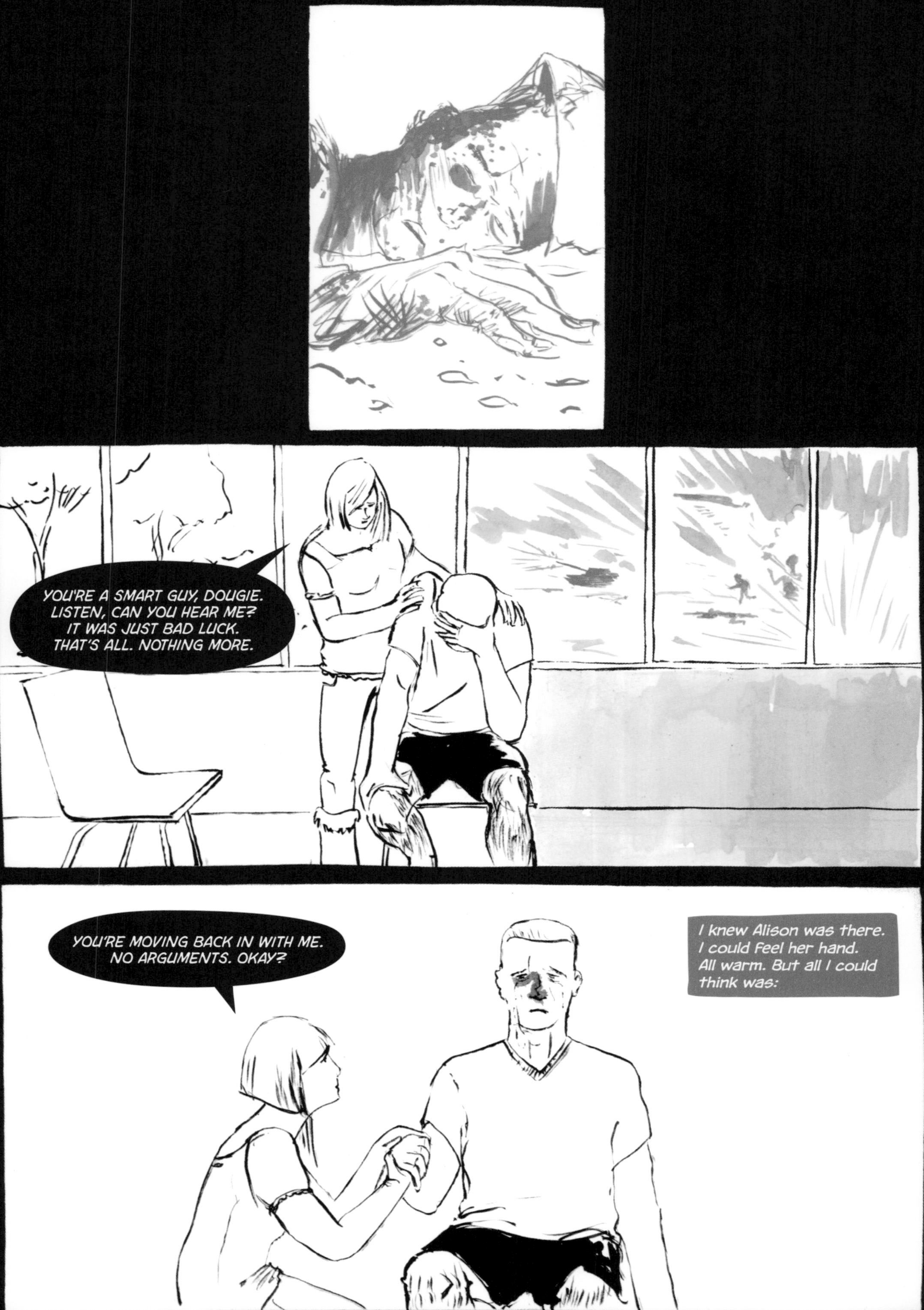
YOU'RE A SMART GUY, DOUGIE. LISTEN, CAN YOU HEAR ME? IT WAS JUST BAD LUCK. THAT'S ALL. NOTHING MORE.
YOU'RE MOVING BACK IN WITH ME. NO ARGUMENTS. OKAY?
I knew Alison was there. I could feel her hand. All warm. But all I could think was:

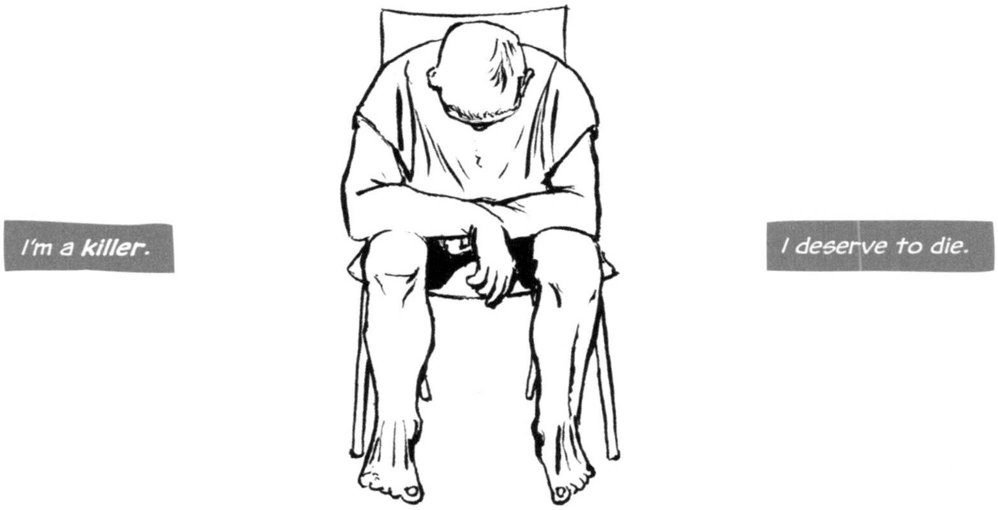
I'm a **killer**.
I deserve to die.

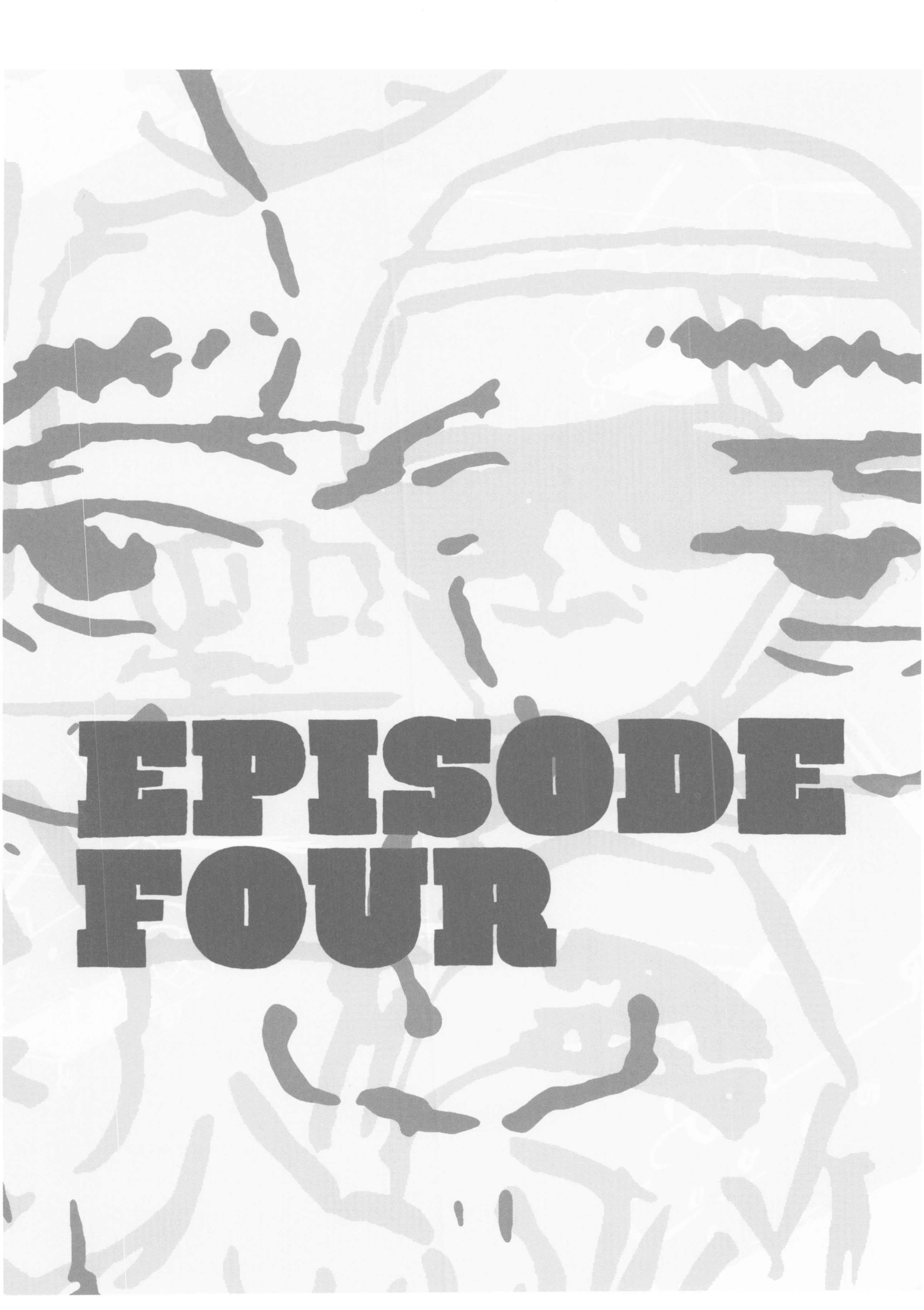

# EPISODE FOUR

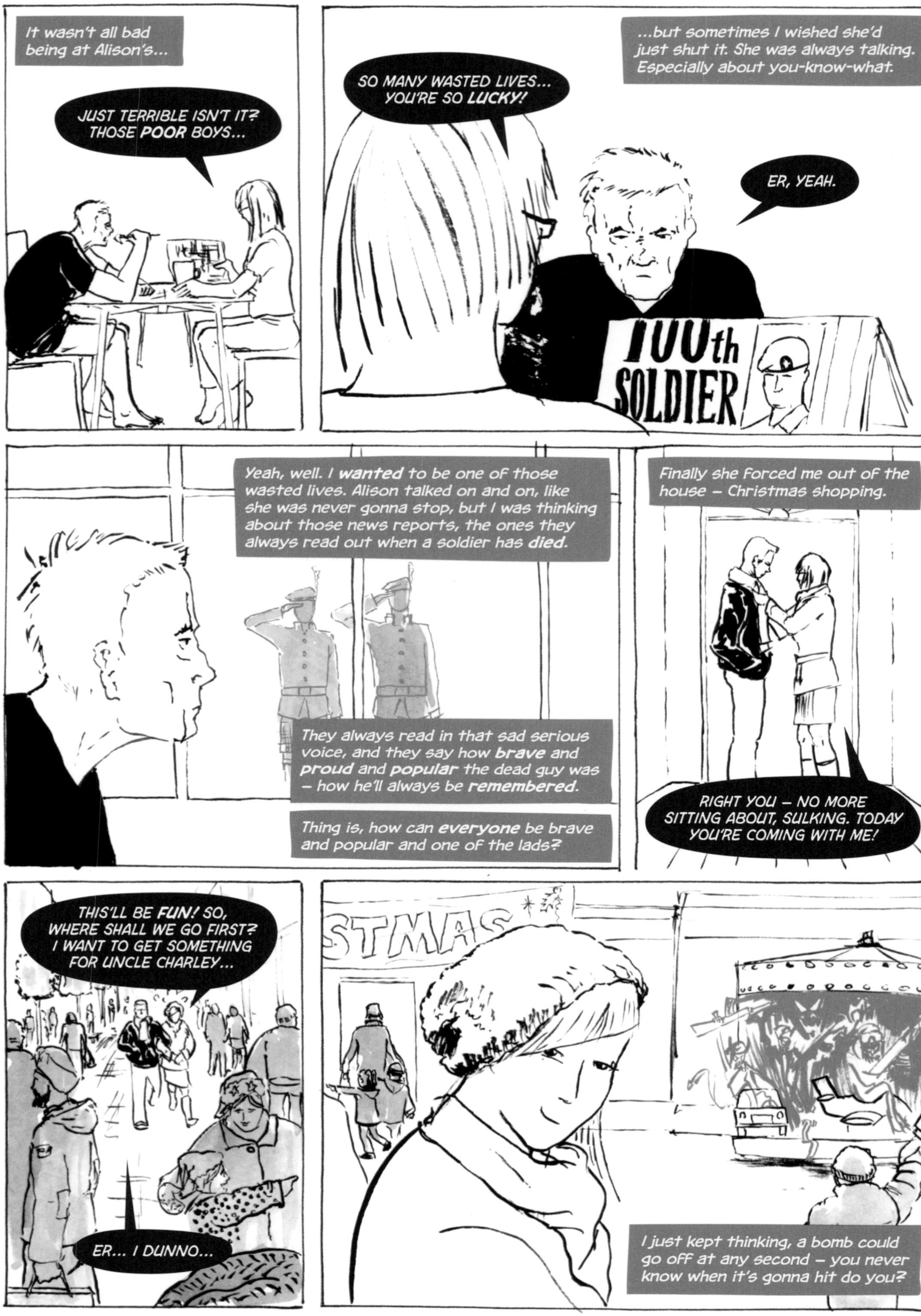
It wasn't all bad being at Alison's...
JUST TERRIBLE ISN'T IT? THOSE POOR BOYS...
...but sometimes I wished she'd just shut it. She was always talking. Especially about you-know-what.
SO MANY WASTED LIVES... YOU'RE SO LUCKY!
ER, YEAH.
100th SOLDIER
Yeah, well. I wanted to be one of those wasted lives. Alison talked on and on, like she was never gonna stop, but I was thinking about those news reports, the ones they always read out when a soldier has died.
They always read in that sad serious voice, and they say how brave and proud and popular the dead guy was – how he'll always be remembered.
Thing is, how can everyone be brave and popular and one of the lads?
Finally she forced me out of the house – Christmas shopping.
RIGHT YOU – NO MORE SITTING ABOUT, SULKING. TODAY YOU'RE COMING WITH ME!
THIS'LL BE FUN! SO, WHERE SHALL WE GO FIRST? I WANT TO GET SOMETHING FOR UNCLE CHARLEY...
ER... I DUNNO...
STMAS
I just kept thinking, a bomb could go off at any second – you never know when it's gonna hit do you?

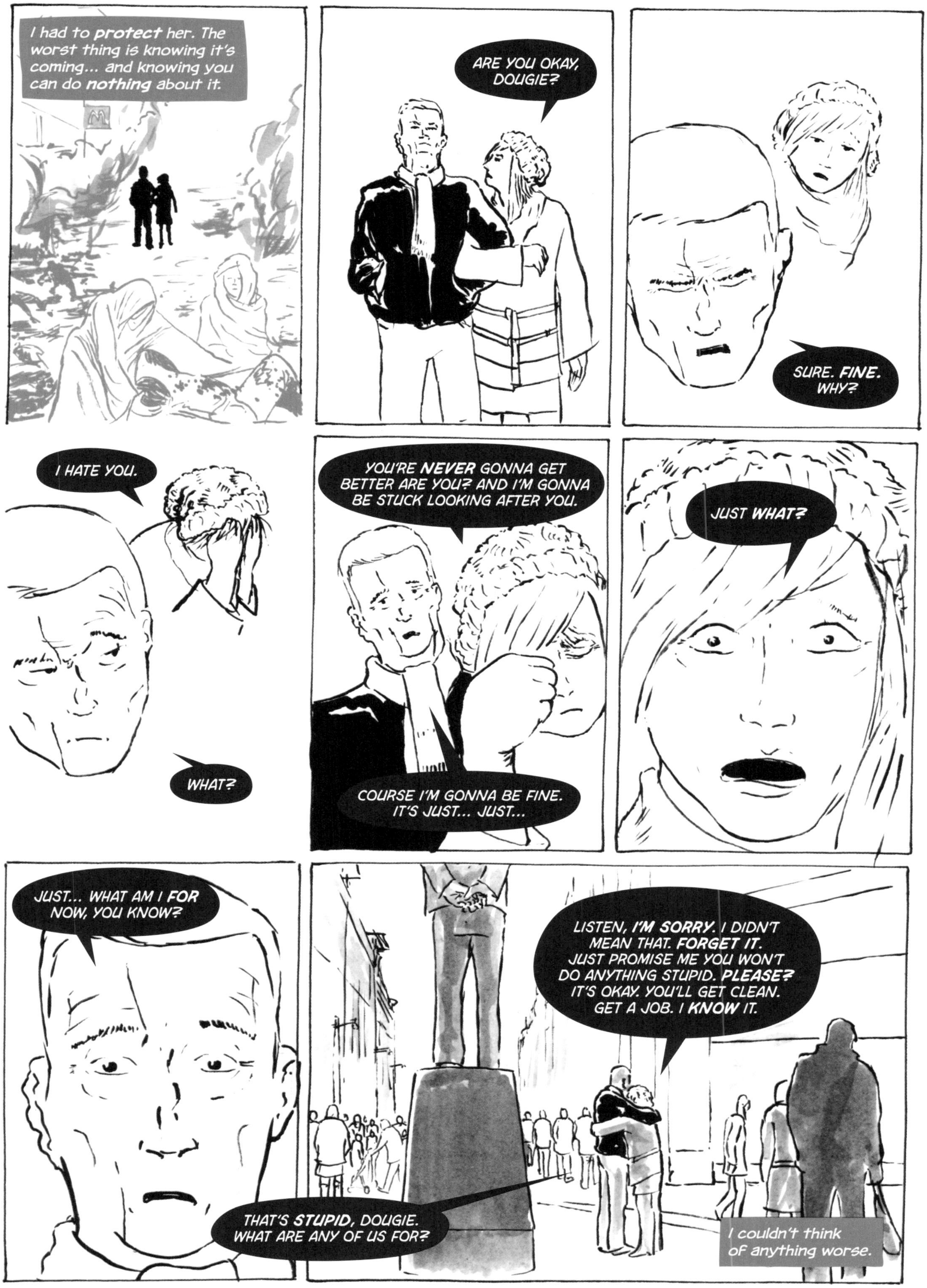
I had to **protect** her. The worst thing is knowing it's coming... and knowing you can do **nothing** about it.
ARE YOU OKAY, DOUGIE?
SURE. **FINE.** WHY?
I HATE YOU.
WHAT?
YOU'RE **NEVER** GONNA GET BETTER ARE YOU? AND I'M GONNA BE STUCK LOOKING AFTER YOU.
COURSE I'M GONNA BE FINE. IT'S JUST... JUST...
JUST **WHAT?**
JUST... WHAT AM I **FOR** NOW, YOU KNOW?
LISTEN, **I'M SORRY.** I DIDN'T MEAN THAT. **FORGET IT.** JUST PROMISE ME YOU WON'T DO ANYTHING STUPID. **PLEASE?** IT'S OKAY. YOU'LL GET CLEAN. GET A JOB. I **KNOW** IT.
THAT'S **STUPID,** DOUGIE. WHAT ARE ANY OF US FOR?
I couldn't think of anything worse.

OKAY, I PROMISE.

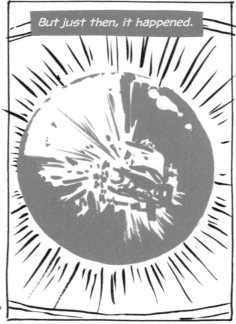

But just then, it happened.

AND TODAY'S HEADLINES:
THIS AFTERNOON DOUGIE CAMPBELL OF GLASGOW WAS GIVEN THE OPPORTUNITY TO START HIS LIFE OVER AGAIN, LEAVING ALCOHOL AND DESPAIR BEHIND AND BEGINNING A *BRIGHTER*, MORE *MEANINGFUL* LIFE.

I heard that *noise* again — I *know* I did.

And I smelt that smell. OF *bodies*, burning. OF *fear*.

At least, I think I did.

PROMISING HIS SISTER HE'D CHANGE HIS WAYS, DOUGIE TOOK UP THE CHALLENGE OF TURNING HIS LIFE AROUND. AND THEN HE *RAN AWAY*.

EX-SOLDIER EXPOSED AS COWARD

I just had to *get out*, you know?

DOUGIE! WHERE ARE YOU GOING? COME BACK!

DOUGIE!!!

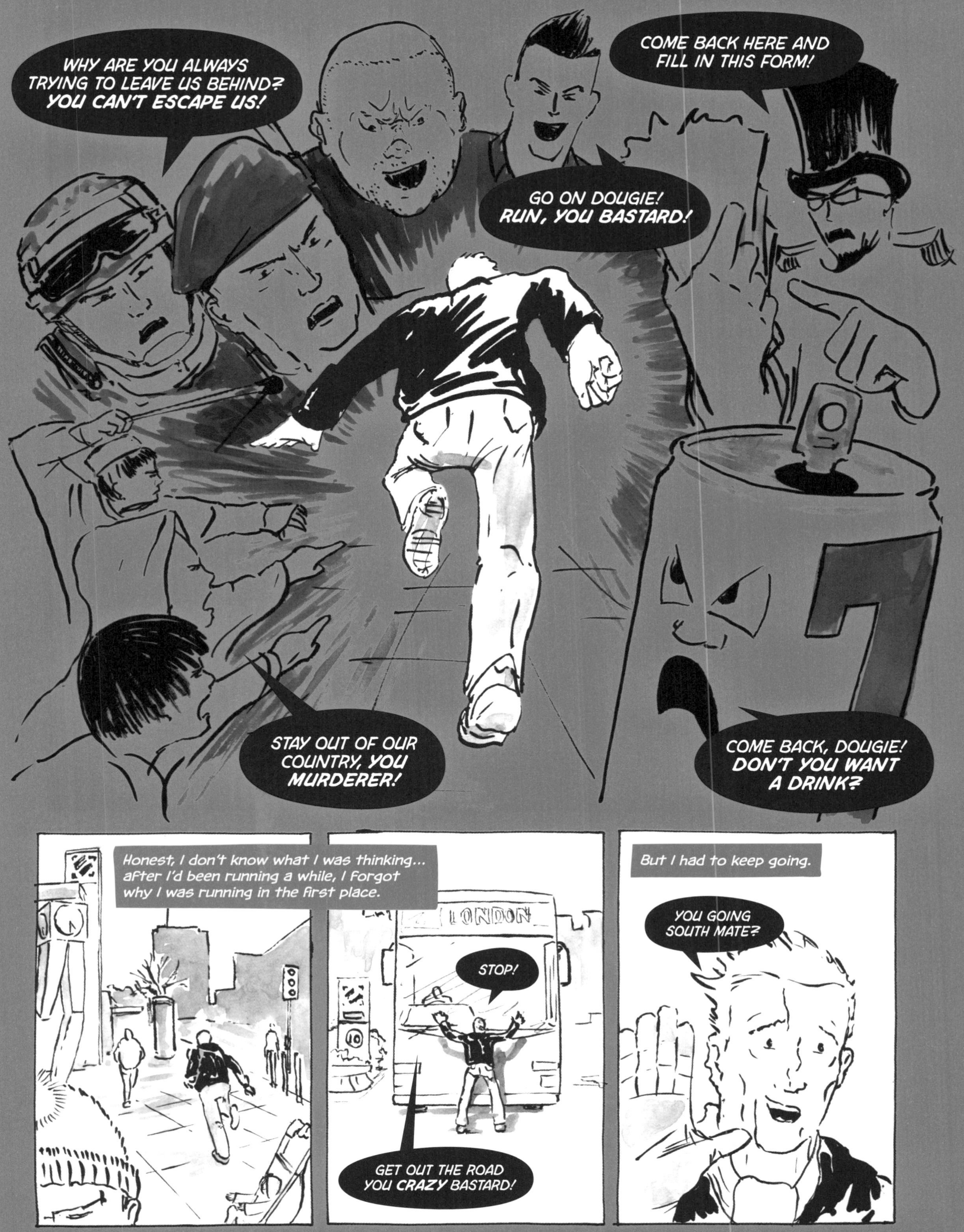
WHY ARE YOU ALWAYS TRYING TO LEAVE US BEHIND? YOU CAN'T ESCAPE US!
COME BACK HERE AND FILL IN THIS FORM!
GO ON DOUGIE! RUN, YOU BASTARD!
STAY OUT OF OUR COUNTRY, YOU MURDERER!
COME BACK, DOUGIE! DON'T YOU WANT A DRINK?
Honest, I don't know what I was thinking... after I'd been running a while, I forgot why I was running in the first place.
LONDON
STOP!
GET OUT THE ROAD YOU CRAZY BASTARD!
But I had to keep going.
YOU GOING SOUTH MATE?

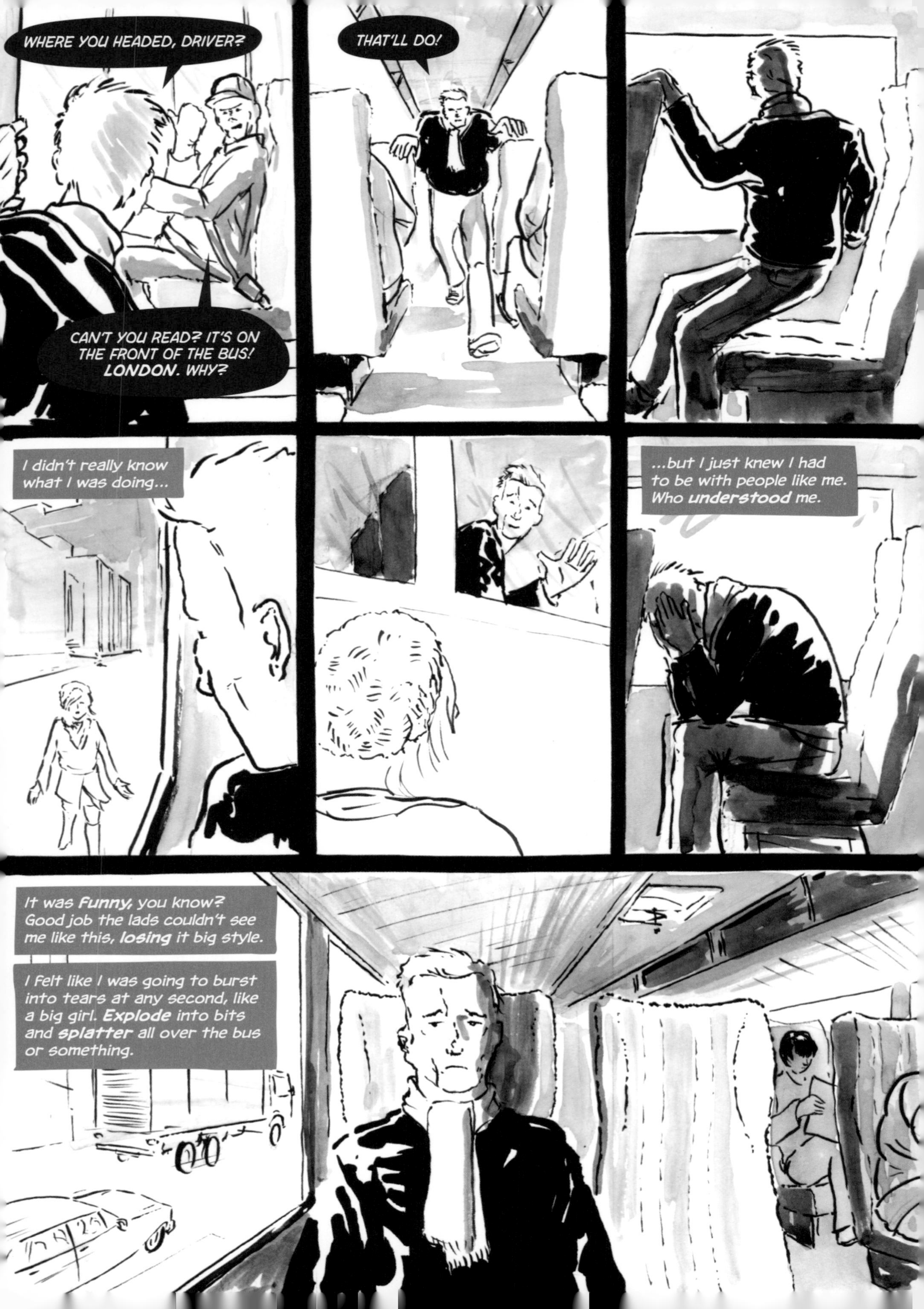
WHERE YOU HEADED, DRIVER?
CAN'T YOU READ? IT'S ON THE FRONT OF THE BUS! LONDON. WHY?
THAT'LL DO!
I didn't really know what I was doing...
...but I just knew I had to be with people like me. Who understood me.
It was funny, you know? Good job the lads couldn't see me like this, losing it big style.
I felt like I was going to burst into tears at any second, like a big girl. Explode into bits and splatter all over the bus or something.

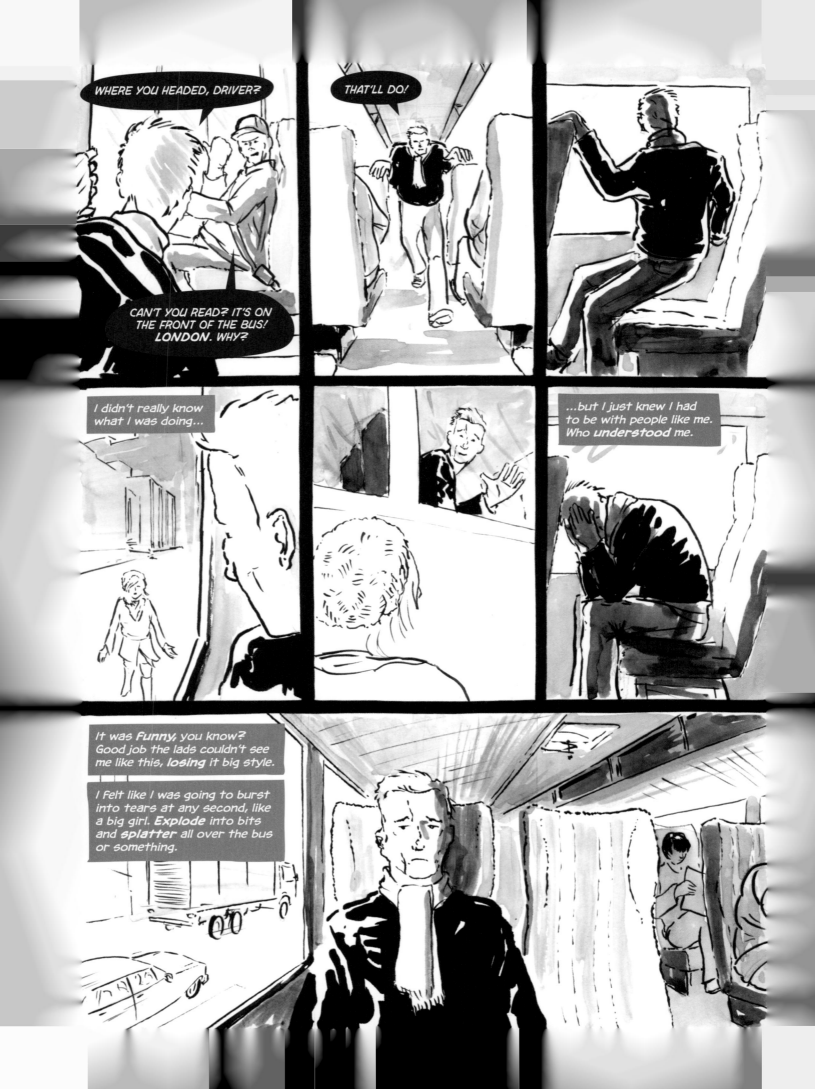

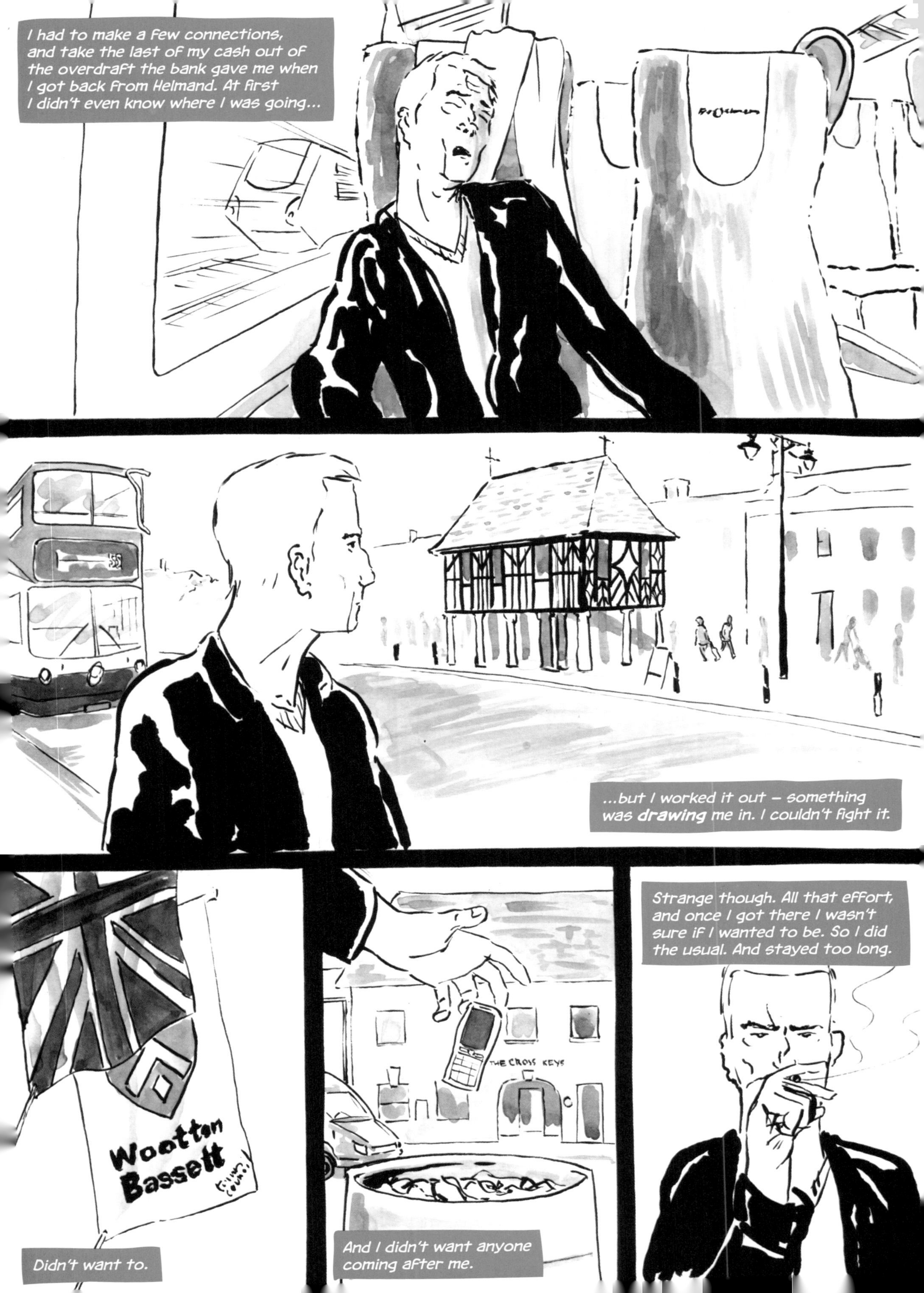
I had to make a few connections, and take the last of my cash out of the overdraft the bank gave me when I got back from Helmand. At first I didn't even know where I was going...
...but I worked it out – something was **drawing** me in. I couldn't fight it.
Wootton Bassett
Didn't want to.
THE CROSS KEYS
And I didn't want anyone coming after me.
Strange though. All that effort, and once I got there I wasn't sure if I wanted to be. So I did the usual. And stayed too long.

**Another** one, barman! I'm having a shot for every dead soldier this year!
And another **hundred** for us fuckers that aren't lucky enough to be in a box!
I don't even **remember** how I got from the pub to the procession, it was like I floated there or something...
...and suddenly I saw it in front of me. All those people standing in silence. The cars crawling by.
IT'S SO **SAD**. WHAT **BRAVE** BOYS.
YES. SO SAD. THEY SAY HE WAS A **BRAVE** LAD. DIED TRYING TO SAVE HIS FRIEND.
YOU KNOW... THAT'SH ME IN THERE. THAT'SH **ME**.
NO, YOUNG MAN. YOU COULDN'T BE MORE WRONG.
WELL, IT WILL BE. **SOON**. I'M GONNA BE **REMEMBERED**...

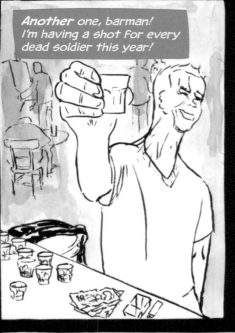

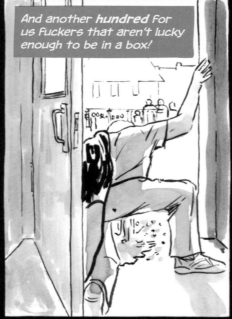

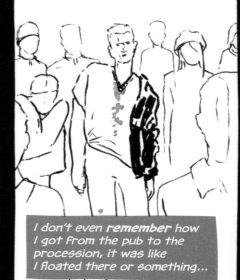

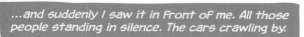

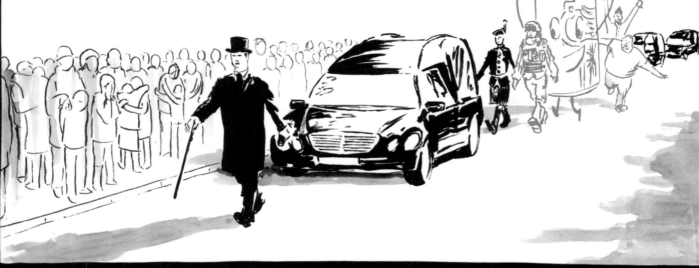

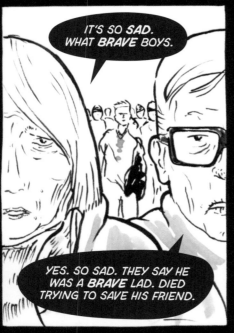

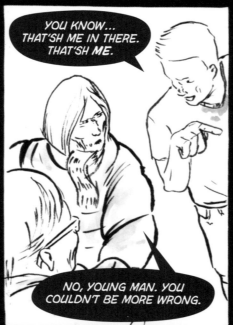

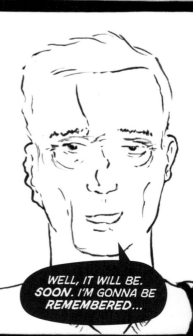

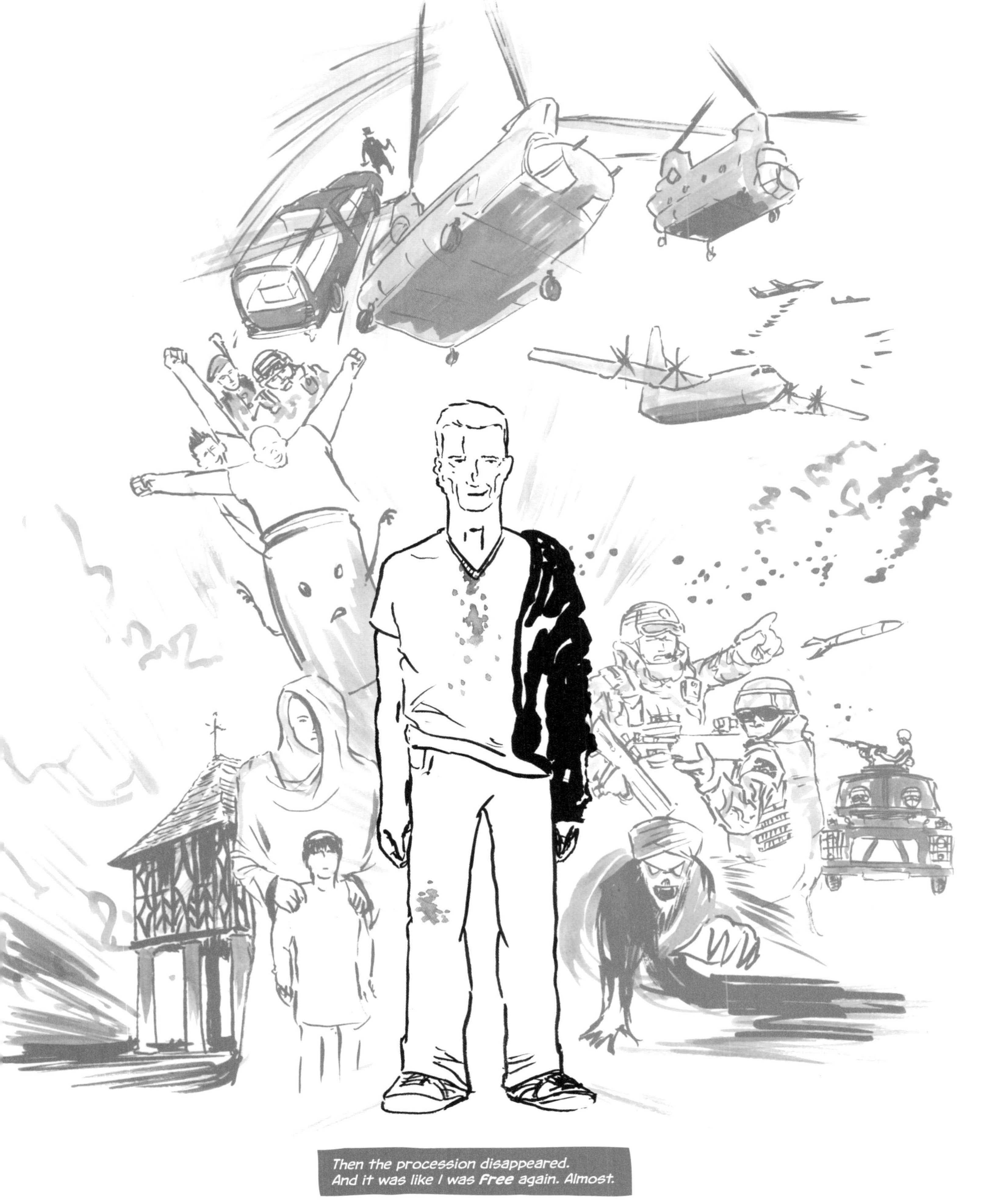
Then the procession disappeared.
And it was like I was free again. Almost.

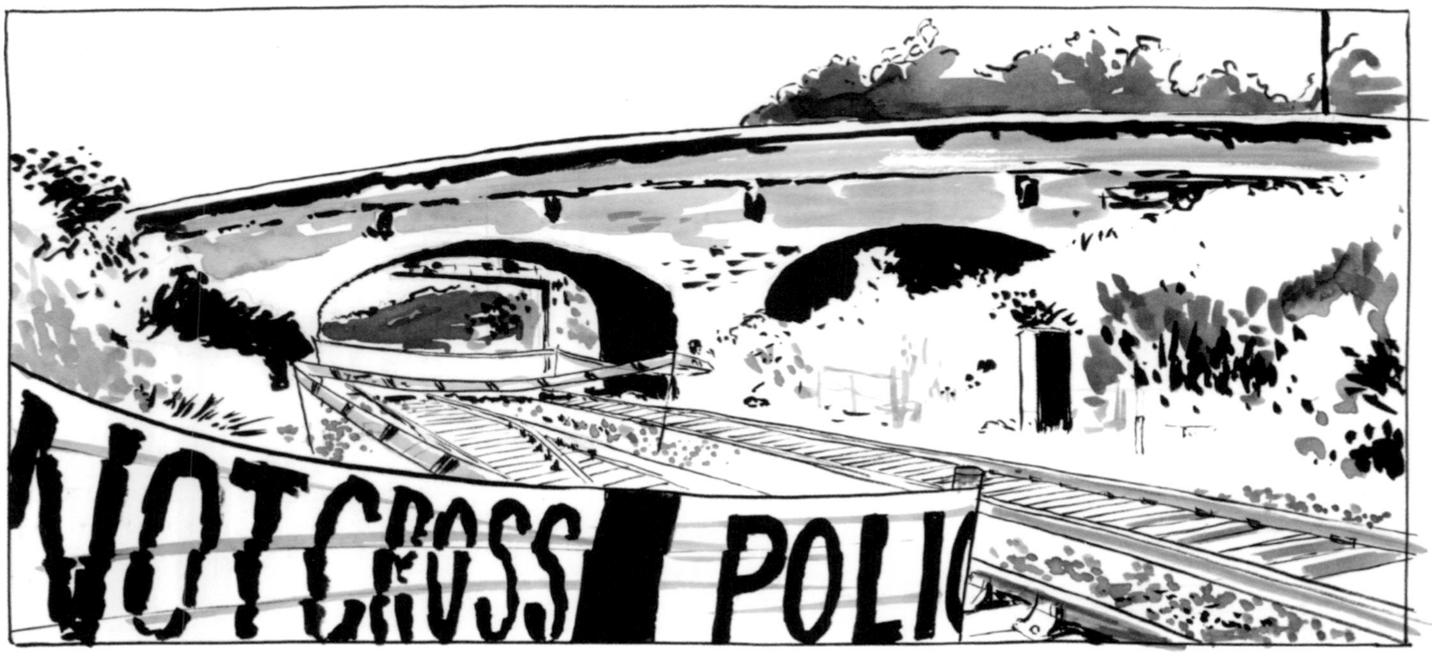
NOT CROSS POLIC

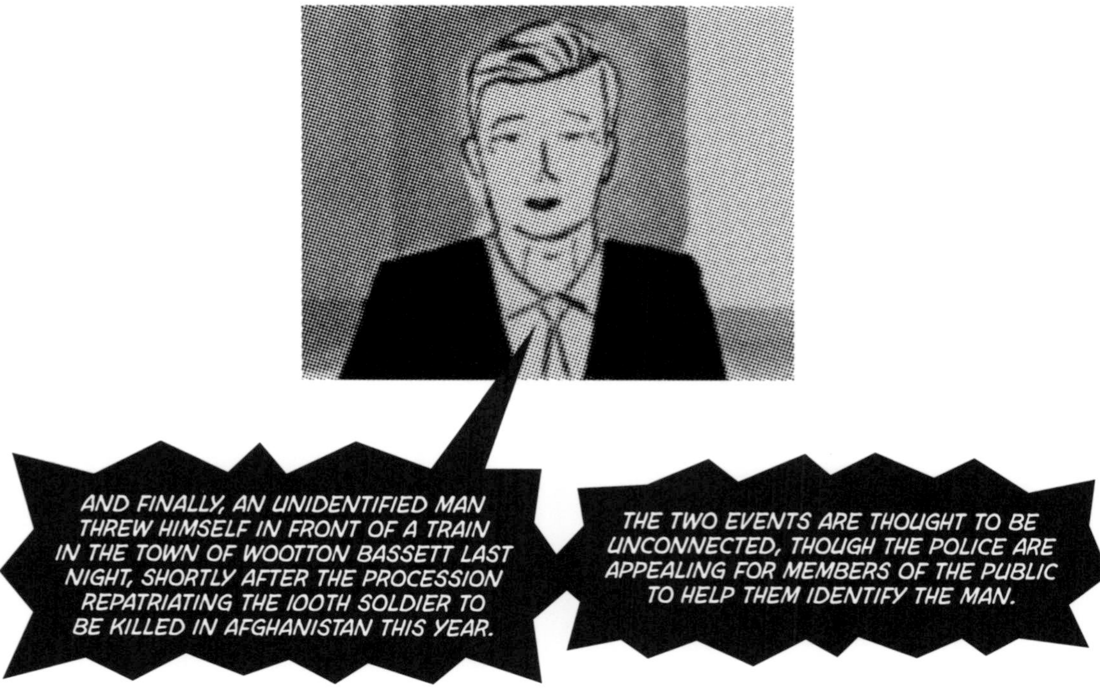
AND FINALLY, AN UNIDENTIFIED MAN THREW HIMSELF IN FRONT OF A TRAIN IN THE TOWN OF WOOTTON BASSETT LAST NIGHT, SHORTLY AFTER THE PROCESSION REPATRIATING THE 100TH SOLDIER TO BE KILLED IN AFGHANISTAN THIS YEAR.
THE TWO EVENTS ARE THOUGHT TO BE UNCONNECTED, THOUGH THE POLICE ARE APPEALING FOR MEMBERS OF THE PUBLIC TO HELP THEM IDENTIFY THE MAN.

*Due to be printed in The Herald newspaper, January 2010**

CUT



# Douglas Campbell

Private, Royal Highland Fusiliers;
Born July 21, 1989;
Died December 19, 2010.

**IN a special dedication, our regular columnist Alison Campbell pays a painfully honest tribute to her brother, local war hero Dougie, who died tragically last week.**

Douglas Campbell was born on July 21st 1989 in the Victoria Infirmary Hospital on the South Side of Glasgow. I should know because I was there—I was seven years old at the time, playing with my toys in the hospital corridor, bored, waiting for him to appear.

Mum had been in labour for nearly 24 hours before Dougie finally joined us here on Planet Earth. While we hung on for news, I remember asking my Dad why it was all taking so long. How hard could childbirth really be? 'It's like he doesn't want to be born at all,' said Dad, quietly, not looking at me. He was thinking out loud, staring at his own shoes: 'I don't blame him really,' he said.

Dougie and I were born into a football-mad family who'd lived in Govanhill since the 1950s. Our grandfather worked in the Clydeside shipyards most of his life and our dad served in the British Army for twenty years, in Northern Ireland, in the former Yugoslavia, in the Falklands, before sinking fast.

Dad never told us about what he saw on active service because as far as he was concerned, real men didn't do that sort of thing. Besides, it was fine. The work, that was fine. His problem was with the rest of the world—and with being what he called 'pissed on' by the society he'd served for so long. After so many nights out on the booze, Dad would stumble home, collapse into his chair and fall asleep muttering 'Why me, eh? Why me?'

Mum saw the world differently. She was a religious woman who was grateful for all she had and rarely said what she was really thinking. She worked part-time in a local supermarket when we were little, though we always said that if she could have worked 24 hours a day, never had a rest, never slept, she would have happily done it. Mum also died too young. That seems to run in the family.

As kids, Dougie and I used to tell each other everything. Sometimes we'd stay up all night, just blethering away. But that kind of thing doesn't last. Meanwhile, Dad's nights out on the booze became more regular, the consequences worse. Sometimes he'd tell us he was going fishing for the day, and disappear for a week. But we reacted differently to that. It made me want to work hard at school, get a good job and get as far away from him as possible. Dougie wanted to hide.

I left home in 2000, saying I wanted to do a course in Dundee (though actually I would have gone anywhere): when I said goodbye, suitcases all around me, my little brother pretended he didn't care I was going. That was an important year, one when Dad's health deteriorated.

The following Christmas, our cousin John returned to Edinburgh after nearly 30 years serving in the Royal Navy. Dougie sent John an email asking what it was like in the Falklands. I remember the reply. John sent back a six word message which read: 'Bloody great. Like sex, only better.' John was always a bad liar. I heard he spent three weeks underwater, expecting to get hit any second. Then his boat turned round and took him home.

In 2003, John came to Dad's funeral, sat in the front pew of the church and cried like a little girl. He's not very well these days. Sometimes it seems like none of us are.

Dougie left school at the age of sixteen, just before his exams, telling Mum he knew what he wanted and nobody could change his mind: he wanted to go to the desert and shoot some terrorists. Then it was Mum's turn to cry—a rare event.

Three weeks before, Dougie brought home a leaflet from school, advertising opportunities for young people, training,

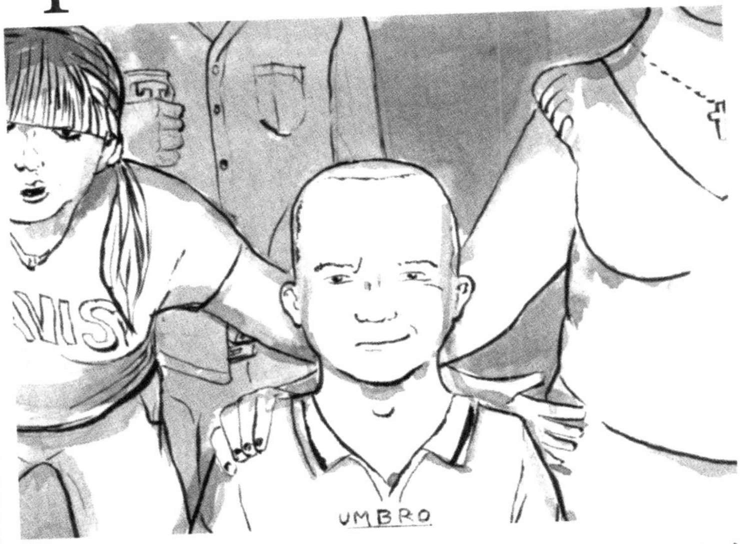
UMBRO

good pay and an exciting life 'exploring the world and serving Queen and country'. The photo on the front was of a smart-looking lad, about Dougie's age, in uniform, under a clear blue sky, looking proudly upwards into the light. Mum had put it in the bin but Dougie spotted it and fished it out again. When I asked him why he wanted to throw his life away fighting other people's wars in the Army, Dougie said: 'Cos I can't join the Navy. I get seasick.'

'But you could get yourself killed!' I told him. I couldn't think of what else to say. 'Aye, maybe,' he replied. 'But what else am I gonna do?' He turned to walk away, and I let him.

Some say if you join up knowing the risks, it's no good complaining afterwards. Especially when there's a war on. Two wars. What kind of idiot joins up when every night on the news there's pictures of dead soldiers, dead kids, and no chance of the whole bloody mess finishing any time soon? Worse: when you know a lot of people back home don't think you should be fighting? Even worse: when according to nearly every poll a big proportion of the public say they don't even know why you're battling away in Iraq and Afghanistan in the first place?

Well, I don't agree with the so-called War on Terror, I think it's making things worse—Dougie and I used to argue about it—but I know courage when I see it. Douglas Campbell was proud to serve in the Royal Highland Fusiliers, and having done a tour in Iraq the year before, he was excited when he was told he was going to be sent out to Helmand Province, Afghanistan in Spring 2008, at just nineteen years old.

Yes, he had no idea what he was doing. Yes, he signed up for the wrong reasons. He felt trapped. He didn't know what else to do with his life. But he risked it, every day, in the heat of the Middle East. And as he always said in our rare phone conversations when he was in Helmand, us journalists like to talk about warfare a lot, but we know nothing about the realities of it, far less about the kind of camaraderie and brotherhood that people like me can only dream of in ordinary civilian life.

I still think of those conversations sometimes. And what do I think of it all now? Now it's taken my little brother away? Well, I think the least we can do is look after our men and women while they're out there, and when they get home.

We didn't look after Dougie at all. His Army career was short because the light-armoured vehicle he was in got blown up on an Afghan street by a roadside bomb. Two other soldiers died in that blast. He survived, just.

Out there he survived on instinct but when he got home, he didn't know how to carry on surviving, and couldn't return to the world he'd left.

Maybe I should have helped him more. If I'm honest, I didn't really know how to. But there's a bigger issue here. In the Falklands War, more young men in the services committed suicide than died on active service. The first Gulf War was the same.

If we don't start supporting them better, many more who return from Iraq and Afghanistan in the years to come will suffer the same fate and, like Douglas Campbell, will choose to end their lives rather than live with the scars of war.

I can't get my brother back, but I can tell people about him.

ALISON CAMPBELL

Poem c

**Tommy**

I went into a
a pint o' beer,
The publican
no red-coats h
The girls be'in
an' giggled fit
I outs into the
myself sez I:
O it's Tommy
an' "Tommy, g
But it's "Thanl
when the ban
The band b
the band b
O it's "Tha
when the b

I went into
could be,
They gave
but 'adn't
They sent
the music
But when
they'll sho
For it's To
an' "Tomn
But it's "Sp
when the t
The troops
the troopshi
O it's "Specia
when the troo

Yes, makin' m
guard you wh
Is cheaper th
an' they're st
An' hustlin' d
they're goin'
Is five times
paradin' in fu
Then it's Tor
that, an' "Tor
But it's "Thin
when the dru
The drums b
the drums b
O it's "Thin
when the dru

We aren't no
we aren't no
But single m
remarkable l
An' if someti
all your fanc
Why, single
grow into pl
While it's T
that, an' "
But it's "
when th
There's
there's
O it's "I
when t

FAMILY ANNOUNCEMENTS

To place your notice in Family Announcements

Telephone 0141-302 600

**This obituary was never actually published. It was scheduled on three separate occasions but was each time replaced when a famous celebrity died and took the space in the newspaper instead. It was eventually put on Alison Campbell's personal website.*

# Tommy

I went into a public-'ouse to get a pint o' beer,
The publican 'e up an' sez, "We serve no red-coats here."
The girls be'ind the bar they laughed an' giggled fit to die,
I outs into the street again an' to myself sez I:
*O it's Tommy this, an' Tommy that, an' "Tommy, go away";*
*But it's "Thank you, Mister Atkins", when the band begins to play,*
*The band begins to play, my boys, the band begins to play,*
*O it's "Thank you, Mister Atkins", when the band begins to play.*

I went into a theatre as sober as could be,
They gave a drunk civilian room, but 'adn't none for me;
They sent me to the gallery or round the music-'alls,
But when it comes to fightin', Lord! they'll shove me in the stalls!
*For it's Tommy this, an' Tommy that, an' "Tommy, wait outside";*
*But it's "Special train for Atkins" when the trooper's on the tide,*
*The troopship's on the tide, my boys, the troopship's on the tide,*
*O it's "Special train for Atkins" when the trooper's on the tide.*

Yes, makin' mock o' uniforms that guard you while you sleep
Is cheaper than them uniforms, an' they're starvation cheap;
An' hustlin' drunken soldiers when they're goin' large a bit
Is five times better business than paradin' in full kit.
*Then it's Tommy this, an' Tommy that, an' "Tommy, 'ow's yer soul?"*
*But it's "Thin red line of 'eroes" when the drums begin to roll,*
*The drums begin to roll, my boys, the drums begin to roll,*
*O it's "Thin red line of 'eroes" when the drums begin to roll.*

We aren't no thin red 'eroes, nor we aren't no blackguards too,
But single men in barricks, most remarkable like you;
An' if sometimes our conduck isn't all your fancy paints,
Why, single men in barricks don't grow into plaster saints;
*While it's Tommy this, an' Tommy that, an' "Tommy, fall be'ind",*
*But it's "Please to walk in front, sir", when there's trouble in the wind,*
*There's trouble in the wind, my boys, there's trouble in the wind,*
*O it's "Please to walk in front, sir", when there's trouble in the wind.*

You talk o' better food for us, an' schools, an' fires, an' all:
We'll wait for extry rations if you treat us rational.
Don't mess about the cook-room slops, but prove it to our face
The Widow's Uniform is not the soldier-man's disgrace.
*For it's Tommy this, an' Tommy that, an' "Chuck him out, the brute!"*
*But it's "Saviour of 'is country" when the guns begin to shoot;*
*An' it's Tommy this, an' Tommy that, an' anything you please;*
*An' Tommy ain't a bloomin' fool – you bet that Tommy sees!*

*by Rudyard Kipling (1865-1936)*

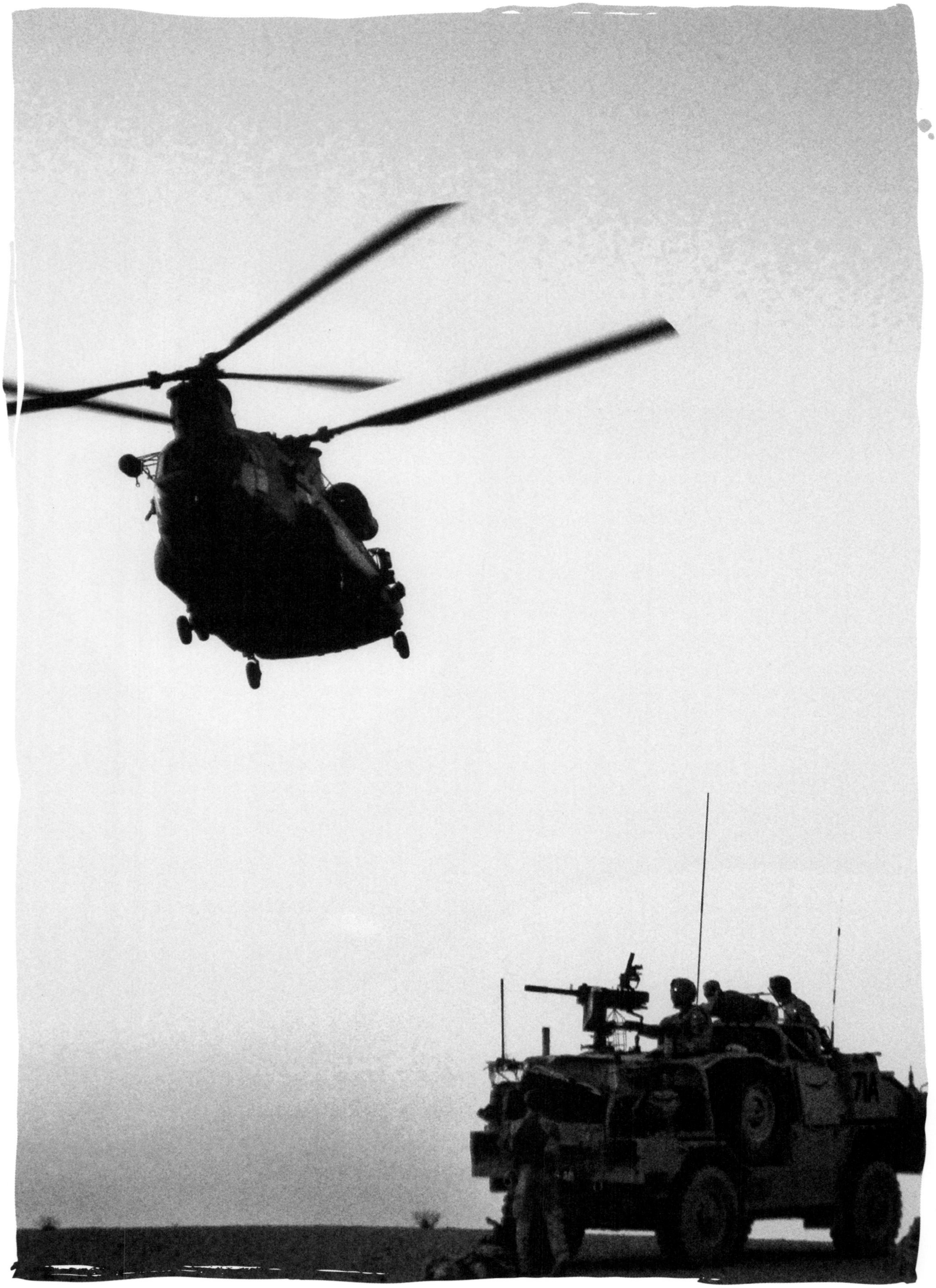

# A War of Attrition

War is a life changing experience for many men and women. The symptoms of Post Traumatic Stress Syndrome can affect individuals, whether combatants or civilians, to greatly varying degrees and at different times in their lives. *Adrian Searle* talked to a number of those who have experienced war first-hand and whose lives have been transformed as a result.

All photography was taken during combat operations in Helmand Province, Afghanistan, by *Sergeant Nick Collins*, Royal Artillery, while a member of 3rd Battalion, Royal Regiment of Scotland (The Black Watch), participating in Op Herrick 10, March – October 2009.

In the late 1960s my grandfather died of pneumonia. It was a premature death brought on by alcoholism. Originally from Darlington, he'd settled in the east coast fishing town of Arbroath and ran a pub in Dundee. My mother remembers him being so drunk he'd wet himself during the short train journey home, humiliating for a man who had always taken great care over his appearance.

*It seems most likely that my grandfather's alcoholism was directly related to his wartime experiences.*

As well as the endless arguments between her parents, she remembers having to flee in the middle of the night in her dressing gown to her Auntie's house as her father, raging drunk, stood in the front garden waving a service revolver and bellowing into the street. The facts have always been sketchy, my mother reluctant to delve too deep into that part of her childhood and adolescence, but I've always had a sense of the over-riding shame that she and my grandmother felt, brought on I think by a sense of helplessness in the face of my grandfather's behaviour.

His name was Arthur Wilson and he spent the majority of his career in the Merchant Navy, joining as a teenager and rising to Captain of an oil tanker during the war. When I was in primary school we still had his Captain's hat, which I used to try on in front of the mirror. It is difficult to imagine the stress of spending the war years in charge of a giant floating container full of thousands of tons of highly combustible liquid. Serving in the Mediterranean, he was torpedoed by a German submarine, probably in 1942 or 1943. The ship broke in half. As Captain, he was duty bound to leave the sinking vessel last. He and his surviving crew were in the water for several hours before being picked up by another ship. Had they been in the North Atlantic they would have been dead from exposure in minutes. He spent the remainder of the war in Egypt, with no way of getting home or contacting his family to let them know he was still alive.

Although I was born only a year before he died, it seems most likely that my grandfather's alcoholism was directly related to his wartime experiences. Not just the torpedoing but also the constant danger he had been in since the outbreak of hostilities, together with the stress of being solely responsible for the safety of his crew. Many, many Scottish families have similar stories: men of my grandfather's generation returning from conflict, unable to talk about their experiences and no understanding of how to find help, instead choosing to self-medicate with alcohol. ›

LEFT PAGE:
Chinook helicopter and Jackal group fire support during airborne extraction of part of the Command Group

'I didn't talk to my wife about it, she had years of it,' he said. 'The neighbours used to think the house was haunted, the screaming. People would be very wary of coming up to me and touching me because I'd just take their heads off. The worst was I had my wife by the nightdress and I was physically dragging her off the bed during the night, saying "get into this trench, get into the trench"'.'

He told me, 'towards the end of my service I sought psychiatric help, saw a nurse. They gave me a tape recorder, but there was nothing there for me, no offer of help. The resources were next to nothing.'

Likewise Norrie, formerly a Major in a Scottish infantry regiment, had a similar experience immediately after the first Gulf War.

'We were brought up to this peak and then nothing,... and then we were dumped back into Fort George [near Inverness]. As a military posting it's in the back of beyond. It was really a stupid thing to do because we weren't wound down in any way. I remember, we used to sit there, there were nine platoon commanders. I know none of us was treated for any mental disorder, but I look back and we were all living life very brightly at that time. An awful lot of heavy drinking. There was nothing else to do there, alcohol was very cheap. There was this race down to Edinburgh every weekend. And before the year was up, I think it was four or maybe five people had been caught drink driving. It's a very serious blot on your record.

Post Traumatic Stress Disorder is a new term for a very old condition. In the First World War it was called shell shock. During and after the Second World War it was called, amongst many other things, battle fatigue. PTSD was a condition first properly recognised through American research with veterans after World War Two, but one that only really penetrated public consciousness after the Vietnam War. Historical references to the psychological effects of war go back

*During an official enquiry undertaken by the War Office in 1922, a Major Adie testified that shell shock 'must be looked upon as a form of disgrace to the soldier'.*

as far as Greek theatre, Shakespeare, and can be found in the black paintings of the Spanish artist, Goya, his response to Napoleon's brutal conquest of Spain. After the First World War, a great deal of art and literature was inspired by direct experience of the trauma of war, from the poetry of Siegfried Sassoon and Wilfred Owen, Erich Remarque's *All Quiet on the Western Front* and R.C. Sherriff's play *Journey's End* to the paintings of Paul Nash, Otto Dix and Georg Grosz.

After the Great War there was conflict between the experience of those suffering the effects of shell shock and the way the military and wider society viewed the condition. During an official enquiry undertaken by the War Office in 1922, a Major Adie testified that shell shock 'must be looked upon as a form of disgrace to the soldier'.

Eighty years later, and military culture didn't seem to have changed. 'You look out for others and you can't display weakness, it's about the role you're in, you've to project an image for people to trust you. I think servicemen are some of the greatest actors in the world. You play this part.' So says Tam, a Glaswegian now living on the south coast, who joined the army as a teenager in the early seventies and rose through the ranks to become a Captain. He was blown up in an attack on Castlereagh Barracks in Northern Ireland and participated in the bloody battle for Mount Tumbledown during the Falklands War, later suffering extreme symptoms of PTSD.

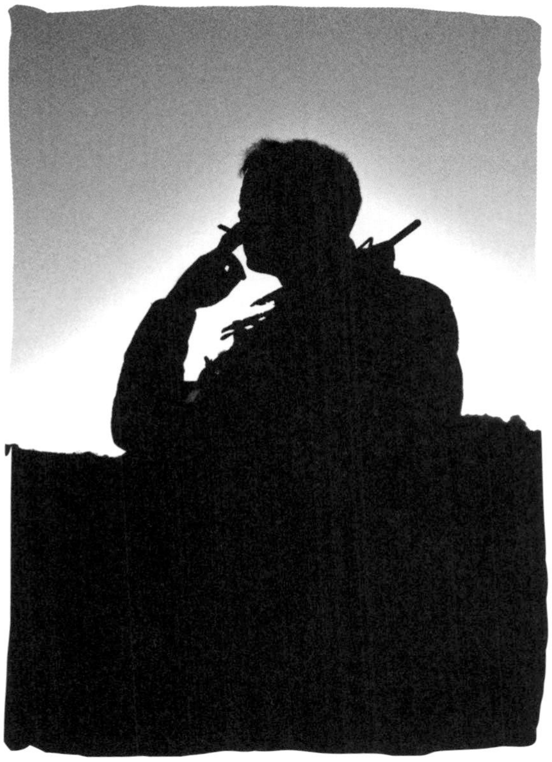

'One of those guys stole a car and was chased across the south of England and was thrown out of the army. One person unfortunately died. He was drunk and fell over a balcony. When you look back, the fact that we'd been in this pressure cooker environment... we were all told that we were to look after the soldiers and we put a lot of effort into that, and no one looked after us.'

Norrie believes that it is particularly difficult for officers to seek help for the effects of PTSD. For officers who admit any form of weakness, 'there'll be a loss of leadership, people will doubt your decision-making in the future. There's absolutely no doubt in my mind there was an issue there.' In the light of this, I couldn't help thinking how isolated my grandfather must have felt, in command of his tanker, vulnerable to attack by roaming U-boats at any time of day or night, responsible for the welfare of his men.

Talking to veterans about their exposure to PTSD, it is clear that some have seen and done things non-combatants cannot come close to imagining, experiences that remain incredibly vivid to this day. Stewart, a Captain in the Royal Green Jackets, also saw active service in the first Gulf War as a twenty one year old subaltern.

'On our battles through Iraq we had some pretty fierce fire fights. As a company we were heading back to join our main battle group when we hit this battalion position. We came under serious fire. We lost a Private who got hit in the chest by an RPG. He'd just deployed out of the back of his Warrior and he took a round in the chest and it exploded on him which also set the Warrior on fire. It was bizarre.

'The fire fight lasted four and a half hours. It was amazing how quickly that went, but it was very confused. It was a big position. A lot of small arms fire coming back at us, RPGs but also white flags as well. Half the Iraqi battalion had decided to fight and half had decided to surrender. Incredibly confusing. Once we'd overrun the position, taking a lot of guys prisoner, treating a lot of casualties, once the euphoria of the battle was over, you realise your thought processes were incredibly clear. But I remember standing at the back of the Warrior, having a fag and that euphoria that I'd felt, I remember it literally going out through my feet and being left with this incredibly empty feeling. I remember looking at hollow faced guys around me, all clearly feeling the same way.'

But it wasn't just the battle that had a profound effect on Stewart, but also seeing its aftermath.

*That euphoria that I'd felt, I remember it literally going out through my feet and being left with this incredibly empty feeling. I remember looking at hollow faced guys around me, all clearly feeling the same way.*

'We had various other skirmishes once we were into Kuwait,' he told me in the office of a London risk management consultancy where he now works. 'After the surrender', he said, 'we ended up on the Basra highway. [We'd seen ›

**LEFT PAGE:**
Impromptu field headquarters in harsh Afghan desert terrain

**RIGHT PAGE:**
Sunrise in Afghanistan: the Tara (Black Watch RSM) winding down after 72 hours on combat patrol

the] Apaches hunting in gangs. I remember coming over a lip of the side of the Basra Kuwait highway. It was early morning. The road was littered with everything; military vehicles, coaches, cars and a huge amount of bodies. We had a few fire fights with little pockets of resistance, and then the next few days we had the gruesome task of trying to find any remaining resistance.

'Quite nerve-wracking, but we were also out looking for bodies, because we were going to end up staying there,

just off the highway for, about three weeks. I remember the first morning when we were able to have a decent breakfast, not having eaten properly for quite a few days and those big fat flies, we subsequently named them corpse flies. They'd probably just come out of some corpse's mouth and then they'd buzz around and land right in the middle of your breakfast, would scrabble around and then take off again. The smell was just shocking. Burnt flesh, everything. It was strange. The smell of burnt rubber, the plastic smell of the burning interior of a vehicle and then the smell of burnt or decaying flesh. The smell of burning plastic, it still makes me retch. Then this amazing smell – because the Iraqis had looted everything out of Kuwait City and had put it into whatever, cars or buses – all this stuff had gone all over the highway. And you'd come across this really pungent smell of cheap scent. There'd be nappies, and then an Armani shirt then video games then a body, a helmet and a rifle. Just surreal.'

The main hostilities during the first Gulf War famously lasted only 100 hours. But according to Stewart, for many the problems continued long after.

*The main hostilities during the first Gulf War famously lasted only 100 hours. But according to Stewart, for many the problems continued long after.*

'We probably didn't have the fight in the end that we thought we'd have, so we were wired. I was wired for months afterwards. Ultimately, we never had that "mother of all battles". I think that there was a huge level of frustration. We'd been there five months and we were needing to have some kind of burst of adrenalin. It left a big hole in me. It had a deep, deep effect. Emotion, anger stayed with me. Because we hadn't had this all-out battle. They'd been predicting 60% casualties.

'When I came back, I went to see a friend who'd been badly injured who was in rehabilitation and then I went straight up to Luing [an island off the West Coast of Scotland], spent a few weeks there just getting my head round what I was feeling, what I'd done. I only once had a nightmare about it, afterwards. For a year there wasn't a day went by when I didn't think about it, what had gone on and what my role in it had been. A lot of people went later to see various psychologists. In the Green Jackets, of the fifteen married guys who'd been out there, every single one of them had ended up spending time apart from their wives afterwards. The one guy who hadn't, he had a real problem being with his kids. I had a similar thing myself. My mother had been my confidante when I was out there. I'd described some things in detail, but when I then got home, I couldn't look her in the eye, although all she wanted was to offer support. I didn't really talk to her properly for a year. As the mother of a child she didn't care, but in my eyes she knew too much. I still think about it.'

Tam, too, was able to recount in graphic detail his experience in the Falklands, although it had taken place nearly thirty years previously. In particular he remembered vividly the terror he felt during the landing operation where he was very nearly killed.

LEFT PAGE:
Ginger on patrol: sometimes Factor 50 just doesn't work

RIGHT PAGE:
Poppy farmer and field retained within the walls of an Afghan compound, being used as a combat patrol base

'They flew us forward to the preparation area. It was like something from Vietnam, everyone in their own world. It was hot, they were shelling us. When we landed we just dug in. We went in for the night attack, it was the most brilliant firework display you'd ever seen. We had point five Browning, we had mortars. There's shells coming in, naval gunfire support. And they were shelling us with one-five-five. And as you're going forward, you see the shells landing and its getting closer and closer. Then suddenly a shell landed in the middle of us and blew us up in the air. It was like a train coming in – bang! Felt myself being lifted, I just saw all red. Up in the air and landed on my back. But because of the peat and the type of terrain, it absorbed it. And I was absolutely terrified. I've never been so scared in my life. I was so close to running away. There was a cigarette paper's width between me doing it and not doing it. It was pure terror. I looked round and I could see some of the guys on the ground. I don't know how long that moment lasts. I could have gone down as the Royal Signals guy who ran away on the battlefield, so easily.

'We're squashed in these landing craft, it's winter in the South Atlantic. All four landing craft take off, flat bottomed, and there's water coming straight over the top, like buckets of ice. Within minutes we're really feeling the effects. There's a guy in the mortar platoon, don't know him from Adam, and it's not long before we have our arms wrapped rounds each other, trying to keep each other warm. Argentinean aircraft come across, drop some bombs. This journey's supposed to take three hours. We've been out there about four hours by this stage, and we're in a state. And suddenly a star shell goes up in the air. We can see a ship there in the distance. All four landing craft start going round in a circle like Cowboys and Indians. And there are cries like "man the machine guns... man the machine guns". Next to me is a Major in the Royal Artillery. A couple more of these star shells go up and he says to me, "they're going to blow us out the water". And I start to say out loud the Lord's Prayer.

'It turned out the ship was HMS Cardiff, they didn't know that we were there. And the skipper tossed a coin to see if they'd blow us out of the water or not. And it fell the right way. We landed at Bluff Cove and about half the Battalion had exposure, we were in bits. The journey took about eight or nine hours.'

Tam was a communications specialist from the Royal Signals attached to the vanguard of the Scots Guards attack on Tumbledown. He described his involvement in the battle.

'We got pinned down for hours. I was doing comms back to Brigade. It was that bad, we couldn't get stretchers forward to our guys. The CO needed to go forward to have a look and he said, "you're coming with me," and I said, "Okay sir," and I was terrified again. I thought I'm dead, I'm absolutely dead,' Tam laughs loudly.

'[There was a] bayonet charge to clear machine gun posts. Then you had to run across two hundred metres of open ground. You get down the other side, and you flop down and you're flopping down on dead bodies. And that is horrendous. ❯

*I was absolutely terrified. I've never been so scared in my life. I was so close to running away. There was a cigarette paper's width between me doing it and not doing it. It was pure terror.*

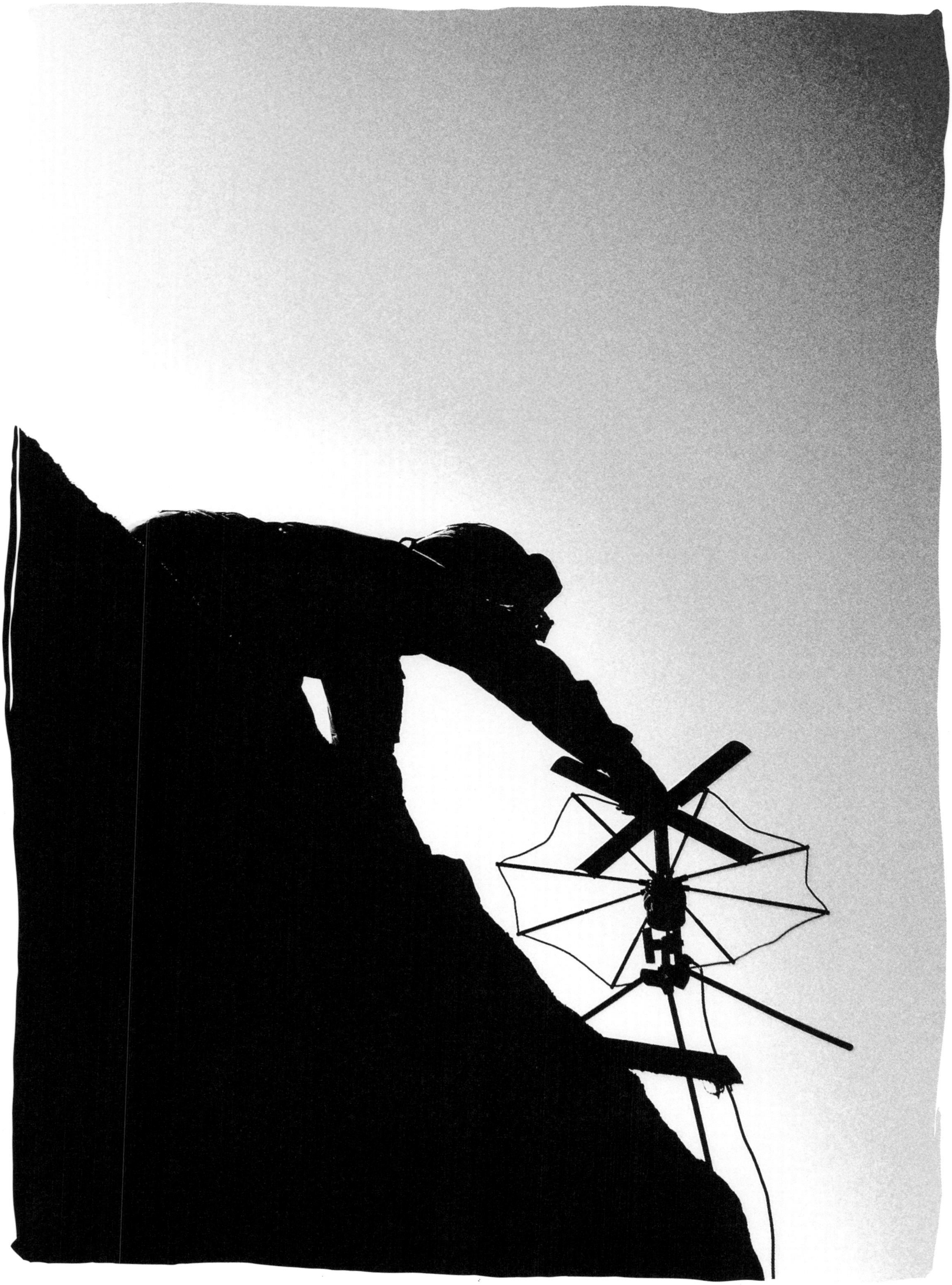

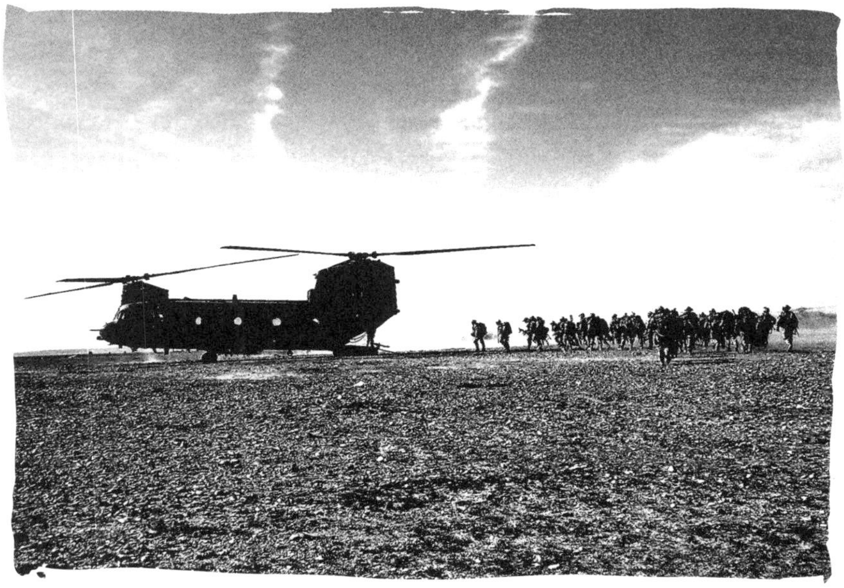

'After the battle, we were up there walking round the positions and there was dead everywhere. I saw sights that were very barbaric.'

> *I remember going out the back of the Warrior and looking and thinking this is just like hell. It was unbelievable.*

Norrie also found he was ill-prepared for the stress of combat.

'As platoon commanders, young officers, we were told, you'll be at the front, don't expect to be coming back. I remember the night before we knew we were going through the breach, sitting in my turret, writing letters home, I was quite sombre at the time. We'd had the talk by the company commander that fifty percent of us were going to die and I remember thinking that I could just say to my driver, let's drive off south. I might spend two years in jail, but I'd probably be alive. Seriously, for an hour I sat there thinking, should I do this? I didn't. You think about your soldiers, but I was quite serious about it.'

Norrie also saw action in Basra during a six-month tour of Iraq, between 2005 and 2006. 'At that time it was very hostile, although it pales into insignificance when what you see happening out in Afghanistan now. You're hearing reports of companies coming back with 40% of people with life changing injuries.

'Fairly regularly we were shot at but you'd just keep driving, just baton down the hatches and ignore it. I was involved in one contact where we were ambushed going across a bridge, quite a hefty ambush going in. I remember going out the back of the Warrior and looking and thinking this is just like hell. It was unbelievable. When you see rounds being fired they seem much slower than they really are. You'd see all the tracers going everywhere, you'd see the RPGs bouncing around. RPGs are very slow. It's a bit like paintballing. You can see a paintball coming at you. Just quick enough that you can't get out of the way. It was really strange.'

However, it is not just combatants that are exposed to the trauma of war. David Pratt, Foreign Editor of *The Herald* and *Sunday Herald* newspapers, suffered severe PTSD after being kidnapped in Bosnia.

'I was kept for four days near Mostar in the final months of the war in the former Yugoslavia,' said David, as we drank tea in a Glasgow cafe. 'By that stage it was very difficult to get access to the front line. A notoriously bad area, run by criminals and gangsters. Some Croat militia I was with just turned on me one day, bundled me into a car along with two other Bosnians, one was a Bosnian Muslim journalist and the other his fixer, and they took us off into the countryside, kept us for four days. The fixer was shot within hours of the kidnapping, in front of us, just feet away. I and the other journalist were kept in this outhouse on a farm. I was beaten. I was weeks in hospital afterwards. I was badly, badly beaten. I'd bust everything imaginable.

'Two days into this experience they shot the other journalist, also in front of me. On the fourth night they came in, very drunk, three guys. They put me in a car again, a brand new BMW, and drove me further into the countryside, got me out, it was pitch black. I was tied, with umpteen broken bones. And then the execution. I was kneeled down in front of a ditch, I remember the sound of a pistol being cocked, the barrel put to my head, then the trigger being pulled: an empty click. And to this day I don't know whether it was a mock execution or whether they just fucked up.

'Then they hit me on the head, I fell into the ditch. When I came to, it was full of people... full of bodies. It took me a day and a half to get out of the hole. I cut myself free on a fence, got to a farmhouse but the woman there wouldn't let me in. I was in and out of consciousness at that point. I got to a nearby road and flagged down the ›

LEFT PAGE:
Dangerous job: tactical satellite radio antenna being erected on the roof of a patrol base

RIGHT PAGE:
Job done: extraction of a company by Chinook at the end of a patrol

were either suffering from PTSD or other psychological problems as a result of the war [with Israel]. And in a long conversation with him, where I virtually broke down in front of him one night after a few glasses of wine, he said, I think you should get this looked at. He said I was showing all the characteristic symptoms of PTSD. He said when I returned to the UK he could put me in touch with people in London who could then in turn refer me to people in Scotland.'

But often, according to those that I talked to, it is not just the major events that cause long term problems. Tam says that living with stress over a long period of time can be just as damaging.

'I used to get nightmares from Northern Ireland. I think it was the heightened tension. I was doing communications and if I got it wrong someone would get killed. Pushing yourself beyond what you're capable of. There's nothing wrong with stretching yourself, but you can raise the bar too high. It's often not other people judging them, it's the servicemen themselves setting standards too high, doing it for themselves. You looked at and examined yourself, when things went wrong you'd look at what you'd done, good and bad, that's the whole ethos of military service. When I got home I found it difficult to settle, wanted that buzz again. It's like two sides of the same coin, when you're there and feel that fear, the adrenalin's running, you don't want to be there, but when you're not there you miss it.'

David agrees. 'It can be a trickle effect, a slow built up, just exposure over a length of time, or it can be a one off incident that completely transforms you. I think in my case it was a combination of both.

'The problems we're talking about never occur in-country or in-theatre. It's when you come back. The sheer frustration of watching people think certain things are important when in actual fact they pale

first vehicle that came along. I knew if I didn't I wasn't going to make it much longer. Two young Croatian guys that I'm still in touch with picked me up and took me to hospital.'

It was only after the physical damage had healed and he returned home that David's psychological scars became visible.

'I went into complete meltdown, became quite reclusive. It was confusion. I distinctly remember walking down a street in Glasgow one afternoon and just bursting into tears. In the evening, if I saw groups of young guys, I'd cross the road, something that just terrified the living daylights out of me. I've described it as like being in a submarine and your air supply being cut off. A sense of suffocation. You don't want to function, you don't want to engage with people. One of the big problems for me at that time was that I was lost in a fug of alcohol. It was a reluctance to face up to what was going on. It was easier to remain in a stupor.'

Help came for David via a chance meeting on a recuperative holiday to Jerusalem.

'The problem was that there was no medical infrastructure [in the UK]. I bumped into this American psychologist, who was working with Palestinians who

*I went into complete meltdown, became quite reclusive. It was confusion. I distinctly remember walking down a street in Glasgow one afternoon and just bursting into tears.*

into insignificance. I remember coming back from a trip to Central America and we'd watched some refugees being mowed down by machine gun fire as they were try to flee over a river and two days later I was on a plane via Madrid coming back to London. This businessman next to me just moaned constantly about everything, his leg room, his food, his tea not being hot enough and whether his driver would be there to pick him up at Heathrow. I felt like strangling the guy. The same thing happens when you come back, but you realise that people's problems are relative. As a journalist, you realise you have to get that perspective. I used to get very angry about it. It would get me into all kinds of problems. I would lose my temper. And that's also part of the stress and the classic symptoms of PTSD. You get angry about nothing, angry with people.'

After over twenty years in the army, Tam suffered a heart attack in the early nineties which prompted a radical change of lifestyle.

'When I went to see the doctor, that was a cry for help. My lifestyle has changed. I've been teetotal for fifteen years, I've been a vegetarian for seventeen years. I don't smoke now either. I don't get nightmares anymore, at least only very rarely when I'm really stressed. No one but me could identify that I had a problem.'

Of his life before he addressed his PTSD, he says, 'You wear masks and you camouflage – [I was] very extrovert, life and soul of the party. I look back and there's so many things that are positive [in military service], but it takes its toll. You look at close friends; there was a friend who was a Warrant Officer, a Regimental Sergeant Major, who eventually joined the TA when he came out, became a Major. Then had a nervous breakdown. Last year, there was a Lieutenant Colonel who'd been through the ranks with me, had served with the SAS, who was medically discharged. All that pressure, bottling it all up.'

> *I look back and there's so many things that are positive [in military service], but it takes its toll.*

Stewart, too, sought medical help ten years after his experiences in Iraq and Kuwait. 'I went to see a psychotherapist in 2002,' he said, 'about one thing but ended up talking about two others, one of which was my experience in the Gulf War.'

With more and more women involved in front line operations, it is not just men that are vulnerable. Julie, originally from Hull, joined the Royal Logistic Corps, where three and half years in Bosnia in the late 1990s, immediately followed by difficult operations in Afghanistan, eventually took their toll.

'The last two years [in Bosnia] were difficult and stressful. During this time, I had to sort out the mess of a corrupt former Detachment Commander. I also once had to mount guard on a mass grave – and clear the blood from the site of a grenade explosion that had killed a soldier and civilians. In May 2002 I found myself in Kabul, and later in Bagram. Death was everywhere – the result of bombings and shootings. The threat and danger was intense. Most things were done at night for safety. Just driving off camp, you always potentially had a price on your head.

'By now, five years of operations were beginning to take their toll. I was having nightmares and losing confidence in myself. I had a permanent 'fed-up' feeling and I asked to be replaced. A CPN (Community Psychiatric Nurse) recommended a week's leave to the UK. On the long flight back I was charged with guarding the remains of two dead soldiers – one of whom was a friend. ❯

**LEFT PAGE:**
Vehicle weapon mounted installation kit (WMIK) General Purpose Machine Gun (GPMG)

**RIGHT PAGE:**
First patrol in Kandahar, April 2009 (mosque in background)

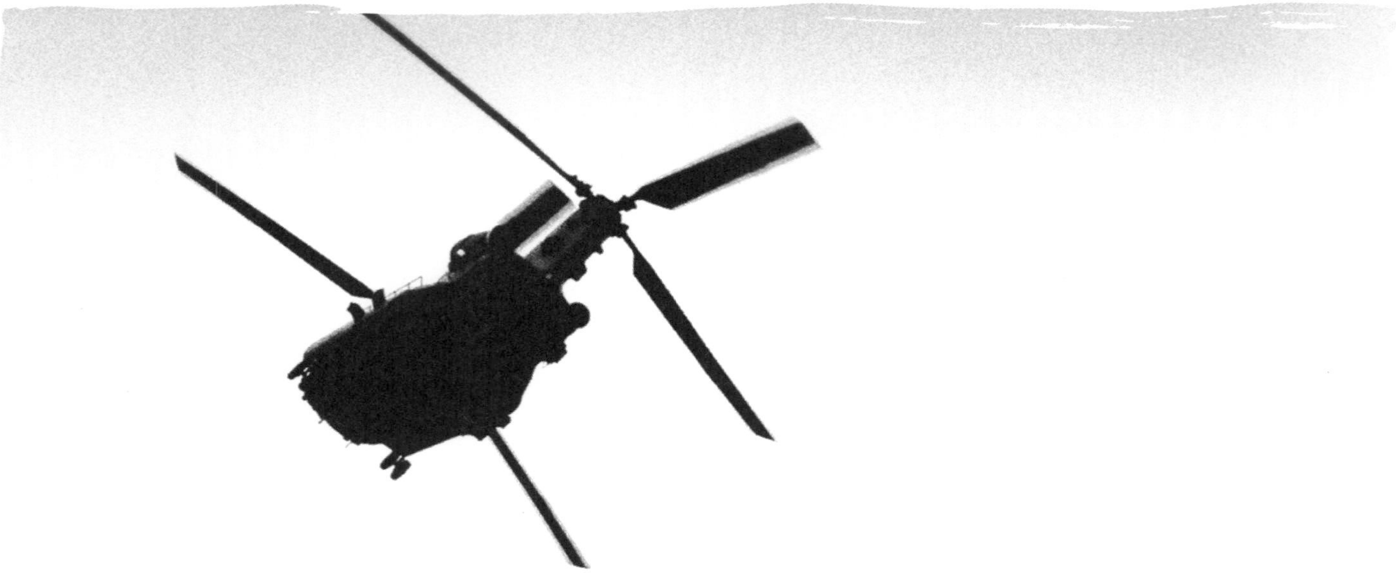

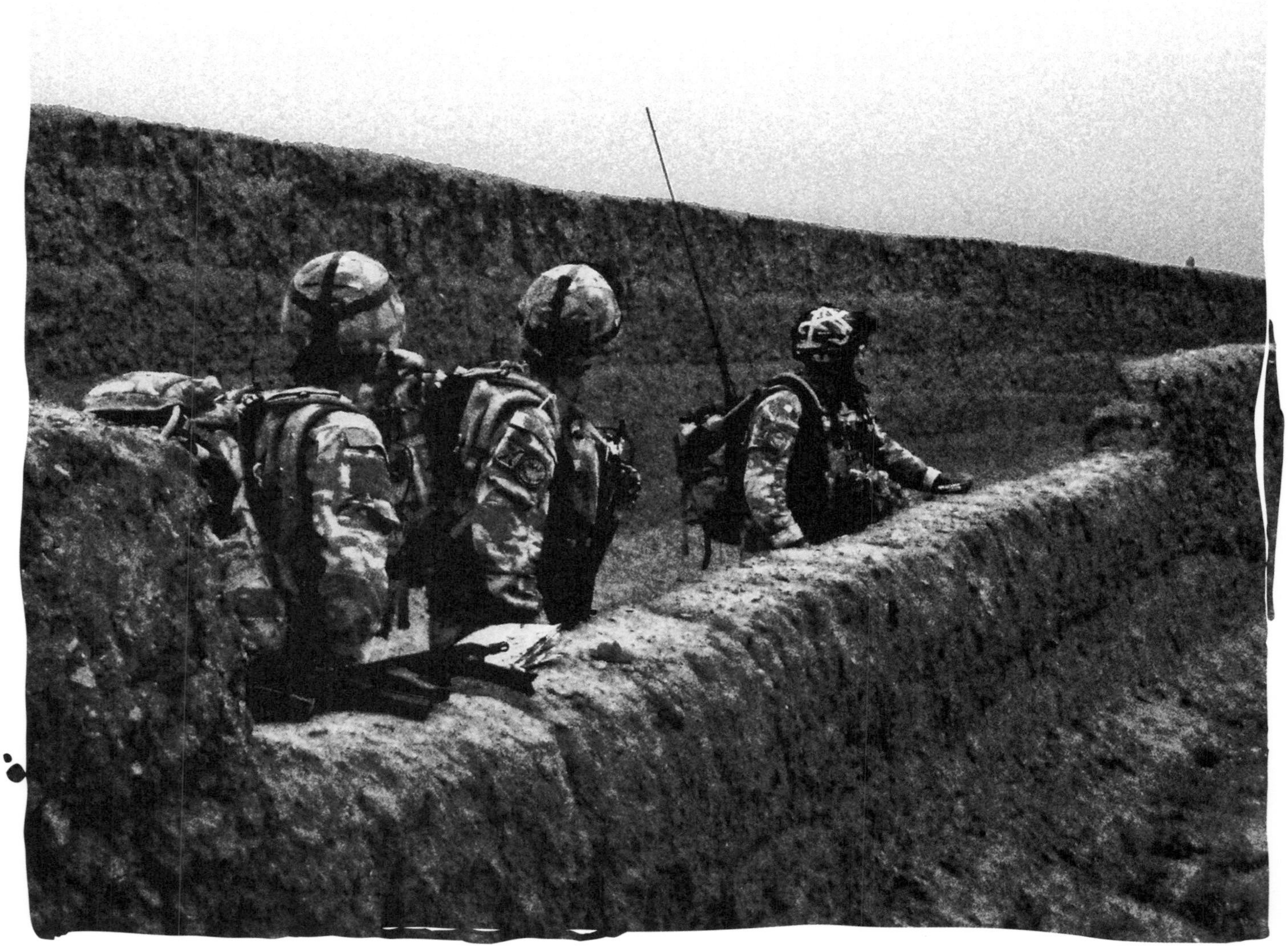

At the time of writing, operations in Afghanistan are resulting in very high numbers of casualties. While combat-related fatalities over the last four years have recently exceeded those during the Falklands (currently 307 deaths compared with an estimated 255 deaths during the South Atlantic campaign), the number of serious combat injuries stand at over 1,280, compared with approximately 770 in the Falklands. Britain has approximately 9,500 troops stationed in Afghanistan but, with the regular rotation of forces, far higher numbers have experienced active service there. With resources stretched, the campaigns in Afghanistan and Iraq have also been the first where large numbers of personnel have completed several tours with less than the Ministry of Defence's own recommended rest and recuperation between. As a result, there is consensus across veterans' charities that Britain faces a 'ticking time bomb' of combat related mental health problems.

David Hill, operations director for Combat Stress, recently said: 'Servicemen and women are exposed to stresses that most people won't be exposed to in their lives. In Afghanistan, they are exposed to them quite early in their careers. There is a general lack of understanding about how intense these stresses can be.'

'It takes an average of 14 years for veterans to ask for help with post-traumatic stress disorder. Many suffer in silence – often harbouring suicidal thoughts – because they are reluctant to admit to their vulnerability.' ❯

---

*I was told I had an adjustment disorder and that in six to twelve weeks I'd be back to normal. I waited for the twelve weeks to end, but they never did. I spent three years like that – not working, not going out of the house, not getting up some days.*

---

'When I returned to Afghanistan there was a notable change in my behaviour and my work was failing, so I was called in to see a CPN. A doctor then had me flown out to Catterick. Within a week I was discharged from the Army, in September 2002.

'It took a long time to sink in. I was told I had an adjustment disorder and that in six to twelve weeks I'd be back to normal. I waited for the twelve weeks to end, but they never did. I spent three years like that – not working, not going out of the house, not getting up some days. I had nightmares, panic attacks and flashbacks.

'It was the Veterans' Agency who told me about Combat Stress [the veterans' charity specializing in the treatment of PTSD amongst ex-service personnel]. My first admission to Audley Court in Shropshire was in September 2006. I didn't want to go at first – I had to force myself because I knew I needed help. At the end of that week I didn't want to go home. I felt safe for the first time since leaving the Army.'

Julie has been four times now. 'The nightmares are still there, though less frequent. And I still have panic attacks. But if my life never improves from now, I know I can cope – whereas before I couldn't even see the next day, never mind the future.'

**LEFT PAGE:**
Resupply to compound area when on patrol, early stage of tour, Kandahar, May 2009

**RIGHT PAGE:**
Supply drop while on operations

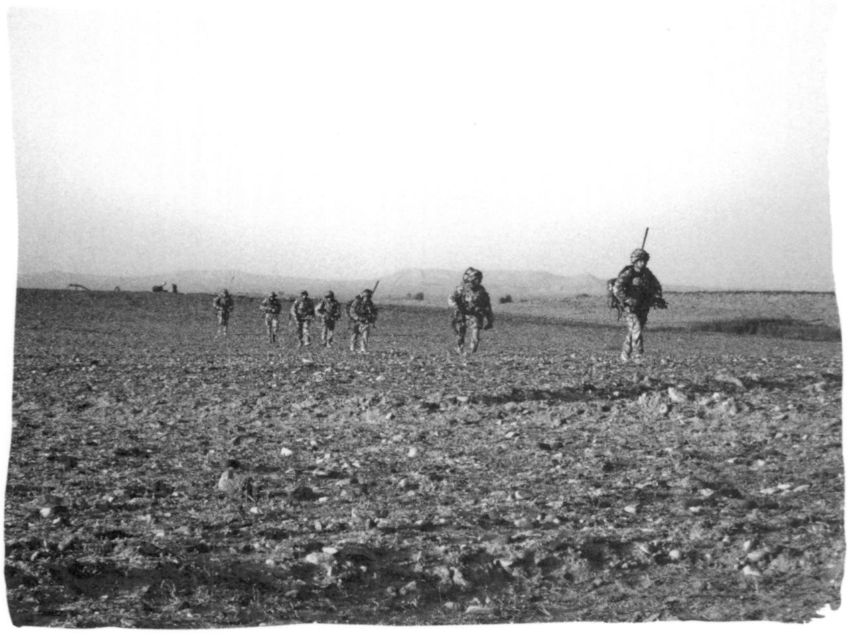

LEFT PAGE:
Returning from a local area clearance patrol

RIGHT PAGE:
The photographer standing-to at last light, manning weapons systems – Landrover mounted GMPG ('the pig')

*With medical understanding of PTSD and its treatment improving all the time, there is no reason why veterans returning from current conflicts should suffer in the same way as those who returned from World War Two or other campaigns.*

'I think a lot more people are identified as having problems and the military is a lot more sympathetic. People are getting fairly lengthy treatment. I don't know about Afghanistan but I suspect there'll be a lot requiring treatment and help.'

But, it is invariably when ex-servicemen leave the forces that they become most vulnerable. Isolation, violence, depression, substance abuse, unemployment and criminal activity have all been identified as key threats facing those suffering from PTSD.

Concern has also been expressed by the veterans' community and politicians that evidence suggests more veterans of the Falklands have died subsequently as result of suicide than were killed during the war itself. If that is true then the implications for those returning from the Middle East are extreme.

A study by Manchester University in 2009 found that ex-servicemen under 24 were between two and three times more likely to kill themselves than men of the same age from outside the forces. Professor Nav Kapur, one of the report's authors, said, 'Young men leaving the armed forces appear to be at a higher risk. That needs to be recognised and action taken.' However, Norrie, who only left the army recently, feels that PTSD is now taken a lot more seriously in the services.

With medical understanding of PTSD and its treatment improving all the time, there is no reason why veterans returning from current conflicts should suffer in the same way as those who returned from World War Two or other campaigns, people who had served their country but received no support, men like my grandfather, Arthur Wilson.

Considering the ferocity of the fighting in Helmand, and in Basra previously, it is clear that in coming years a great strain will be placed on specialist mental health services supplied by veterans' charities. It is certain that the public will continue to support these organisations, through the Poppy Appeal and many other ways of giving. But it is undoubtedly vital that veterans, the families of veterans, mental health and charity workers, and ordinary men and women of all ages, actively lobby their elected politicians (parliamentarians who most likely supported the decisions to send our troops to these conflicts) to ensure there is adequate government funding to help ex-service men and women, and their families, cope with the consequences of the hell they have had to experience on our behalf.

*Adrian Searle*

***Sergeant Nick Collins*** was born in Yorkshire. He joined the army at the age of 15 in 1989. He has seen active service in Northern Ireland, Bosnia, Iraq and Afghanistan. He has represented the Army at sailing and played football for his regiment. He currently lives in Glasgow with his Scottish wife and dog.

PLEASE NOTE:

All names have been changed at the request of interviewees.

Julie's testimony was first published in the Combat Stress Annual Report 2009.

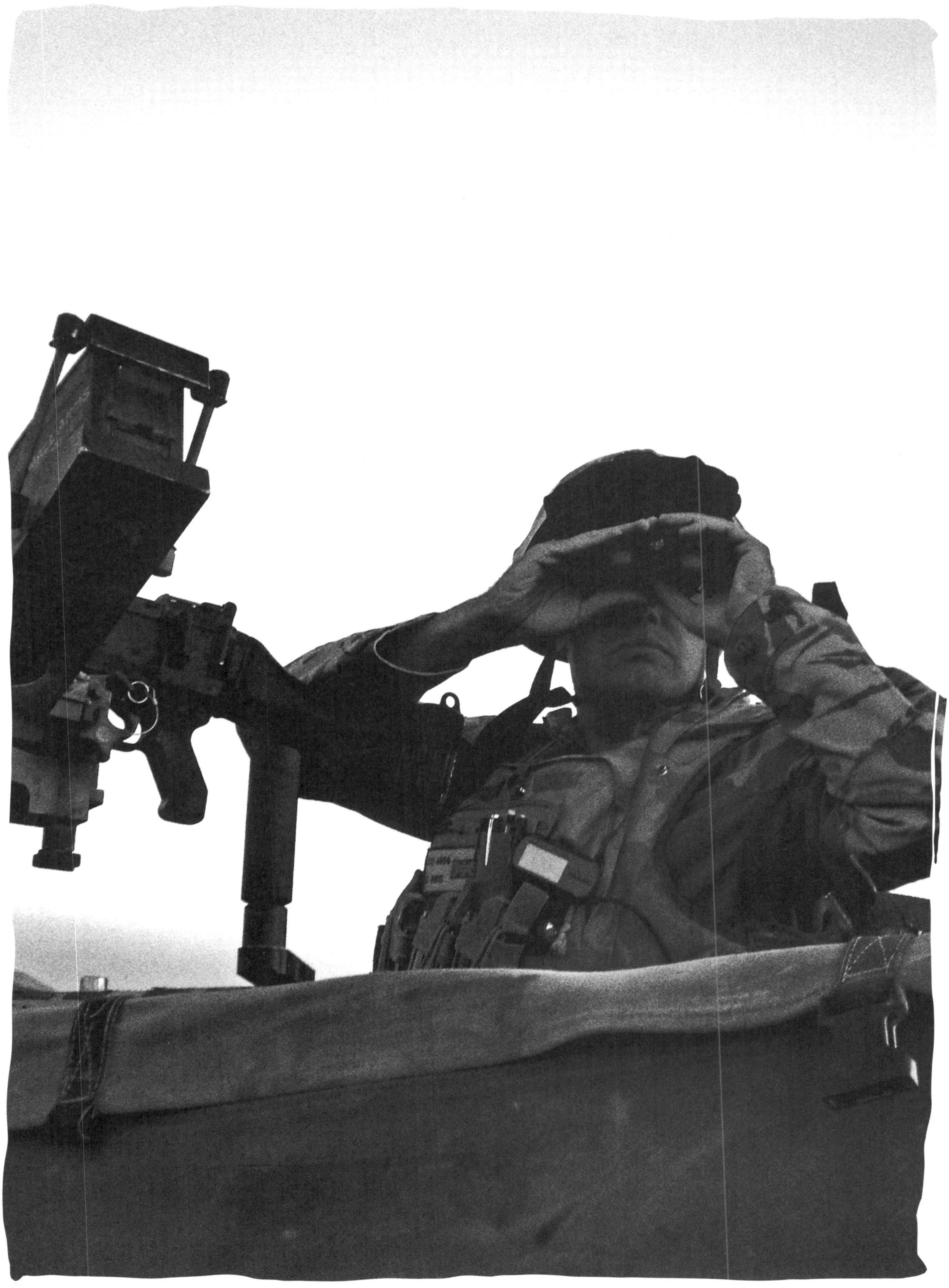

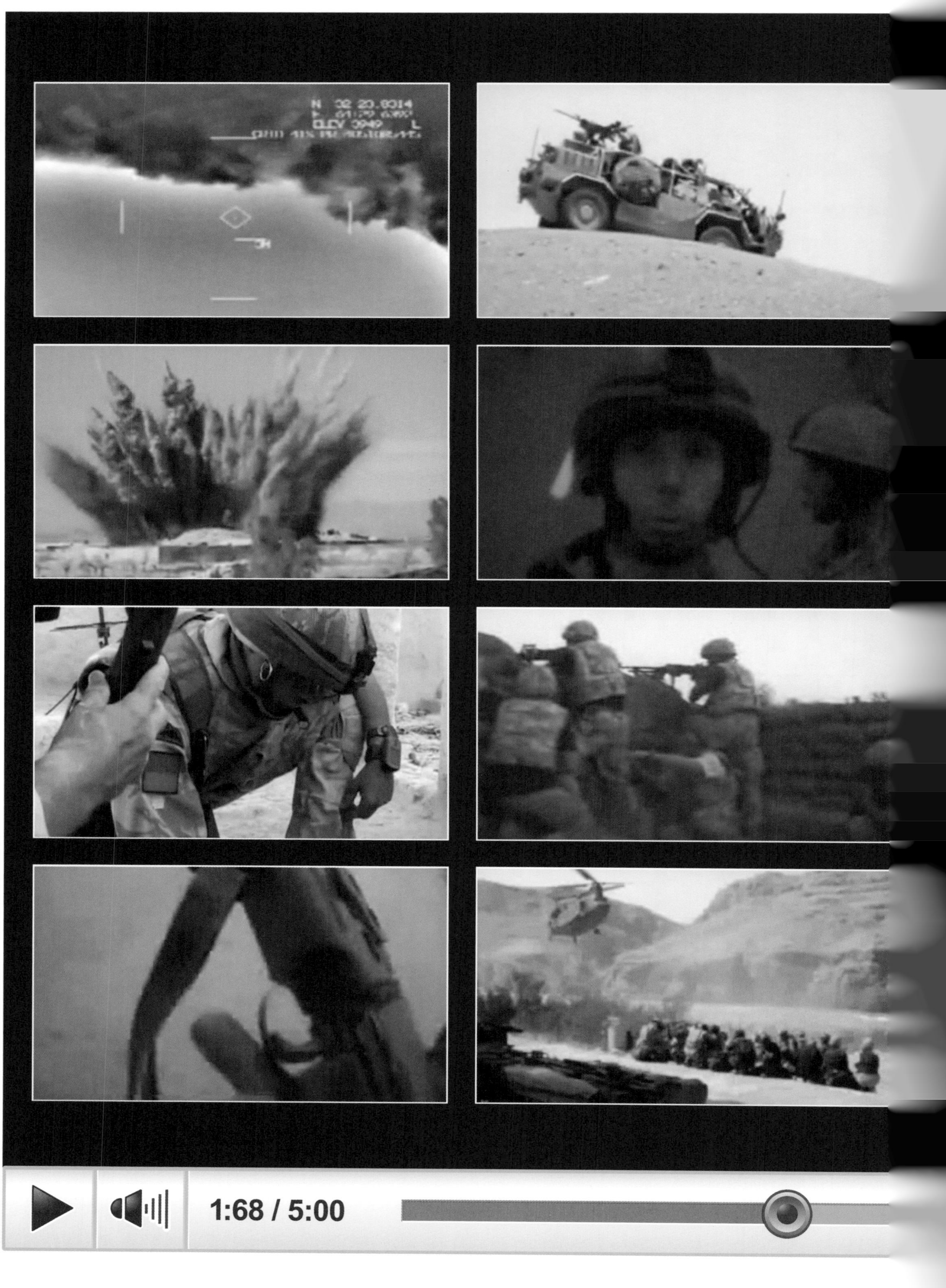
1:68 / 5:00

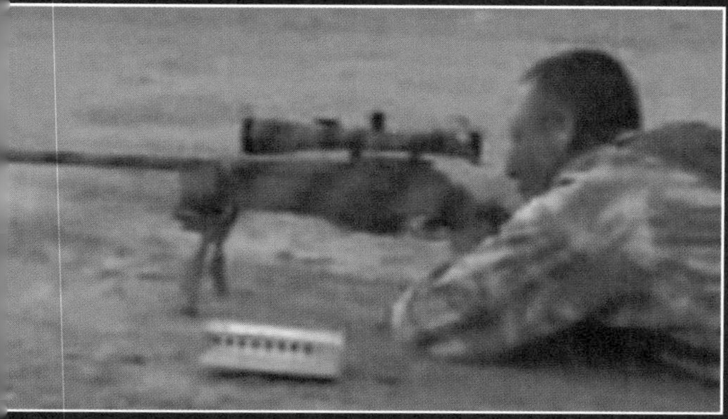
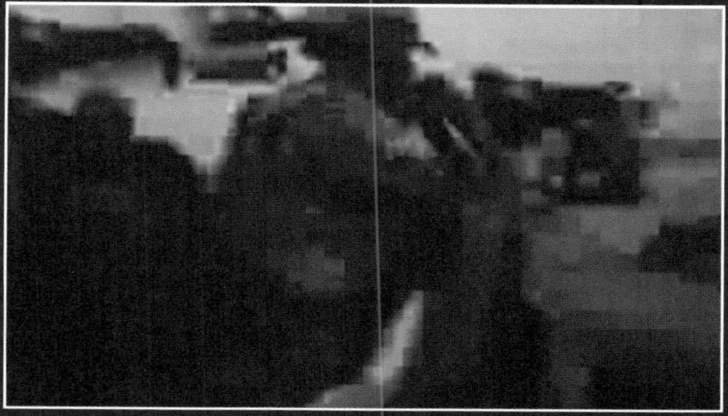
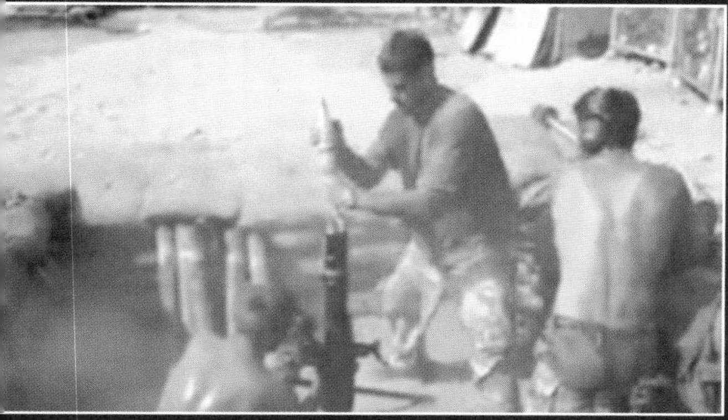
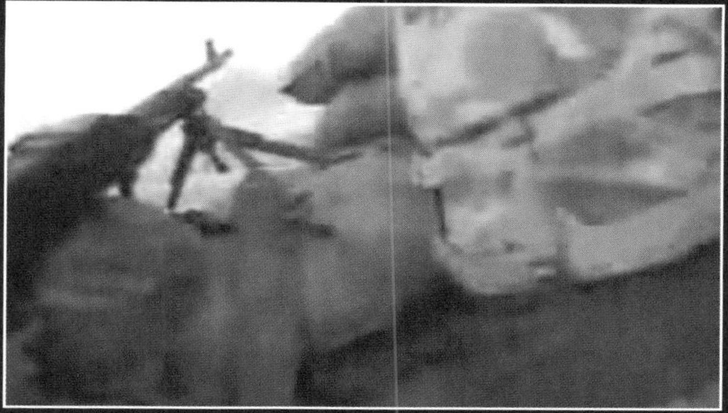
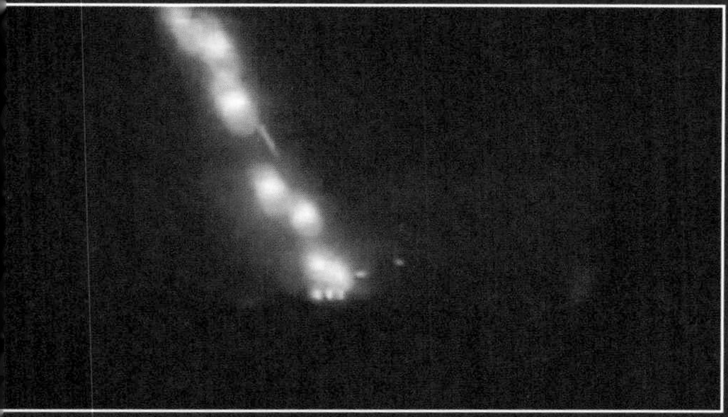
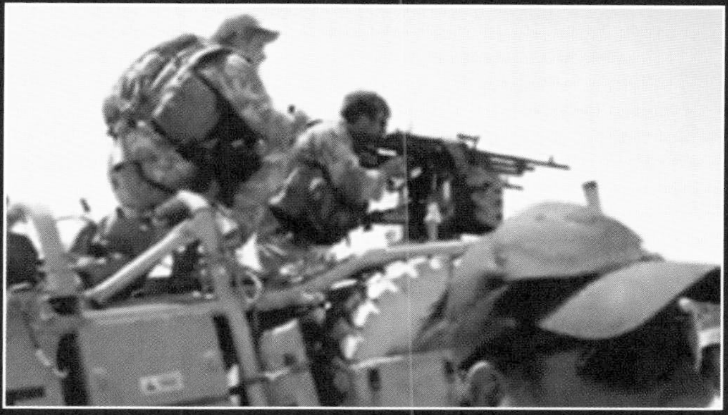
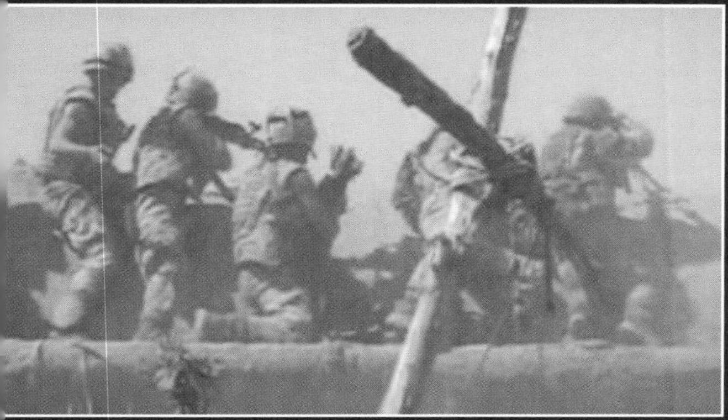
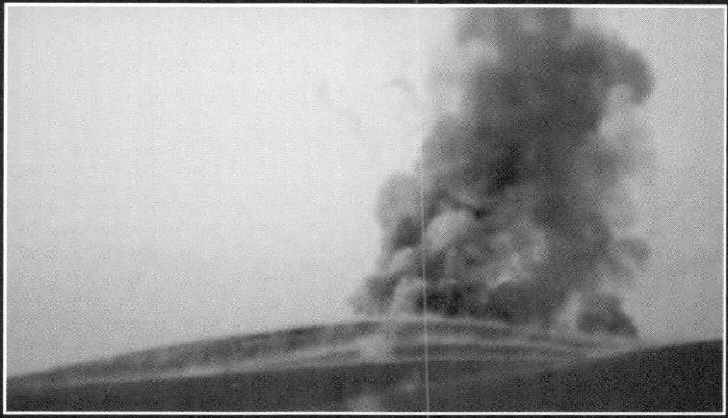

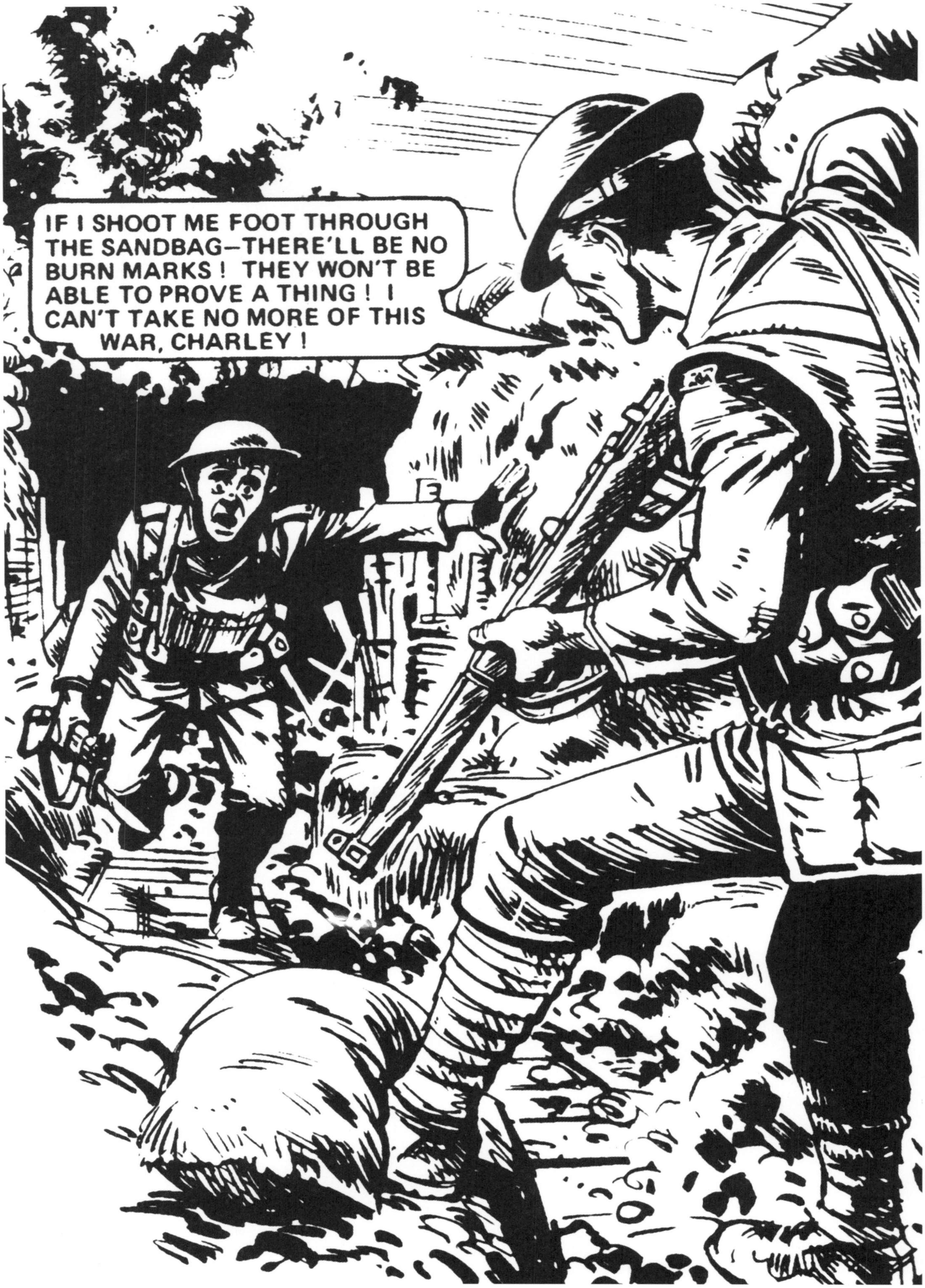
IF I SHOOT ME FOOT THROUGH THE SANDBAG—THERE'LL BE NO BURN MARKS ! THEY WON'T BE ABLE TO PROVE A THING ! I CAN'T TAKE NO MORE OF THIS WAR, CHARLEY !

# A Boy's Own Story

**C**harley's War was a starting point for this graphic novel. It first appeared in January 1979. I was already a subscriber to *Battle Action* and, aged 11, it gripped me from the very first episode. I used to cycle up to Bruce's Newsagent's on the High Street on a Wednesday evening on my Raleigh Grifter, pocket money in my jeans. *Battle* was supposed to come out on a Thursday but Bruce's took delivery late on a Wednesday and I always wanted to get my copy as soon as I could. It had built its reputation on publishing grittier, more irreverent storylines like *Hookjaw*, *Major Easy* and *Johnny Red*. And, on the whole, *Battle's* artwork was better than the competition, so it was already the choice of the discerning pre-pubescent comic consumer.

Several things immediately struck me as different about *Charley's War* in comparison to the stiff upper lip tales of derring-do I was used to in *Commando* and other traditional comics, like *Warlord* and *Valour*.

The first was that it felt real. By real I mean it felt historically accurate, warts and all. It was clear a great deal of research had gone into Pat Mills's stories. They were jammed with facts and I, like most young boys, loved facts, particularly about war. I was learning something…

> With such dark, unflinching scripts, Charley's War brought out an innate expressionism in Colquhoun's stark black and white artwork.

Beginning just before the Battle of the Somme, as Charley Bourne, an under-age volunteer arrives at the front aged 16, *Charley's War* was also about a period rarely covered by previous comics. And the drawing was stunning. I'd grown to love the work of artist Joe Colquhoun (who had drawn *Roy of the Rovers* in the 1950s) from his time on *Johnny Red*, a strip about an RAF pilot fighting on the Russian front. But with such dark, unflinching scripts, *Charley's War* brought out an innate expressionism in Colquhoun's stark black and white artwork that later I'd recognise in the likes of Hieronymus Bosch, Goya, Der Blaue Reiter and Georg Grosz. Writer and artist together took *Charley's War* to a place that no other British comic had gone before, trailblazing a path for realism-driven graphic novels of the future, those like the Frank Miller's series *Batman: The Dark Knight Returns* or anti-war stories like Art Spiegelman's *Maus* or, more recently, Ari Folman's *Waltz with Bashir.* ❯

Extract 1
Published February 1979:
It's 16th June 1916 and Charley's friend Lucky is suffering under the pressure of knowing a 'big push' is coming.

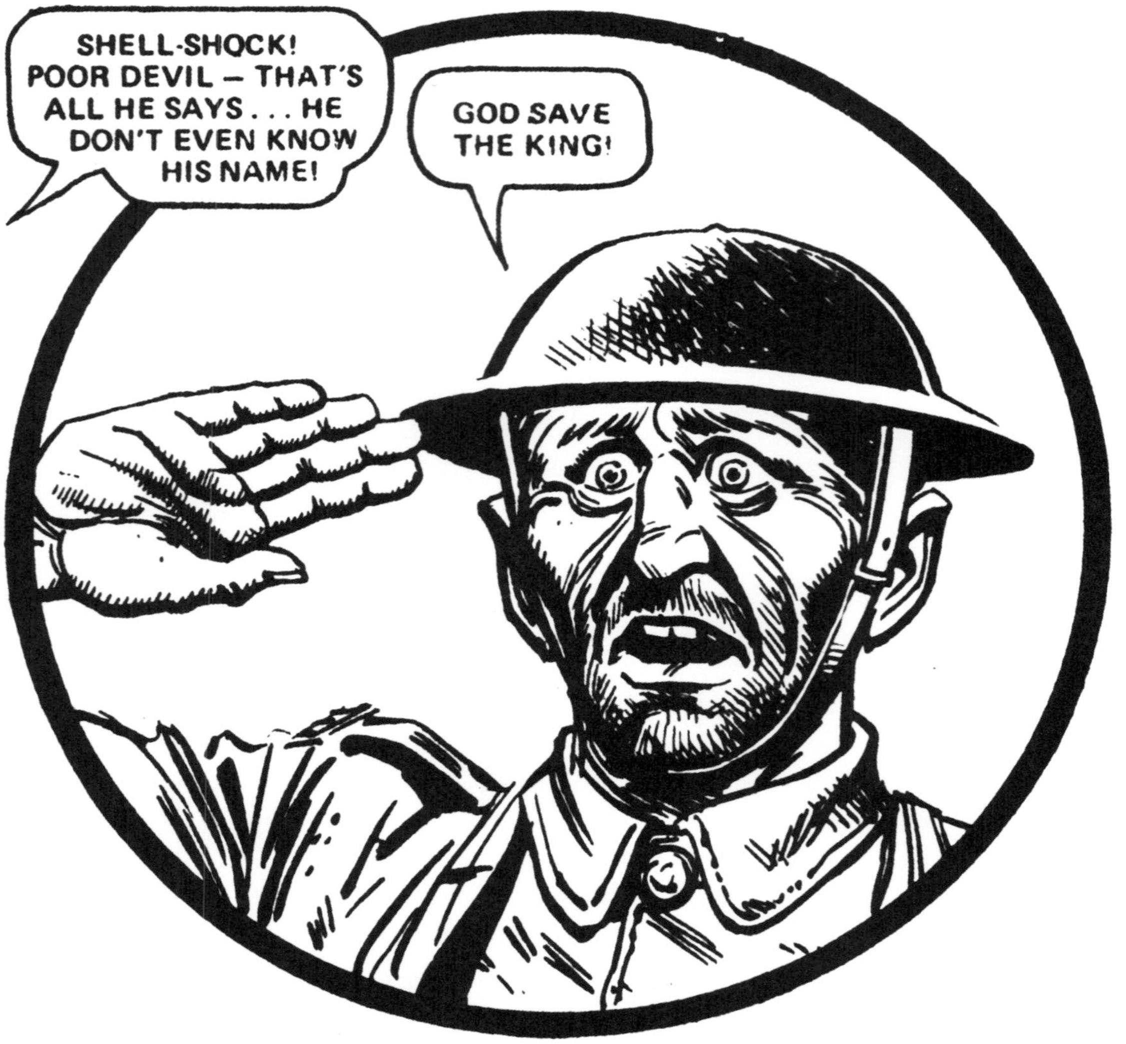
SHELL-SHOCK! POOR DEVIL – THAT'S ALL HE SAYS . . . HE DON'T EVEN KNOW HIS NAME!
GOD SAVE THE KING!

**Extract 2** (left)
Published July 1980:
In October 1916 the German Offensive 'Operation Wotan' is raging. Charley has received a head injury but, together with a soldier so traumatised he can only repeat one phrase, he is passed fit for service.

Most importantly, *Charley's War* didn't feel sanitised in the way that every other comic strip had. To my mind, Mills and Colquhoun were the first to completely reject talking down to their young comic reading audience. Everything was in there, war in all its grotesque horror, madness and gallows humour.

Perhaps the single most memorable element of Charley's story for me, and why it pushed at the boundaries back in the early eighties, was the way it represented shell shock, a condition I'd heard of but knew almost nothing about. The following panels are just some of the references Colquhoun and Mills made to what we now call combat stress or Post Traumatic Stress Disorder, whose effects were first catalogued by the medical profession during the Great War.

*Perhaps the single most memorable element of Charley's story for me…was the way it represented shell shock.*

These sections not only brilliantly dramatise the mental cost to soldiers – living daily with the incompetent tactics of their superiors, squalid conditions, relentless bombardment, going 'over the top' into the face of German machine guns and brutal, bloody death – but they also took the war comic into previously unchartered territory. The use of fantasy within such a realist form was particularly shocking and effective and it was these sections that stayed with me the longest.

I followed Charley Bourne's story for at least five years, buying *Battle* long after interest in any other comic strips has faded. I had no idea that it was so highly regarded in the British comic scene. From my own point-of-view, it was no coincidence that I ended up studying First World War history at the University of Edinburgh. Much of the two year course covered subjects and themes I'd first encountered in *Charley's War*.

*Adrian Searle*

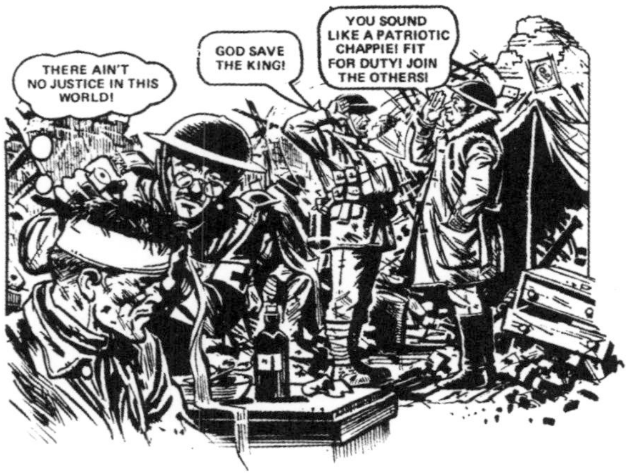
THERE AIN'T NO JUSTICE IN THIS WORLD!
GOD SAVE THE KING!
YOU SOUND LIKE A PATRIOTIC CHAPPIE! FIT FOR DUTY! JOIN THE OTHERS!

**Extract 3** (right)
Published September 1979: It's August 1st 1916 and Charley celebrates his Seventeenth birthday. Pop, one of the members of his platoon, who has lost both his sons earlier in the war, is showing signs of battle fatigue.

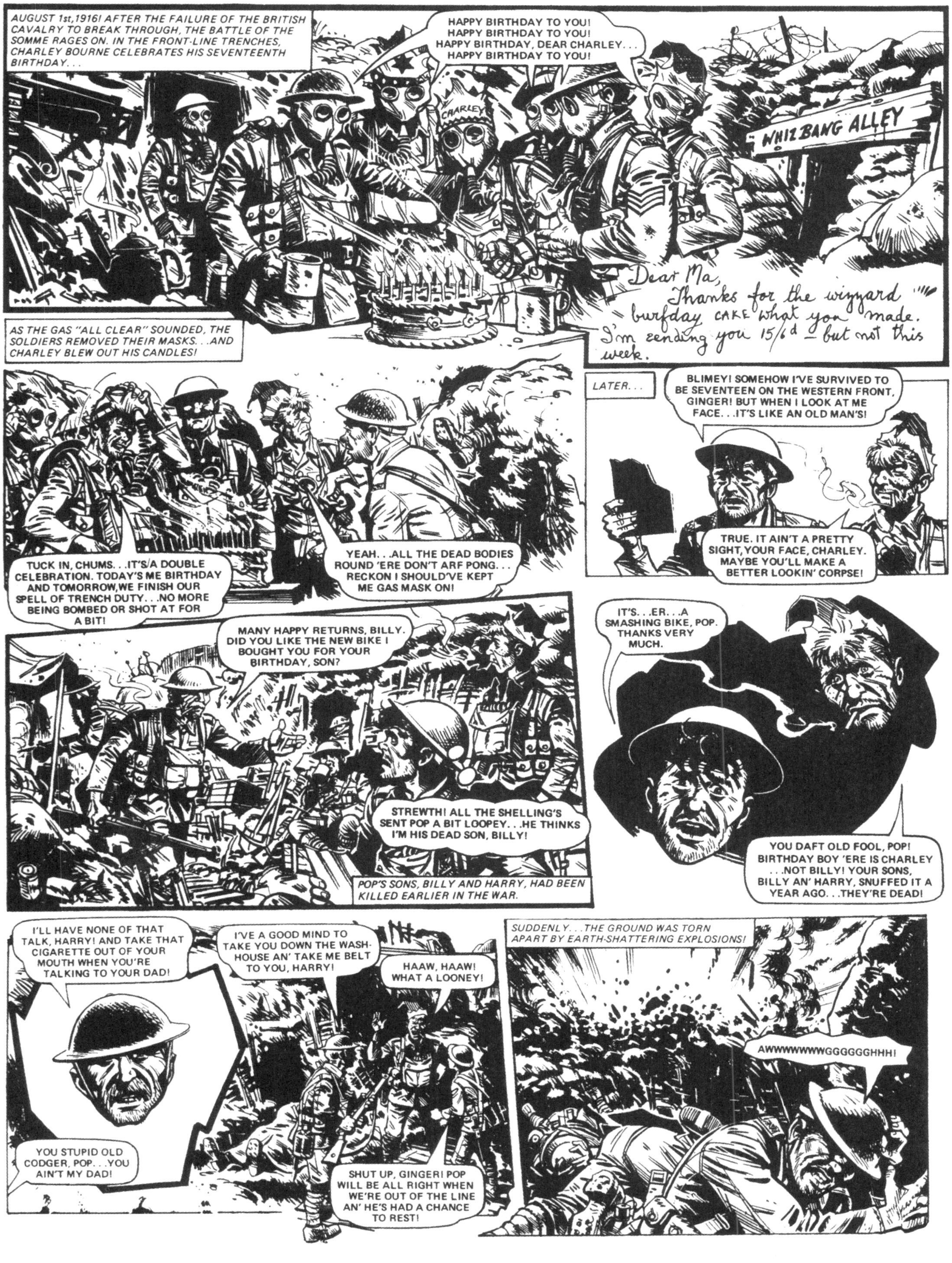
AUGUST 1st,1916! AFTER THE FAILURE OF THE BRITISH CAVALRY TO BREAK THROUGH, THE BATTLE OF THE SOMME RAGES ON. IN THE FRONT-LINE TRENCHES, CHARLEY BOURNE CELEBRATES HIS SEVENTEENTH BIRTHDAY...
HAPPY BIRTHDAY TO YOU! HAPPY BIRTHDAY TO YOU! HAPPY BIRTHDAY, DEAR CHARLEY... HAPPY BIRTHDAY TO YOU!
CHARLEY
WHIZ BANG ALLEY
Dear Ma, Thanks for the wizzard burfday CAKE what you made. I'm sending you 15/6d – but not this week.
AS THE GAS "ALL CLEAR" SOUNDED, THE SOLDIERS REMOVED THEIR MASKS...AND CHARLEY BLEW OUT HIS CANDLES!
TUCK IN, CHUMS...IT'S A DOUBLE CELEBRATION. TODAY'S ME BIRTHDAY AND TOMORROW, WE FINISH OUR SPELL OF TRENCH DUTY...NO MORE BEING BOMBED OR SHOT AT FOR A BIT!
YEAH...ALL THE DEAD BODIES ROUND 'ERE DON'T ARF PONG... RECKON I SHOULD'VE KEPT ME GAS MASK ON!
LATER...
BLIMEY! SOMEHOW I'VE SURVIVED TO BE SEVENTEEN ON THE WESTERN FRONT, GINGER! BUT WHEN I LOOK AT ME FACE...IT'S LIKE AN OLD MAN'S!
TRUE. IT AIN'T A PRETTY SIGHT, YOUR FACE, CHARLEY. MAYBE YOU'LL MAKE A BETTER LOOKIN' CORPSE!
MANY HAPPY RETURNS, BILLY. DID YOU LIKE THE NEW BIKE I BOUGHT YOU FOR YOUR BIRTHDAY, SON?
STREWTH! ALL THE SHELLING'S SENT POP A BIT LOOPEY...HE THINKS I'M HIS DEAD SON, BILLY!
POP'S SONS, BILLY AND HARRY, HAD BEEN KILLED EARLIER IN THE WAR.
IT'S...ER...A SMASHING BIKE, POP. THANKS VERY MUCH.
YOU DAFT OLD FOOL, POP! BIRTHDAY BOY 'ERE IS CHARLEY ...NOT BILLY! YOUR SONS, BILLY AN' HARRY, SNUFFED IT A YEAR AGO...THEY'RE DEAD!
I'LL HAVE NONE OF THAT TALK, HARRY! AND TAKE THAT CIGARETTE OUT OF YOUR MOUTH WHEN YOU'RE TALKING TO YOUR DAD!
YOU STUPID OLD CODGER, POP...YOU AIN'T MY DAD!
I'VE A GOOD MIND TO TAKE YOU DOWN THE WASH-HOUSE AN' TAKE ME BELT TO YOU, HARRY!
HAAW, HAAW! WHAT A LOONEY!
SHUT UP, GINGER! POP WILL BE ALL RIGHT WHEN WE'RE OUT OF THE LINE AN' HE'S HAD A CHANCE TO REST!
SUDDENLY...THE GROUND WAS TORN APART BY EARTH-SHATTERING EXPLOSIONS!
AWWWWWWWGGGGGGHHH!

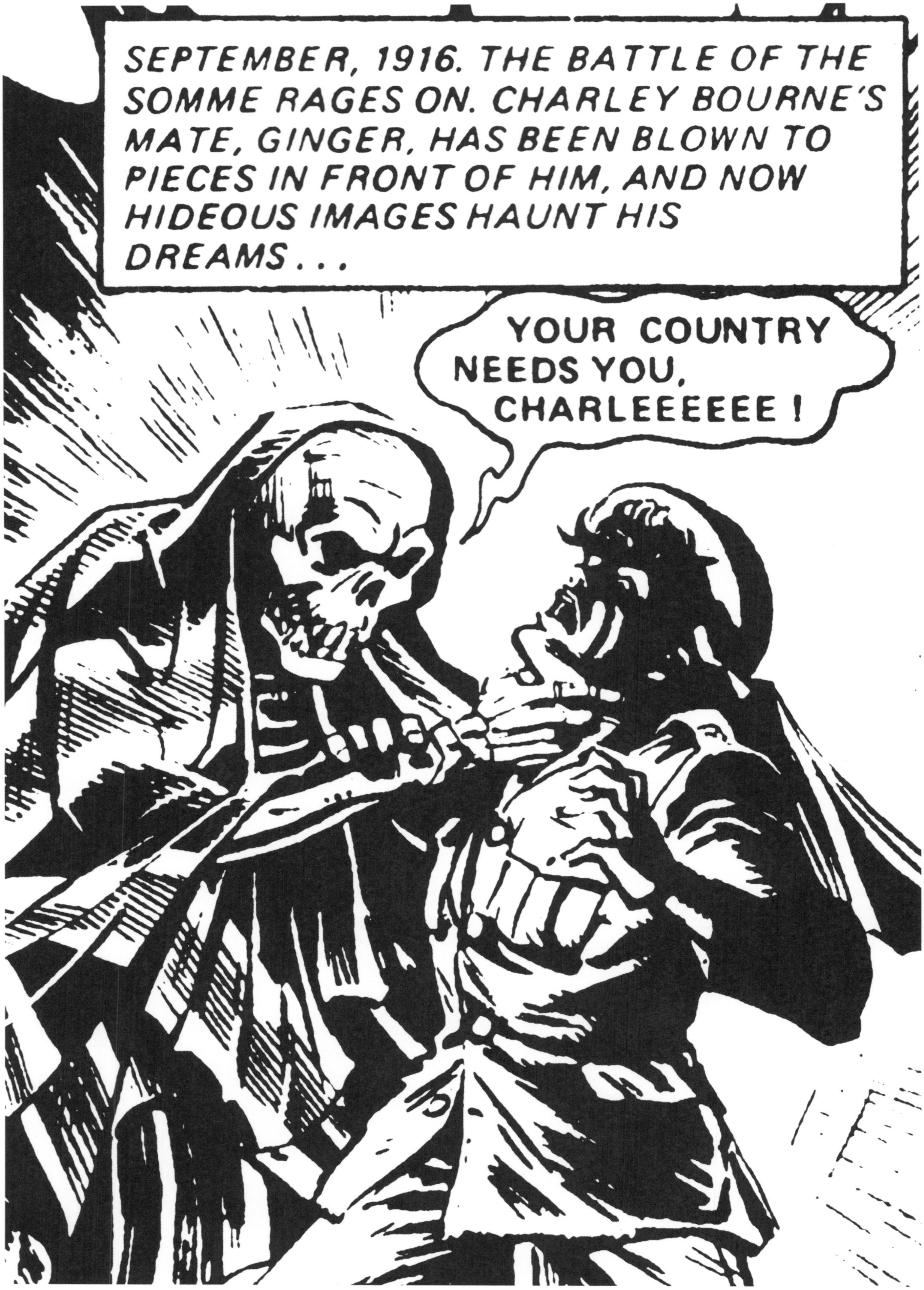
SEPTEMBER, 1916. THE BATTLE OF THE SOMME RAGES ON. CHARLEY BOURNE'S MATE, GINGER, HAS BEEN BLOWN TO PIECES IN FRONT OF HIM, AND NOW HIDEOUS IMAGES HAUNT HIS DREAMS . . .
YOUR COUNTRY NEEDS YOU, CHARLEEEEEE !

Extract 4

Published October 1979: In September 1916 Charley's friend Ginger has been blown up by stray artillery fire and Charley has collected his remains in a sack. Charley is now showing symptoms of shell shock.

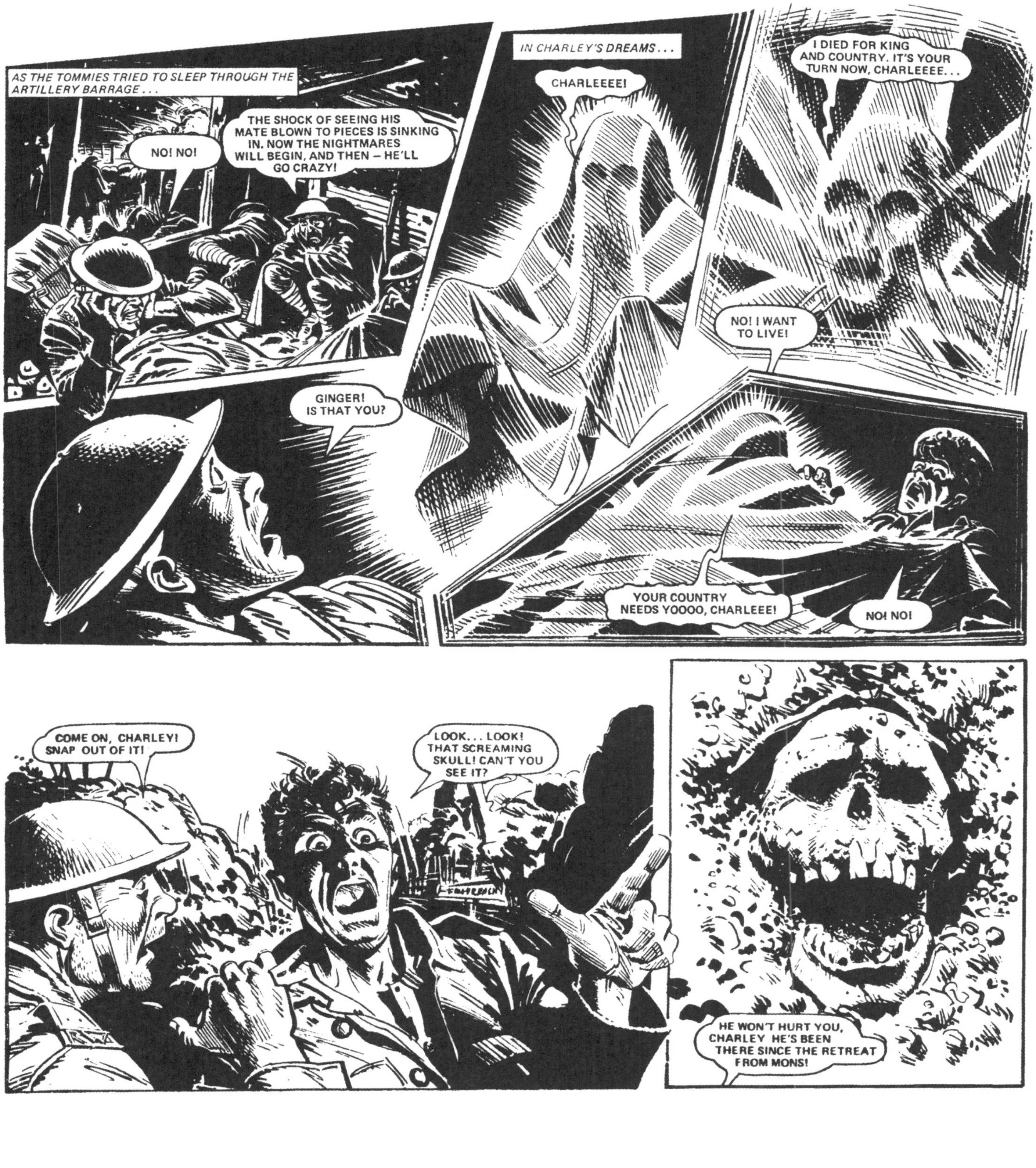
AS THE TOMMIES TRIED TO SLEEP THROUGH THE ARTILLERY BARRAGE . . .
NO! NO!
THE SHOCK OF SEEING HIS MATE BLOWN TO PIECES IS SINKING IN. NOW THE NIGHTMARES WILL BEGIN, AND THEN – HE'LL GO CRAZY!
GINGER! IS THAT YOU?
IN CHARLEY'S DREAMS . . .
CHARLEEEE!
I DIED FOR KING AND COUNTRY. IT'S YOUR TURN NOW, CHARLEEEE. . .
NO! I WANT TO LIVE!
YOUR COUNTRY NEEDS YOOOO, CHARLEEE!
NO! NO!
COME ON, CHARLEY! SNAP OUT OF IT!
LOOK. . . LOOK! THAT SCREAMING SKULL! CAN'T YOU SEE IT?
HE WON'T HURT YOU, CHARLEY HE'S BEEN THERE SINCE THE RETREAT FROM MONS!

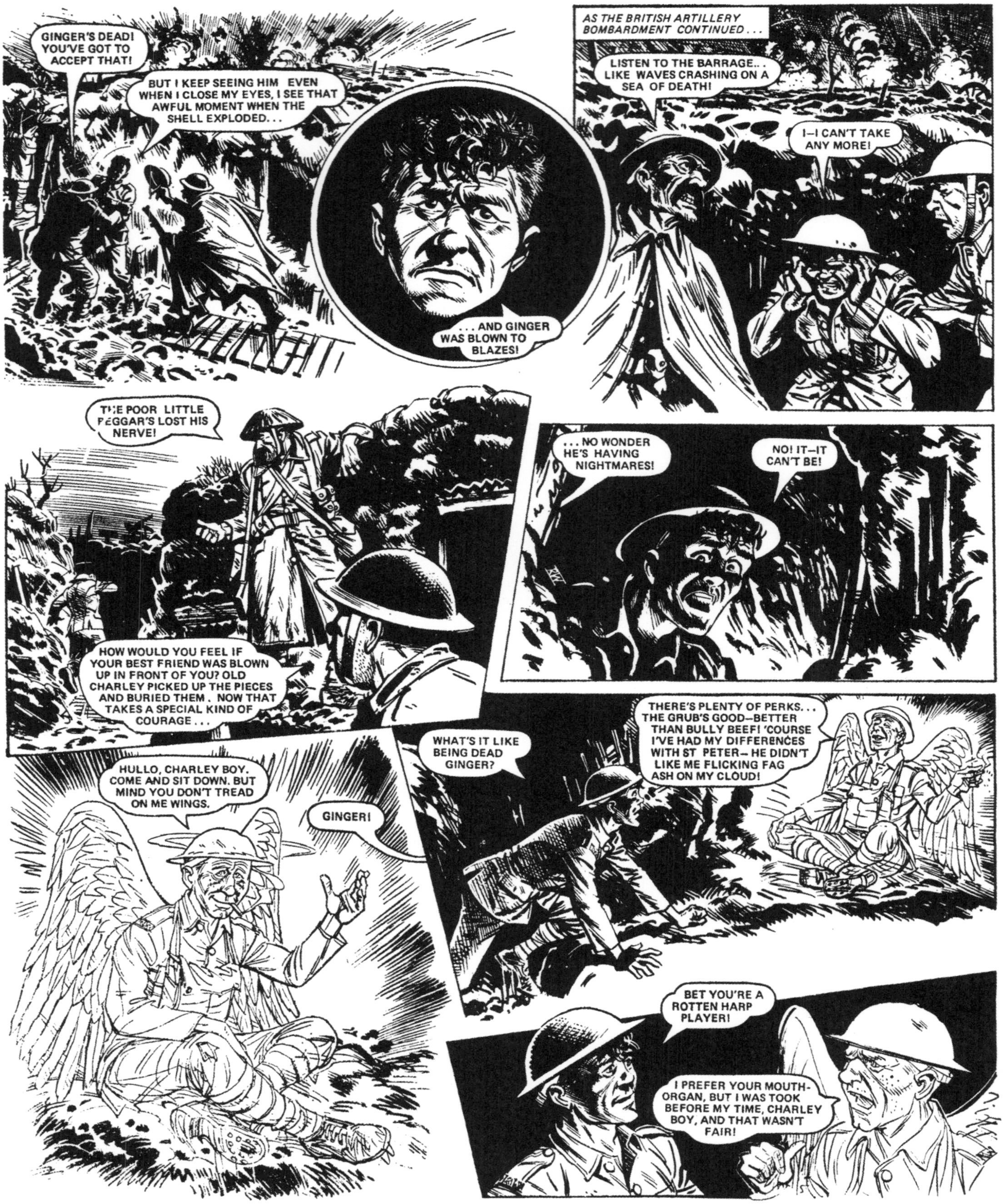
GINGER'S DEAD! YOU'VE GOT TO ACCEPT THAT!
BUT I KEEP SEEING HIM EVEN WHEN I CLOSE MY EYES, I SEE THAT AWFUL MOMENT WHEN THE SHELL EXPLODED . . .
. . . AND GINGER WAS BLOWN TO BLAZES!
AS THE BRITISH ARTILLERY BOMBARDMENT CONTINUED . . .
LISTEN TO THE BARRAGE.. LIKE WAVES CRASHING ON A SEA OF DEATH!
I—I CAN'T TAKE ANY MORE!
THE POOR LITTLE BEGGAR'S LOST HIS NERVE!
HOW WOULD YOU FEEL IF YOUR BEST FRIEND WAS BLOWN UP IN FRONT OF YOU? OLD CHARLEY PICKED UP THE PIECES AND BURIED THEM. NOW THAT TAKES A SPECIAL KIND OF COURAGE . . .
. . . NO WONDER HE'S HAVING NIGHTMARES!
NO! IT—IT CAN'T BE!
HULLO, CHARLEY BOY. COME AND SIT DOWN. BUT MIND YOU DON'T TREAD ON ME WINGS.
GINGER!
WHAT'S IT LIKE BEING DEAD GINGER?
THERE'S PLENTY OF PERKS. . . THE GRUB'S GOOD—BETTER THAN BULLY BEEF! 'COURSE I'VE HAD MY DIFFERENCES WITH ST PETER— HE DIDN'T LIKE ME FLICKING FAG ASH ON MY CLOUD!
BET YOU'RE A ROTTEN HARP PLAYER!
I PREFER YOUR MOUTH-ORGAN, BUT I WAS TOOK BEFORE MY TIME, CHARLEY BOY, AND THAT WASN'T FAIR!

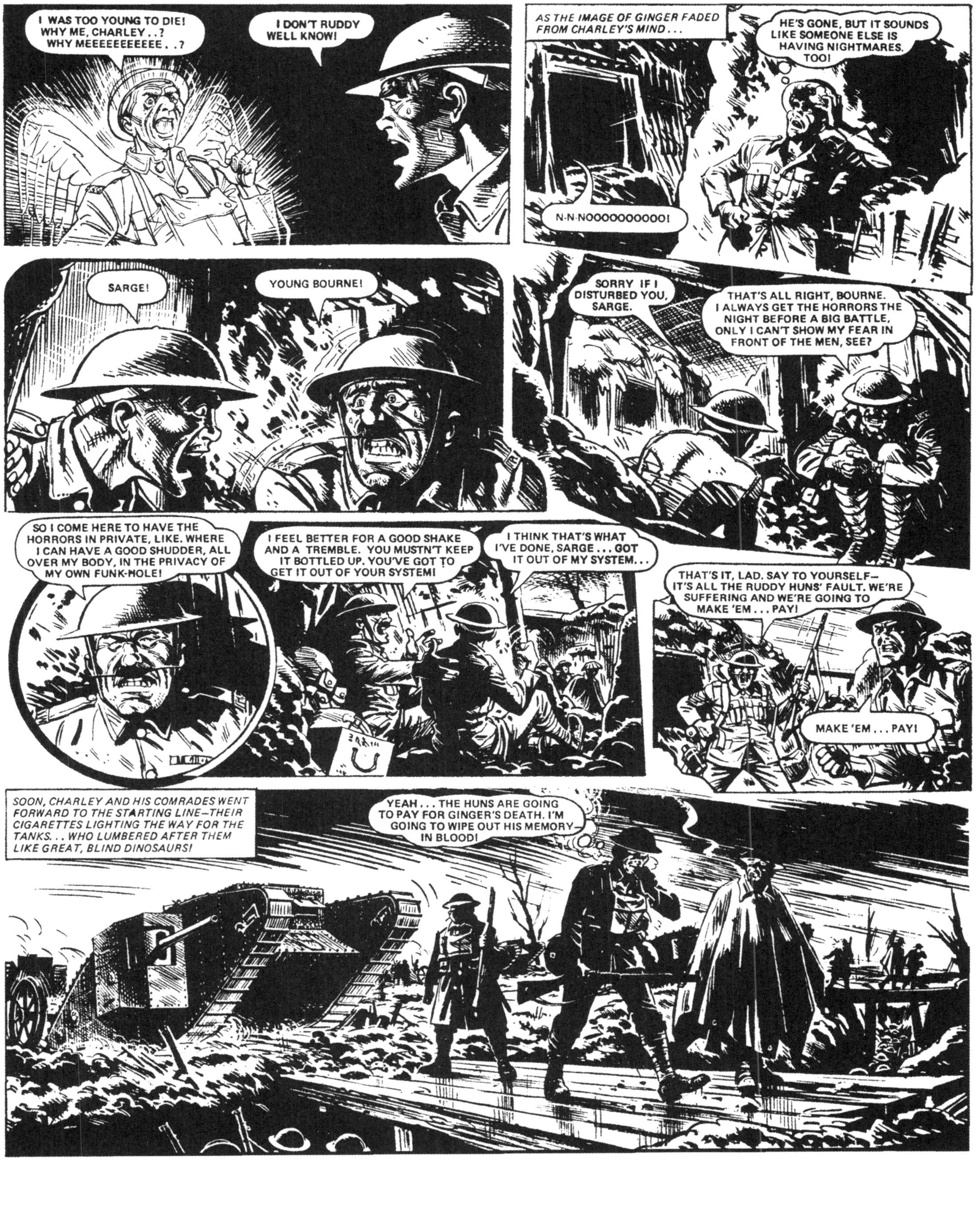
I WAS TOO YOUNG TO DIE! WHY ME, CHARLEY..? WHY MEEEEEEEEEE..?
I DON'T RUDDY WELL KNOW!
AS THE IMAGE OF GINGER FADED FROM CHARLEY'S MIND...
HE'S GONE, BUT IT SOUNDS LIKE SOMEONE ELSE IS HAVING NIGHTMARES, TOO!
N-N-NOOOOOOOOOO!
SARGE!
YOUNG BOURNE!
SORRY IF I DISTURBED YOU, SARGE.
THAT'S ALL RIGHT, BOURNE. I ALWAYS GET THE HORRORS THE NIGHT BEFORE A BIG BATTLE, ONLY I CAN'T SHOW MY FEAR IN FRONT OF THE MEN, SEE?
SO I COME HERE TO HAVE THE HORRORS IN PRIVATE, LIKE. WHERE I CAN HAVE A GOOD SHUDDER, ALL OVER MY BODY, IN THE PRIVACY OF MY OWN FUNK-HOLE!
I FEEL BETTER FOR A GOOD SHAKE AND A TREMBLE. YOU MUSTN'T KEEP IT BOTTLED UP. YOU'VE GOT TO GET IT OUT OF YOUR SYSTEM!
I THINK THAT'S WHAT I'VE DONE, SARGE... GOT IT OUT OF MY SYSTEM...
THAT'S IT, LAD. SAY TO YOURSELF— IT'S ALL THE RUDDY HUNS' FAULT. WE'RE SUFFERING AND WE'RE GOING TO MAKE 'EM... PAY!
MAKE 'EM... PAY!
SOON, CHARLEY AND HIS COMRADES WENT FORWARD TO THE STARTING LINE—THEIR CIGARETTES LIGHTING THE WAY FOR THE TANKS... WHO LUMBERED AFTER THEM LIKE GREAT, BLIND DINOSAURS!
YEAH... THE HUNS ARE GOING TO PAY FOR GINGER'S DEATH. I'M GOING TO WIPE OUT HIS MEMORY IN BLOOD!

Extract 5
Published November 1979: It's July 1916 and Private Lonely is the only survivor of a platoon previously commanded by Charley's nemesis, the psychotic Lieutenant Snell.

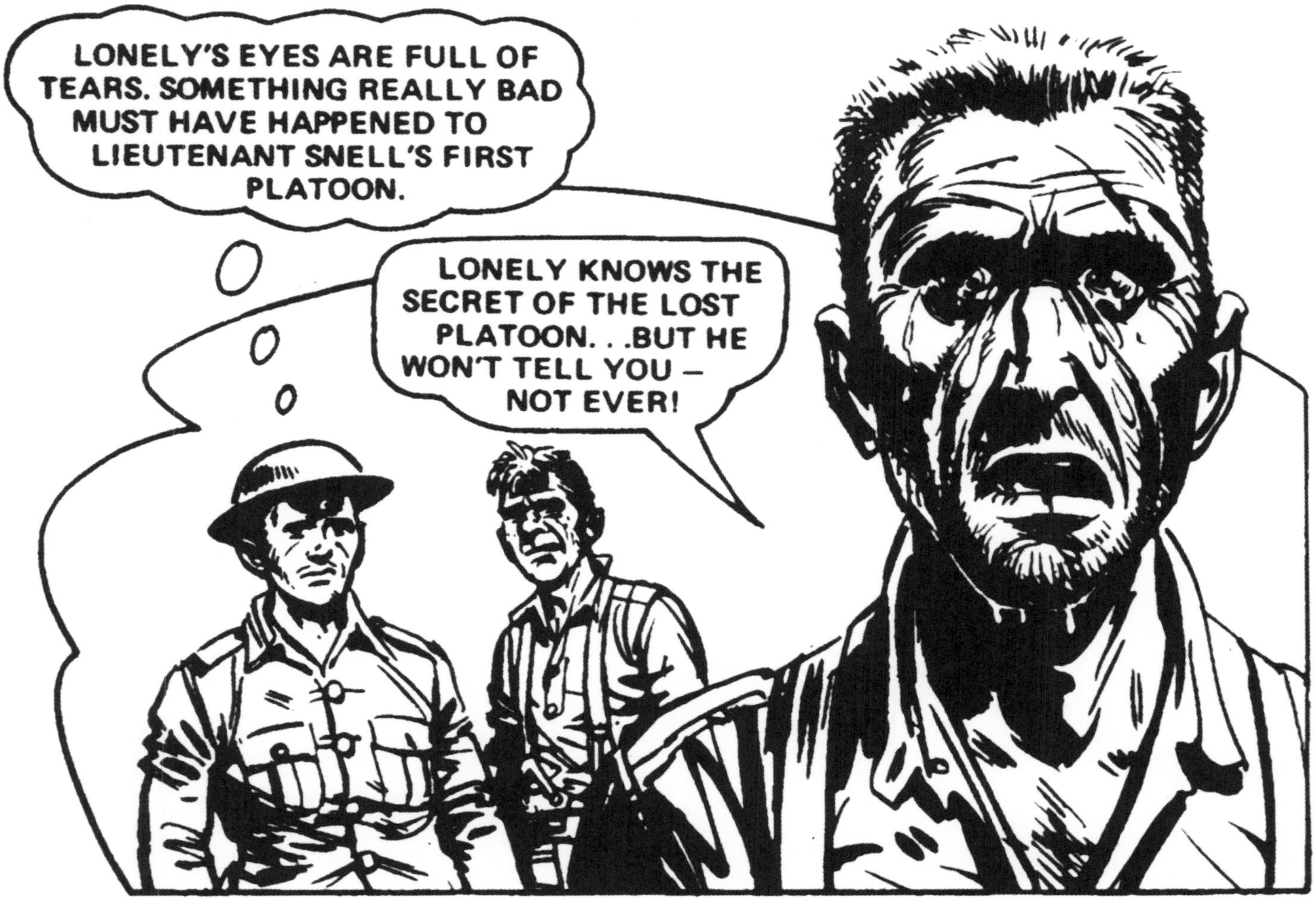
LONELY'S EYES ARE FULL OF TEARS. SOMETHING REALLY BAD MUST HAVE HAPPENED TO LIEUTENANT SNELL'S FIRST PLATOON.
LONELY KNOWS THE SECRET OF THE LOST PLATOON. . .BUT HE WON'T TELL YOU – NOT EVER!

I CARE ABOUT MESELF FIRST – THEN ME MATES. NO-ONE ELSE! 'COS I WANT TO SURVIVE!
YES, THAT'S WHAT LONELY THOUGHT. HEE, HEE!. . .HE COULD HAVE STOPPED A MASSACRE ONCE – BUT HE DIDN'T, DID HE?
BUT MAYBE. . . THIS IS HIS CHANCE TO MAKE HIS SON PROUD OF HIM!
DUE TO LONELY'S ACT OF COWARDICE SOME MONTHS PREVIOUSLY, HIS PLATOON HAD BEEN WIPED OUT. SINCE THEN, THE SOLDIER HAD TORMENTED HIMSELF WITH HIS LACK OF COURAGE.
GOODBYE, GINGER. . . CHARLEY! I'VE GOT TO GO NOW. . .THEY'RE HERE ALREADY!
WHO? I – I CAN'T SEE NO-ONE!
IT'S A LONG WAY TO TIPPERARY, IT'S A LONG WAY TO GO. . .
ALL MY DEAD MATES THAT I BETRAYED – THE LOST PLATOON . . .THEY'VE COME BACK! THEY'VE FORGIVEN ME!
WAIT FOR ME, MATES! WAIT FOR OLD LONELY!
FALL IN THEN, LONELY LAD! ROOM FOR ONE MORE IN THE LOST PLATOON!
IT'S A LONG WAY TO TIPPERARY, TO THE SWEETEST GIRL I KNOW!
TO THE TRAGIC, HAUNTED LONELY, THE SOLDIERS OF HIS IMAGINATION WERE VERY REAL. . .
CAN'T YOU SEE THEM? CAN'T YOU SEE THEM?
GHOST-SOLDIERS IN THE SKY!
PICK UP THE SONG, LONELY LAD! WE KNOW YOU WON'T LET US DOWN THIS TIME!
GOODBYE, PICCADILLY . . .FAREWELL, LEICESTER SQUARE. . !

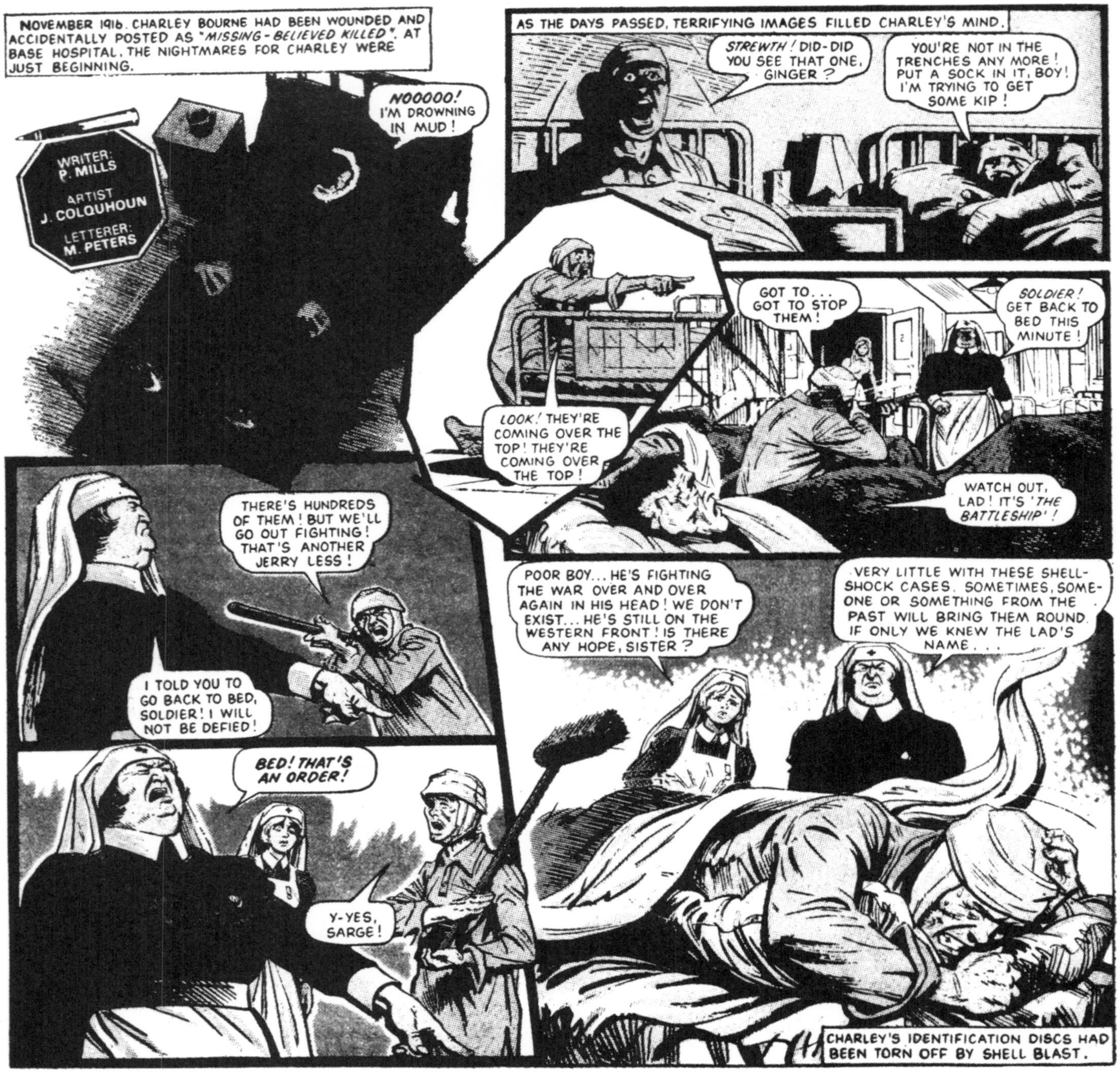
NOVEMBER 1916. CHARLEY BOURNE HAD BEEN WOUNDED AND ACCIDENTALLY POSTED AS "MISSING - BELIEVED KILLED". AT BASE HOSPITAL, THE NIGHTMARES FOR CHARLEY WERE JUST BEGINNING.
WRITER: P. MILLS
ARTIST J. COLQUHOUN
LETTERER: M. PETERS
NOOOOO! I'M DROWNING IN MUD!
AS THE DAYS PASSED, TERRIFYING IMAGES FILLED CHARLEY'S MIND.
STREWTH! DID-DID YOU SEE THAT ONE, GINGER?
YOU'RE NOT IN THE TRENCHES ANY MORE! PUT A SOCK IN IT, BOY! I'M TRYING TO GET SOME KIP!
LOOK! THEY'RE COMING OVER THE TOP! THEY'RE COMING OVER THE TOP!
GOT TO... GOT TO STOP THEM!
SOLDIER! GET BACK TO BED THIS MINUTE!
WATCH OUT, LAD! IT'S 'THE BATTLESHIP'!
THERE'S HUNDREDS OF THEM! BUT WE'LL GO OUT FIGHTING! THAT'S ANOTHER JERRY LESS!
I TOLD YOU TO GO BACK TO BED, SOLDIER! I WILL NOT BE DEFIED!
BED! THAT'S AN ORDER!
Y-YES, SARGE!
POOR BOY... HE'S FIGHTING THE WAR OVER AND OVER AGAIN IN HIS HEAD! WE DON'T EXIST... HE'S STILL ON THE WESTERN FRONT! IS THERE ANY HOPE, SISTER?
VERY LITTLE WITH THESE SHELL-SHOCK CASES. SOMETIMES, SOMEONE OR SOMETHING FROM THE PAST WILL BRING THEM ROUND. IF ONLY WE KNEW THE LAD'S NAME...
CHARLEY'S IDENTIFICATION DISCS HAD BEEN TORN OFF BY SHELL BLAST.

Extract 6
Published August 1980: In November 1916 Charley is wounded and is hospitalised suffering from trauma-induced amnesia. He undergoes quack treatments typical of the early years of military psychiatry.

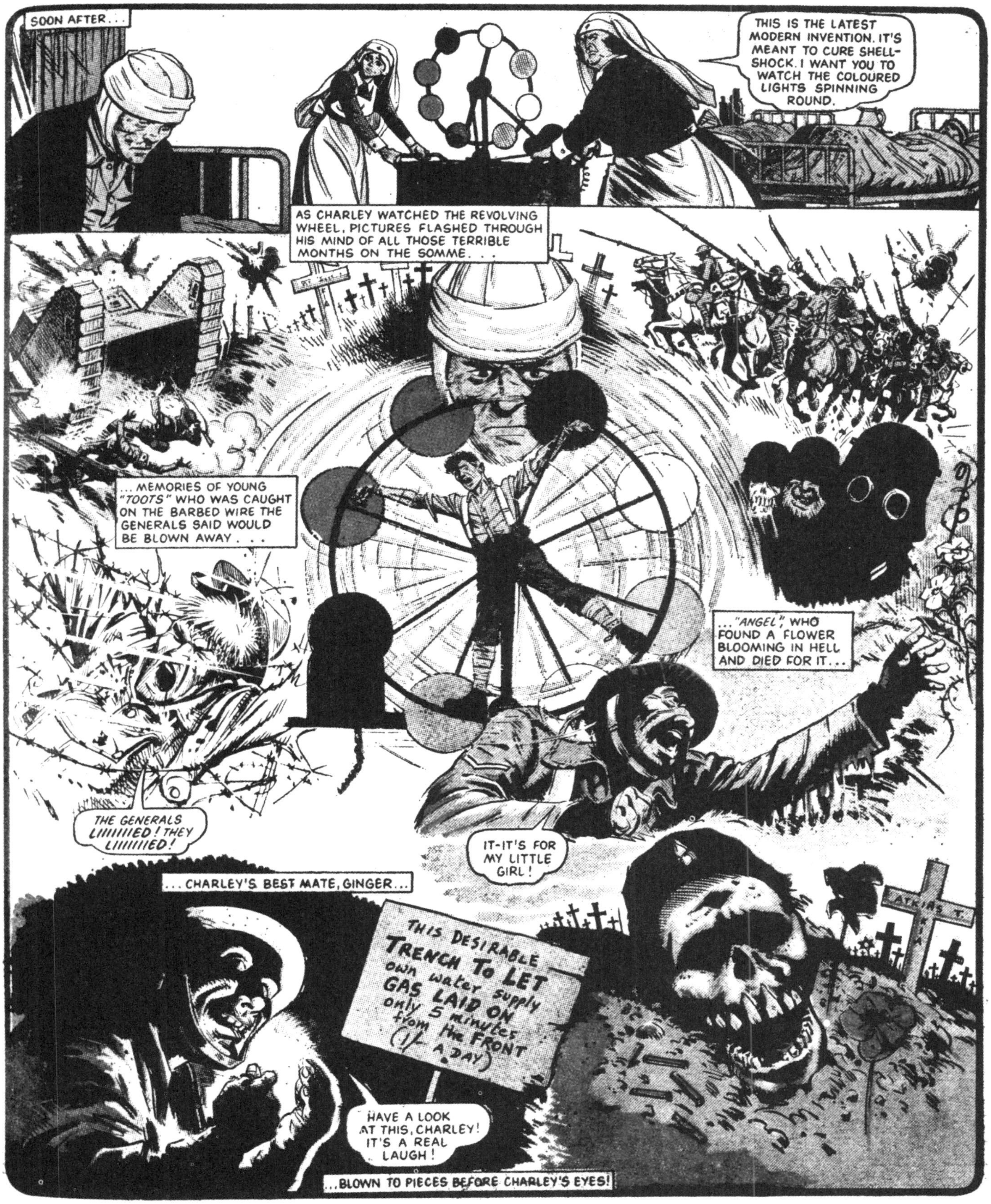

SOON AFTER...
THIS IS THE LATEST MODERN INVENTION. IT'S MEANT TO CURE SHELL-SHOCK. I WANT YOU TO WATCH THE COLOURED LIGHTS SPINNING ROUND.
AS CHARLEY WATCHED THE REVOLVING WHEEL, PICTURES FLASHED THROUGH HIS MIND OF ALL THOSE TERRIBLE MONTHS ON THE SOMME...
...MEMORIES OF YOUNG "TOOTS" WHO WAS CAUGHT ON THE BARBED WIRE THE GENERALS SAID WOULD BE BLOWN AWAY...
THE GENERALS LIIIIIIED! THEY LIIIIIIED!
..."ANGEL", WHO FOUND A FLOWER BLOOMING IN HELL AND DIED FOR IT...
IT-IT'S FOR MY LITTLE GIRL!
...CHARLEY'S BEST MATE, GINGER...
THIS DESIRABLE TRENCH TO LET own water supply GAS LAID ON only 5 minutes from the FRONT (1/- A DAY)
HAVE A LOOK AT THIS, CHARLEY! IT'S A REAL LAUGH!
...BLOWN TO PIECES BEFORE CHARLEY'S EYES!

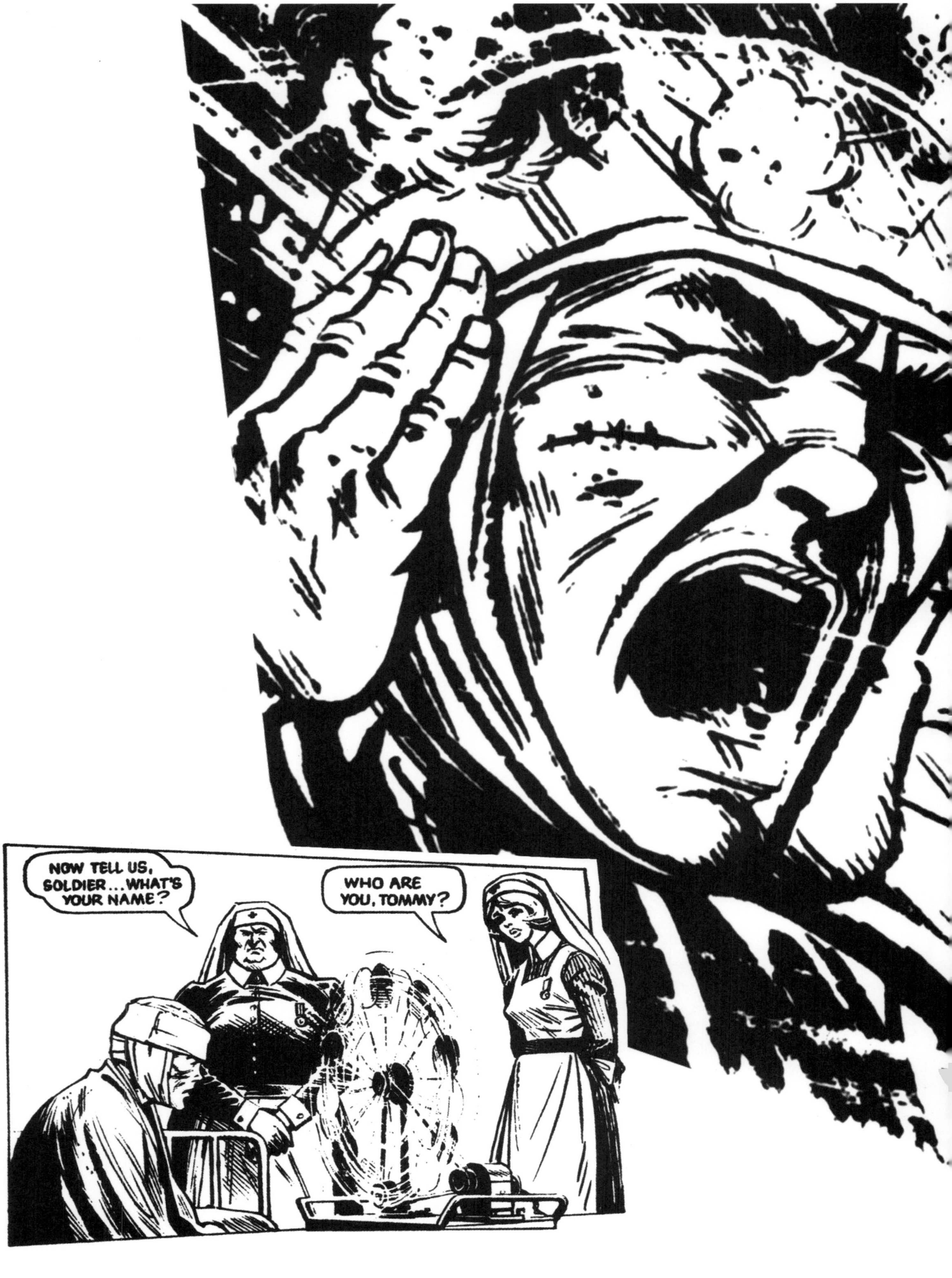
NOW TELL US, SOLDIER... WHAT'S YOUR NAME?
WHO ARE YOU, TOMMY?

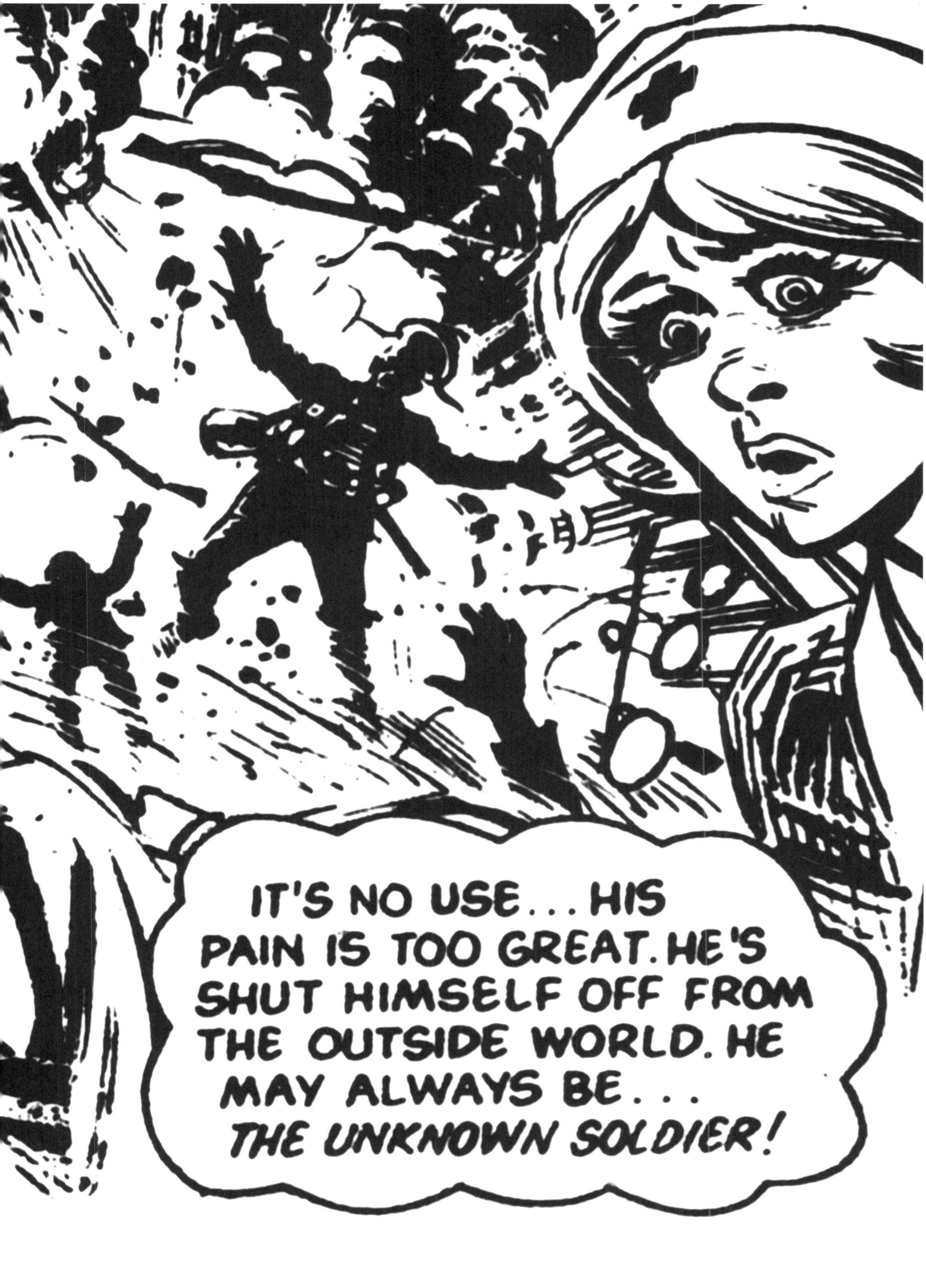
IT'S NO USE... HIS PAIN IS TOO GREAT. HE'S SHUT HIMSELF OFF FROM THE OUTSIDE WORLD. HE MAY ALWAYS BE... *THE UNKNOWN SOLDIER!*

# Afterword

When Adrian Searle asked me to write the script for what is now *Dougie's War*, I'd just finished a biography which took me four years to complete, and I really needed a change. Writing can be quite a solitary business, and sometimes you can get isolated from the world around you, and totally consumed by projects that often take a fat chunk of your life to complete. When working on them, it's hard to imagine ever doing anything else. Days disappear unaccounted for. Loved ones suffer. Friends give up on you. But once each mountain is finally conquered, you're sometimes left not quite knowing what to do, with a vague sense of anti-climax. There's a strange void than needs filling, and fast. Then, before you know it, you suddenly find yourself at the bottom of a different, scarier-looking mountain, thinking about another big climb and not knowing how to go about it, or whether you're capable of it at all. When Adrian got in touch I was trying out several new book ideas, but none were working yet. So I was grateful to be able to have something totally new and different to throw myself into, on a topic I was passionate about. Besides, I wanted to learn more about graphic novels and this gave me a good excuse to slouch around for a while, reading comics and taking notes. Which was a lot of fun.

Inspirations for these pages, aside from *Charley's War* itself, came from the likes of Brian K. Vaughan and Niko Henrichon's beautifully rendered *Pride of Baghdad*, about lions who escape from Baghdad zoo at the beginning of the Iraq War in 2003. Other inspirations were Marjane Satrapi's revolutionary Iranian tale *Persepolis*, Ari Folman and David Polonsky's *Waltz with Bashir*, based in Israel and Lebanon, another soldier's story of guilt and mind games, and especially Garth Ennis's dark, intense *War Stories* collections. One particularly keen shop assistant in Forbidden Planet told me I needed *War Stories* in my life and that if I didn't like them I was an idiot. This was the kind of obsession I was looking for! And he was right, I loved them. The Ennis volumes showed me there was plenty of scope for a storyteller like me in the graphic novel world, a real energy and immediacy to the form and content of what I was discovering, and plenty of space to experiment too. That instinct for experimentation is why I brought Dave Turbitt on board. I've known Dave's artwork for a decade; we worked together on my last novel *Hope for Newborns* (which was about three generations of an Army family) and knew I could trust him with this potentially difficult story. But exactly what story were we going to tell?

Before I started writing, I spent a few months doing research. During that time I met with a number of ex-Army, Air Force and Navy men and women who had served in various conflicts over the last fifty years, and I felt that *lots* of their voices deserved to be heard. So rather than directly tell one person's real life tale, I wanted to attempt to echo the experiences of lots of those I came across. That means *Dougie's War* is based on facts, but is a complete fiction. It appears to be about one person, but is really about hundreds of them. On one level it's about conflict in Afghanistan, but it's informed by tales of Scots who have served all over the world: in Iraq, the Falklands, Northern Ireland, the former Yugoslavia. All the places I heard about. On my travels I met people who told me about what it was like to be stationed in Berlin before the fall of the Wall there, or in Hong Kong before the handover to the Chinese in 1997, or in Burma in 1942, and I was struck by just how much the mental after-effects of these experiences and conflicts had in common with each other. No matter the setting, many of these people had felt well equipped to deal with life in the Services, and many enjoyed the energy, the camaraderie, the sense of purpose that it gave them. It was their identity and they were proud of it. Some of them looked on weaklings like me with pity, as I could never understand what it is like to know you can trust the man standing next to you with your life. But these same people struggled to adapt to civilian life when they left active service. The rules of civilian relationships are different to those needed in a war zone. The skills are different. It can be tough to adapt, and just as tough to leave bad experiences behind. These tend to linger in the mind afterwards,

> *Dougie's War is based on facts, but is a complete fiction. It appears to be about one person, but is really about hundreds of them.*

sometimes only becoming a serious threat to daily life many months or years after the original trauma. The question is, how do you cope?

Here in Scotland there are those trying to help ex-Services Personnel with Post Traumatic Stress Disorder, now a much more recognised problem than it was twenty or even ten years ago. Member organisations of Veteran Scotland are regularly involved in that difficult work, including Combat Stress and a number of others whose job it is to reach those that need assistance. But there's still much about the condition we don't understand, and there are a huge amount of people who desperately need practical help but don't know how to go about getting it. The situation is complicated by the current political climate, with some of those I spoke to feeling that support for the Armed Services is not as strong as it should be. A sizeable chunk of the public, and a fair proportion of those taking part in current conflicts aren't sure whether they believe in the causes being fought for in Iraq and Afghanistan at all. Neither do I – and I found that difficult to admit to people who had put their lives at risk for those causes – but that doesn't mean I don't believe we should properly support those we send out to the desert or the mountains of the Middle East to fight in our name. On the contrary, I think it makes it more important.

In early 2010, in the last days of Gordon Brown's government, there was much talk about "communicating more effectively" why we are in Afghanistan in the first place. After nearly a decade of presence there, hundreds of deaths of British soldiers, and many thousands of civilian Afghan deaths we don't (to our shame) even bother to count, it's depressing to think that case still needs to be made. And it's equally depressing that some of those who serve in these conflicts struggle to re-enter society when they return home, with so many slipping into alcoholism, addiction, homelessness or even ending up in prison. I can't pretend to understand what it's like to fight those demons, but I have listened to those who have. Hopefully *Dougie's War* gives a flavour of the horror, the frustration and the struggles of ordinary people who we, as a society, (as one ex-Army man told me) "turn into killing machines, then don't do enough to help turn back into people again". In that sense, the world of *Dougie's War* is similar to that of *Charley's War*, the original inspiration for this project.

In *Charley's War*, a young boy entered World War I having lied about his age to sign up, and readers watch him adapt to being thrown into the Battle of the Somme. Dougie also signs up young, too young perhaps, and also gets a shock when he arrives in a war zone, with little prospect of imminent victory and little understanding of what it's all for. But in this story we focus more on what was only hinted at in *Charley's War* – the idea that another very real struggle begins after you leave the battlefield. Dougie is unable to fight any more, which strips away his reason for being. Feeling he is not properly understood or recognised by the State or by his family and friends, he begins to believe the only way he will be remembered is if he dies, like the two friends he lost in Afghanistan. The life he lives after his return to Glasgow brings death closer much faster than he imagines. We hope that Dougie's story makes for a good read, but also highlights some of the issues we are only now beginning to understand about the human consequences of war.

**With thanks to:** *The Scottish Veterans Fund, Fife Veteran's Association (especially David Cruickshanks, Sean Davidson and Andy Laker), and everyone at the Earl Haig Poppy Factory in Edinburgh. Thanks also to all ex-Services men and women who would rather not be named but deserve to be acknowledged here. You know who you are. For advice on how to turn a novelist into a graphic novelist, big thanks to Denise Mina. For help understanding the issues, and for his powerful film, thanks to SB. Also, thanks to Steven Turner for directing me towards Rudyard Kipling's poem, 'Tommy'.*

*A graphic novel is a joint effort.*

*Rodge Glass*

**Enormous thanks** *to my beautiful wife Mary-Anne, for all her love and support. Thank you also to Rob, for sharing combat experiences and technical detail, to the Six Fingers Of Fate, for encouragement through strenuous days at the drawing table, and thank you to all my family and in-laws. Finally, massive thanks to Rodge and Adrian for opening the door. Seriously, thanks. It was raining outside.*

*Dave Turbitt*

# Help

If you are a veteran or know a veteran in need of help you can contact:

**GENERAL ENQUIRIES**

## Soldiers, Sailors, Airmen and Families Association

Our telephone support line is available 365 days a year and provides a service which is outside the chain of command.
The line is open from 10.30am – 10.30pm. Free phone lines operate from Germany, Cyprus and the UK:

**From the UK (Main Line):**
0800 731 4880

**From Germany:** 0800 1827 395

**From Cyprus:** 800 91065

**From the Falkland Islands:** # 6111

**From anywhere in the world (Call-back):**
+44 (0)1980 630854

From Operational Theatres, to enable access through Paradigm's phone system, dial the appropriate access number then enter *201 at the PIN prompt.

**www.ssafa.org.uk**

**MENTAL HEALTH**

## Combat Stress

We have people in your area ready to take your call 8.30am – 4.30pm, Monday to Friday. Veterans do not have to have seen active service in order to qualify for our help – but if you are in any doubt, just ask us.

**Scotland and North of England**
01292 561352
outreachscotland@combatstress.org.uk

**England North East**
01952 822755
outreachnorth@combatstress.org.uk

**England North West**
01952 822756
outreachnorth@combatstress.org.uk

**North Wales**
01952 822754
outreachnorth@combatstress.org.uk

**South Wales**
01952 822757
outreachnorth@combatstress.org.uk

**Central England**
01952 822753
outreachnorth@combatstress.org.uk

**Anglia**
01372 841686
outreachsouth@combatstress.org.uk

**England South**
01372 841684
outreachsouth@combatstress.org.uk

**England South East**
01372 841683
outreachsouth@combatstress.org.uk

**England South West**
01372 841687
outreachsouth@combatstress.org.uk

**Ireland**
02890 269990
outreachireland@combatstress.org.uk

**www.combatstress.org.uk**